KILLING KINSLEY

ALLY LEE

CONTENT WARNING

This book contains
graphic content and
sensitive material
that may be
disturbing
to some.
Read with caution.

With the warmest heart,

Ally Lee

This one is for those who are dealing with trauma. You know who you are you. This story belongs to you.

ONE

WILLOW

I kill with my bare hands. Professionally. But I don't only use the obvious methods such as strangulation or asphyxiation, to apprehend my targets. I also use weapons. Of course, at my clients' discretion. Clients that hire me to carry out a civic duty, a civic duty that avenges the hearts of the scorned and the scorned that unwittingly subject themselves to extreme misogyny. My heart belongs to them. And so do my services.

I'm a hit woman. A trained assassin. The Siren Assassin. And the hallmark of every good assassin is the lack of remorse. To set aside any fear of transgressions that may sliver its way through your psyche. You see, killing isn't for the faint of heart. And if there's anything I learned through my ten years of bloodshed, it's that the world lacks empathy. Me, Willow Harding, case in point.

My trusted accomplice, Meredith McKinley, sits in the passenger seat of my 2014 Cadillac Escalade and passes me the necessary details of my fourth mission of the day.

"Benji Lockson, 27, mayor's son. Prick sits on Daddy's mountain of cash," she snarls, yanking out a white handkerchief, wiping any residue from my previous kill job off my pistol, and handing it to me. "Have to hurry 'cause it's election night for Mr. Mayor," she warns. "This'll make headlines within hours."

I take another hasty puff of my cigarette and drop it out the window, watching it impale the asphalt with smoke and ashes. I mockingly give her the two-finger salute and slip out of the car unnoticed. A hop, skip, and a jump later, I'm in the alleyway of Benji's two-story condominium. Boston winter stabs through my flesh as I dispose of my usual garb of a black turtleneck, black jeans, and combat boots, stuffing the ensemble in my black bookbag. I replace it with a white laced bustier corset, fishnet stockings, black skirt, and pink heels. A sex worker at her finest. Top it off with a platinum blond wig, and I'm golden. I pull out my compact mirror from my bookbag, do a quick primp in the mirror, and when I'm satisfied with my new role for the night, I toss the mirror in my bag and skip up to Mr. Benji Lockson's front porch.

Benji Lockson, the eldest son of Richard Lockson, trust-fund baby with a passion for causing emotional suffering. Cheated on his girlfriend, Marissa Moore, numerous times on presumed business trips to Cancun. A mild offense, you say? If he wasn't an obsessive drunk that would incidentally indulge in physical abuse, I'd say absolutely. And might I not forget, textbook manipulators typically disguise a sex trip as such and, in part, demand their partner not participate in infidelity. I pull out the photos that Marissa's private investigator took of Benji and his mistresses at a beach resort. Nightly, he would meet an island local and bring her to his suite. Classy, to say the least. *My heart belongs to the scorned.*

Mr. Benji Lockson not only employs sex workers when he's on vacation. He even goes as far as inviting them into his personal domain. Throughout my search for Benji's background, I found out that he doesn't just meet random girls and invite them to his luxury townhome for a night of fun under the guise of playing a few rounds of Jenga. He makes a few calls, specifically to his personal assistant, to hire a superficial pillow talk partner for the night, while Ms. Moore is away. Three knocks later, the devil himself opens the door, a Cheshire grin on his face.

"There she is," he slurs, the stench of bourbon on his breath. "I've been waiting for you all night, baby."

It takes all of me to not shiver in disgust. But I manage a ditzy persona, twirling a fake blond strand around my finger. "That's me," I giggle. "I'm Sidney."

"Yes, you are," he says, his gaze inching up and down my body. "You fancy a drink?"

I walk in without responding, and he shuts the door behind me. I muster an exaggerated sigh at the privilege that threatens to assault my eyes. His living room stands in its glory, and it's exactly how I imagined it. Wood panels line the ceiling and walls, and empty bottles of Old Forrester sit on his white fiberstone coffee table. A 98-inch flat screen TV hangs on the wall with a basketball game going. The entire living room looks like it's been decorated and set up by Marissa as it has a feminine touch to it. A white sheepskin rug lies on the hardwood floor underneath the coffee table and gray sectional. It alarms me to notice the large window—with the curtains open—that looks out onto the backyard and another townhouse whose curtains are also open. A compromising position for the kill. We don't need any witnesses.

Before I can think of a way to get the curtains closed, Benji becomes handsy, one large hand cupping one butt cheek and the other wrapping around my hip. "You thinking what I'm thinking?"

"A round of Jenga?"

Anything to find my way to the curtains without drawing suspicion from him. The way I see it, the Jenga box is probably secretly hiding in a closet somewhere. And since he doesn't know I'm aware this is a ruse to get sex, I'm guessing the box isn't opened yet. There's also the chance that he doesn't even have the game.

His eyes are still dilated, but I can see that I just brought him out of his drunken, horny daze. "Jenga sounds good. The box is in the coat closet by the stairs. I can go grab it."

"That'd be amazing. I'll just stay here," I say, putting my hands behind my back.

He gives me another sexual once-over before disappearing around the corner to the coat closet. I watch for a few seconds before silently dashing to the window. The closer I get to his expansive window, the more I see his neighbor across the way prancing around her living room. Chuckling at the dancing queen, I give her a gentle wave when she eyes me, and I close the thankfully opaque white curtains.

"Sarah, Sarah, Sarah," his voice singsongs around the corner. Bastard can't even get my fake name right. But I'm momentarily distracted when he appears with a jumbo bag, presumably filled with jumbo Jenga blocks. Huh. Touché.

"I'm ready whenever you are." I put on a flirty mask. He gives me a wink, drops the bag on his couch, and consumes me in a big embrace, making me yelp.

His nose is already in the crook of my neck, taking in my scent. "You smell like heaven, Sally," he breathes.

"It's Sidney." I pry his arms from around my waist. "And I thought we were playing Jenga."

His torrid gaze up and down my body is back, his eyes dilated with desire. "Jenga can wait for a bit. Care to see my room?"

"Well, I usually engage my clients in small talk. You know, a bit of getting to know each other," I say truthfully, making him laugh.

"We can make small talk in my room. What's the harm in getting a little comfy?" Willow Harding would be unamused with his incessant flirting. But Sidney the Sex Worker is a glutton for a good time.

I twirl another pathetic strand of hair around my finger. "Well…okay," I giggle. "We can talk in your room. Let me get changed into something more comfortable."

He's immediately interested. "Yeah? You brought a change of clothes?"

"Of course I did. I always try to stay prepared when I'm meeting with my clients. I think you'll like it."

He winks at me again. "I'm thinking I will, too, babe. Just be careful where you change. My girlfriend set cameras up around the house, and she's the only one with access to the footage. So try not to get caught."

"Oh, you have a girlfriend?" I feign unaware.

"Yeah. That's okay, right?"

"Of course, that's okay. Thank you for letting me know," I say, blowing him a kiss as he pantomimes catching it. I watch as he scurries up his spiral staircase, and when he disappears around the corner, I pull my black leather gloves from my backpack and begin canvasing the living room for items I may have touched. The curtains are the main thing. I can't dispose of the curtains quite yet because it's still early in the night and his neighbor is most likely still awake, watching TV or trying to figure out why the hell a girl in a bustier and blond wig closed the curtains. I notice a small window in the kitchen looking out onto the backyard. I make quick steps to it and look out, trying to find her house.

And I was right. She's no longer dancing, but she is watching TV, a mystery man having joined her, his arm wrapped around her shoulders. Data point.

"Oh, Sandra! I'm ready whenever you are!" Benji shouts from upstairs.

"I'll be just a second! These panties really are tight, they're hard to get on!" I don't have to see him to know that makes him excited because I can hear an excited squeal. Suddenly amused, I then look around for the cameras Marissa set up. I find one in the kitchen, one in the living room, and one hanging out in the hallway, and I remember seeing one outside in the alleyway and the front of the house. Since the townhomes are designed to be conjoined, it doesn't take long for me to figure out that I have my work cut out for me.

A few touch points later, I cut the cord to all but one of the cameras and send a quick text to Meredith, making sure she can only see through the one camera on a monitor that Marissa helped us link up to. My phone rings, and it's the accomplice in question.

"I can see you pretty clearly on this monitor," Meredith affirms. "Big ups to Marissa for letting us see him do his dirty work."

I glance in the direction of the stairs. "Yeah, well, he thinks he's in for a good fuck. How much time do I have left?"

"Fifty minutes. Make it snappy," she directs. With that, I hang up and quickly change into my lingerie for the night—a fuchsia lace bustier and a lace thong to match. Step one is setting the scene for the kill. Canvasing the room for fingerprints—done. Now it's time to indulge a little bit. Step one is far from over.

I slip my heels back on, pull out a plastic bag from my backpack, and stroll up the twirling staircase. The hallway to his room is an endless one. And yet again, it reeks of sex parties and prestige. I don't miss the bizarre wall art depicting images of nude women and risqué scenes.

Waltzing into their master bedroom, I find a shirtless Benji lying on a king size bed, mischievously smirking up at me. His gaze scours my body, pupils dilating. "You're a sight for sore eyes, Sidney."

"You remember my name," I point out, noting that he acted as if he couldn't care less earlier.

He gets up and crawls to the edge of the bed, prompting me to move closer to him, and a new persona seems to take shape. From clueless drunk to calculated prick, I make another mental note of the duplicity.

"Just keeping you on your toes, darling. Now who gave you permission to look so hot? For fuck's sake, that pink looks amazing against your skin."

"Don't worry about that. When are we making small talk? Jenga's calling my name."

"In a second." His gaze refuses to leave my ensemble. He reaches for my waist, but suddenly the dominating Willow Harding makes her appearance, blocks his hand, and pushes him back onto the bed. His gray boxers tent up in excitement. I've got him where I want him. I reach for the band of his boxers and slowly pull them down, his eyes continuing to dilate in arousal as I throw them across the room.

"Would you say you're a Dom or a sub?" I whisper, cringing inwardly as I ask.

"Depends on what you're in the mood for," he says seductively.

"I was in the mood for small talk, but now you've got me going a little bit." That makes him even more excited.

He tries to reach out to me again, but I'm already off the bed. "I guess we'll see which one you are," I challenge.

Enamored, he watches me take a roll of duct tape out of my bookbag. I make a show of unrolling a strip, and he leans his head on his arms against the headboard, smiling up at me appreciatively.

"Has your girlfriend ever used duct tape before?"

Red splotches trace his cheeks as he rolls his eyes, annoyed that I mentioned her.

"Marissa's too much of a prude to do anything fun in bed," he says with contempt.

I cock an eyebrow. "Marissa's her name? That's pretty."

He shrugs indifferent. "She's okay. Not as stunning as you, Sidney." I try with every ounce of my being not to kill him right now.

"I'm sure that's not true. You're just being nice." I attempt to be coy.

"I'm not. You're really beautiful, Sidney," he says with sincerity, and I almost believe it. The look he's giving me makes me a bit uncomfortable. It's almost as if he's trying to enchant me. I can't fall for it. He's a cheater and an abuser. There's always a charm about most men, which is how I got here in the first place. *My heart belongs to the scorned.*

Little does he know duplicity is my entire alias. So I give him a kiss on the lips. The taste of bourbon and cigarettes envelops my senses. When he tries to deepen it, I quickly pull back.

"Lie back." Like an obedient puppy, he lies down. I grab the roll of duct tape and rip off two long strips.

"What a naughty girl. You're already my favorite call girl." It would be a slap in the face if I didn't deal with men like this as a career. All of the *you're beautifuls* and *if I were singles* are only sweet nothings when dealing with men like this. It's crucial to not give in.

I pull his legs down violently, and he yelps. Trailing kisses up his stomach, I wrap one arm in a long strip of duct tape. "Tug a few times for me."

He looks at me skeptically. "Why?"

"Because we can't have you escape, remember? That's an easy way out," I cajole. His shoulders lessen in tension as he tugs, the tape staying in place. "Good boy."

He gives me a boyish grin as I revel in the fact that it's strong enough…for now. I wrap his other arm with the same amount of duct tape, once again asking him to tug to test the strength of it.

I give him another kiss as encouragement, and this seems to ease him—but only a smidge. When I'm confident he trusts me a bit more, I pull out my sleep mask from my bookbag.

"Uh…what are you planning to do?"

I give him a sexy smile. "Wouldn't you like to know. Do you trust me, Benji?"

"I'm not sure anymore."

Rolling my shoulders back, I lean in. "I'm not going to hurt you. This is supposed to be fun. You wanted to have fun, right?"

He stares at me skeptically for a few seconds before nodding.

"Just making sure this is in good fun. Do your worst, Sidney."

I wink at him and put the sleep mask over his eyes. He clears his throat, and a guttural breath escapes him.

"Do you trust me?" I give him a kiss on the cheek and the lips again to try to ease him. The bastard probably knows he's about to die, but I have to try to steer him away from that thought to avoid too much of a struggle.

"Yes, ma'am, I trust you," he says, attempting to shake out any fear that's left in his body by blowing a raspberry and shaking his legs.

Now that he can't see me, I grab a roll of Gorilla tape from my bag and begin wrapping his arms tighter, making him yelp again. With both duct tape and Gorilla tape wrapped around his wrists, he won't be able to escape at all. I wrap gorilla tape around his legs so he can't wrestle me at any point either.

"Let's set the mood a bit. Do you have any music to play?" I need to drown out any struggle because I can already see he'll be ready to put up a fight when it comes to it.

"I have Alexa. Alexa, play some sexy music!" he shouts as I roll my eyes.

Sultry music fills the bedroom, but the volume isn't loud enough.

"Ask her to turn up the volume a smidge."

He's once again obedient, and the volume goes up. The music seems to comfort him more as he slowly dances through his constraints.

Setting the scene for the kill is done. He's in the mood, and he's right where I want him. I quickly grab my phone out of my bag and see a text from Meredith. Forty minutes left.

Step two. Set up the kill. It's simple. As I've said before, I don't only use methods such as strangulation or asphyxiation. But in this specific kill, either is necessary.

I give him a chaste kiss on the cheek before whispering, "She's still not loud enough. Ask her to turn up the volume a bit?"

He laughs in response, telling the speaker to turn up the volume again.

"Not quite in the mood yet, Sidney?" But I don't answer him. Instead, I take the plastic wrap from before out of my bag and silently place it on an end table beside the bed.

"I'm already in the mood, lover boy." I give him a kiss, and since I disposed of his boxers a while ago, I sit on his length. He mutters a curse when he feels my flesh touch his.

Set up the kill? It's that simple. The method used for course of action is placed where it needs to be, a mere foot away from me. A feral growl escapes the mayor's son, and it momentarily scares me. My fear paces, however, when I notice that it's just a sign of arousal and not an attempt to attack me.

I've rid him of his ability to see and attack me. Now that the setup for the kill is over, you know what happens next. And it's the most enthralling, thrilling step of the kill sequence.

I give his length a tug, causing his hips to jut out.

"Go slow, baby," he growls again.

I lean down and kiss his temple. "Aye, aye, Captain."

To get him even more excited, I slide forward and slowly begin undulating against him. He lets out a satisfied groan, lifting his hips to meet me in arousal. The sensual music filling the bedroom seems perfect for Mr. Benji Lockson.

Reaching for his phone on the side table, I tap the screen. Luckily, he doesn't have it locked with the requirement to put in a passcode. Rookie mistake. I quickly find the Alexa app on his phone and use the slider function in the app to turn up the volume, music once more surrounding at a fuller volume.

I continue riding him, and he grows more aroused. His fingers grip the wraps of tape around his wrists in an effort to tear them off, but the Gorilla tape is no small feat. My phone screen lights up in my peripherals. I try to continue riding him while reaching slowly for it.

"Did you turn the volume up again?"

But I don't respond. Meredith's text quickly grabs my attention.

MEREDITH: T - 30 minutes, Low.

Challenge accepted. The easiest way for this to work is perfect timing. Timing is everything for executing the kill. You don't want to put the target off by any unconventional behavior. Setting up for the kill consisted of making him feel at ease and exploit exactly what he gets off on: control. My heartbeat speeds up in anticipation as always in this stage. His groans fill the room as I reach for the plastic bag neatly placed on the table next to me.

I use the slider function in his app to turn up the volume again as I brace for the kill. I do a hard, calculated ride against him, and his groan clashes with the music.

"Sidney?" His voice becomes worried through the groans. "How are you turning the volume up?"

I slowly prep the plastic wrap in my hands, lean down and whisper, "What do you know about the Mississippi River?"

"What?"

"It takes about three months for one drop of water to travel the Mississippi River's length." His movement slow as confusion etches his eyebrows.

"Sidney?"

Ignoring him calling my name, I slide the volume up yet again. I lean down to his ear again. "Do you think it'll take that long for the police to find your body, Benji?"

He shakes his head in confusion and tries to tug on the wraps around his wrists, but he's not fast enough. I thrash the plastic wrap over his head as his entire body begins wailing in horror. His muffles are suffocated by the music.

"Let's do this times 10, okay?" He shouts in response as his struggle becomes more vicious. "One Mississippi."

His skin turns a shade of pink, and I know it'll be quick work. My guess is he's already dehydrated. Which means he's lacking a bit of oxygenation.

"Two Mississippi." Plastic goes in and out of his mouth as he tries to search for air, but it's no use. I quickly pull up the app again and slide the volume up to 10.

Music blasts the room, and his struggles only become a far cry. As far as I am concerned, my work here is done. Now there's some time to change the kill execution a bit. The bastard's stuck in plastic wrap. He can't unwrap himself from the scourges of tape around his wrists and ankles. However, with him thrashing across the bed in mayhem, executing the kill is far from over.

Leaving him to his convulsing attempts to break free from his restraints, I jump off his body and throw everything in my bookbag as his cries fill the room. I canvas the room for fingerprints again and dash downstairs. All his curtains are closed, so there are no witnesses. I look through the kitchen window yet again to see if his neighbor is awake, and she's no longer in the living room. Given that the lights are off, it's safe to assume she's turned in for the night. Cleansing is an early step for this kill job, but this has taken longer than I anticipated.

I yank the curtain down, shove it in a large garbage bag, and peek around the corner to change into my black turtleneck, black jeans, and black combat boots. I stuff both Sidney ensembles into my bookbag, take down the cameras around the house, stuff them into the garbage bag, turn off the lights, and rush out of the house. His cries stopped awhile ago. Executing the kill and cleansing are done.

Meredith gets out of the Escalade and walks up to me, satisfaction plastered across her face.

"Thirteen minutes to spare. It amazes me to see your talent on these kills."

I shrug in indifference, throwing the garbage of evidence in the backseat. "He stopped breathing not too long ago."

She chuckles and shakes her head, jumping back into the passenger seat as I walk around to the driver side.

I drive to the city river's overlook, park, and dispose of the garbage bag of evidence. The river breeze oddly provides a sense of calm and rebirth. My tenth kill of the week, and it's only Wednesday. And while it's another successful kill, something seems to be missing. The thrill is cheap. I need something worthwhile.

"Valerie will be here any minute. Let's get back in the car," Meredith warns.

Contemplating will have to wait. My decoy, Valerie, is an ex-convict who…to put it in simplest terms, has nothing to lose. All she's been instructed to do is to be a decoy for when the police investigate Benji's death and explain that she killed him in self-defense at his townhouse. Whatever may come of the crime is fine with her. She's supposed to be meeting us here so I can pay her and give her the Sidney ensemble. Since we had nearly fifteen minutes to spare for the job, though, she's not quite here.

When she does arrive at the river, I hand her the payment and the outfit and give her the list of instructions. When I remind her that it's not promised she won't go to jail, all she says is, "What happens happens," and then she's gone as fast as she came.

Meredith and I agree to have a meeting tomorrow for my next scheduled kill job, and then I drop her off at her condo.

My mission is complete. The last step of the sequence is to cleanse, and it's far from over. And there's no better way to cleanse than a drink.

TWO

WILLOW

The check clears faster than I expect it to. When the notification that Marissa sent me $7,000 flashes across my phone's screen, I take an even happier sip of my Manhattan. I'm finishing my cleanse of the night at my usual place, The Tacky Sand Bar.

"You still good, Low?" the bartender, Vinny, asks.

I give him a lazy nod, holding up my nearly finished Manhattan. "I'll take another. It's been a tiring night."

His crooked grin is something I've come to get used to in the last twenty-five years. Vinny DeMarco was a friend of my father's. Vinny and his wife, Kara, have been co-owners of the bar for forty years. Dad was also part owner until he died when I was twenty years old.

"Doing the Lord's work again?"

I shrug. "What do you think, Vin? $7,000 isn't something to ignore."

He sighs, tossing his dish rag on the bar. "How many jobs have you done this week already? You said it's your tenth job."

"Your point?"

"I've seen you grow up, Low. Your dad told me to take care of you. I remember you as the happy-go-lucky little girl, and now"—he looks around to make sure no one hears him—"you're a killer."

"Okay?"

There it is. The look. The 'disappointed dad' look that I haven't seen in a decade. Ten years ago, my dad died from pancreatic cancer and didn't think to tell me he even had it. He claimed the reason he waited so long to talk about it was because I was busy at college. But that didn't stop me from stonewalling him. I wish I hadn't. The last time I saw my dad alive was that argument. Six months later, July 9th, he took his last breath. The aftermath? It's a long fucking story.

"Your dad wouldn't want—"

"—me to be a professional vigilante. We have this conversation all the time."

"And nothing seems to change."

"Vinny, I get it. I promise," I snap.

"Kara and I are all you have left, honey. Your mom's married to a jerk-off. You don't have a man in your life to take care of you…"

"I don't need a man to take care of me. You're all I need."

He gives me a humorous look. "I'm not a man now?"

That little quip breaks the tension. "You know what I mean," I say, refusing to let my imminent smile slip out.

A hearty laugh escapes him as his eyes crinkle at the sides.

"I can't stop you because you're a grown woman. But how long until you're no longer contracted with this criminal organization?"

"Kill Elite Inc. isn't a criminal organization. And I'm not contracted with them anymore. I'm a killer for hire."

Usually, an admission of something like this would cause someone to raise their eyebrow. But this is Vinny. And he knows my story. A story that haunts me every fucking day.

"I think I'll take it from here, Vinny," a masculine voice says beside me, making my shoulders tense.

A look of disbelief surfaces across Vinny's face. "I think you're barking up the wrong tree, son," he says, chuckling.

"I think the beautiful lady can speak for herself."

Already annoyed with the asshole trying to get my attention, I make a horrible mistake that I know I'll regret and turn to see who the fuck he is. And the bastard is so beautiful it hurts.

A man with a chiseled jawline and strikingly hazel eyes is grinning at me like I'm his prey. The same man I had a glimpse of when I first sat at the bar, talking to another woman across the bar. Trauma threatens to slip through the cracks, and I'm prepared to put on a shield when looked at like I'm defenseless.

"I'm okay, Vinny. We'll continue this talk later, all right?"

He doesn't look convinced as his gaze wavers between me and the man still looking down at me. When I give him a reassuring nod, he grabs his dish rag, gives the sexy prick a once-over, and continues his rounds with other guests at the bar.

I turn again to the man who rivals a true Viking, and the smirk is still on his face.

"Is there something I can help you with?"

His perfect eyebrows shoot to the sky. "Is that an invitation, honey?"

"It's a genuine question, love," I say, impassively.

"We're already at the 'love' stage. I was hoping you'd treat me to a drink first, but hey, I'll bite," he says, winking.

I tilt my head, trying to figure him out. He's flirty, handsome, and cocky. But I don't detect anything sleazy about him. I'm generally good at determining how sleazy someone is.

"What's your name, mystery girl?" He takes a seat next to me, with growing interest.

Almost on time, Vinny sets my third Manhattan down. I take a quick sip.

"Willow."

Vinny hands him an Old Fashioned. "Willow. Like the graceful tree."

"I didn't know I was talking to a tree connoisseur."

A hearty chuckle feels like velvet on my skin. "Everyone knows about the willow tree." He leans on his elbows, gaze still examining me like a lab dissection. "Willow. I like it."

What the hell is this dude's deal? I don't talk to men for recreation. I usually hate male attention. But this doesn't feel…awful.

"I'm assuming you want something."

He shrugs, stretching his arms, his tight sleeves riding up, exposing his biceps.

"I don't want anything, darling. I just wanted to talk to you."

I scoff in disbelief. "You wanted to talk to a stranger?" I look around the bar, eyeing the beautiful women either sitting in lounge chairs or chatting with their friends at the bar. I'm wearing a black turtleneck and black jeans, and I'm sure I smell like cheap bourbon and lethal musk.

"Are you blind?"

His eyes crinkling at the sides tells me he has to be at least five years my senior.

"How do you know Vinny?" he asks, taking a sip of his Old Fashioned.

And there it is. The small talk meant to break down my walls and leave me exposed. Lots of men use this tactic, and I have to recognize it as a data point, even when it's not for a kill.

"Just a family friend." I keep it short and sweet. But the gleam in his eyes doesn't relent. The dastardly charming man remains his persona, and I'm not sure how to feel about it.

"I see how it is, gorgeous. Not much of a talker?"

"Not after a kill."

This catches his attention. I feel his gaze on me, as well as a change in demeanor. I sneak a look at him, and he's visibly confused.

"After a kill?"

"Exactly."

"That sounds like a good conversation starter." He shifts, seemingly more interested in talking. "Because either you're fucking with me, or you're the woman of my dreams."

I snap my head back to him. "Come again?"

"Again? I didn't do it the first time yet, gorgeous."

I shift in my barstool, feeling my core heat. "You're kinky. And cheesy."

Another guttural chuckle vibrates through him. "Sorry, I guess I'm just a cheesy guy. Now what is it with you and killing?"

I've spoken too much. What was meant to be a deceptive attempt to get him the fuck away didn't work.

"Nothing. I was kidding."

"Odd joke," he remarks.

"I'm an odd girl. Now go away."

But he doesn't let up. "I have time to chat. Leif."

"What?"

"I'm Leif. Leif Mattson. Figured we'd get the names out of the way before we dive deeper into the *getting-to-know-each-other* stage."

I look at him.

Really look at him.

Again, all I see is sincerity. When you're me, you know the signs to look for. Arrogance. Malice. Sadism. Manipulation. Easy characteristics to spot in my line of work and history with men. It's par for the course.

But with Mr. Leif Mattson…my radar is certainly malfunctioning.

"Why don't we cut the bullshit, eh, Mr. Mattson?"

His brows furrow in confusion. "What?"

I look across the room at the woman he was talking to as she scowls at me. *I'm not the one you need to be angry at, honey.*

"I'm not sure what kind of game you're playing here, all right? Usually, my radar is pretty good at detecting bullshitters, and for whatever reason, it's malfunctioning. Your suave approach was cute, nonetheless, but suspicious. Why are you over here?"

I render him speechless, dumbstruck evident on his face. "That's a mouthful, darling."

"Not hardly. What do you want?"

"I already answered this question. I wanted to talk to you."

"You magically got that epiphany while you were chatting with Pippi Longstocking?" I nod to the redhead in question, eyes still piercing into the side of my face.

His perfect, chiseled cheeks have the audacity to redden as his gaze follows. "Caught me red-handed, would you say?"

I stare at him again, dumbfounded. The playful smirk he's giving me is affecting me in ways I haven't felt in a long time, and it pisses me off.

"What would she say about you bouncing from woman to woman in a bar?"

He shrugs as if it's a silly question. "Who cares about what she would have to say about it?"

"Don't be a dick."

"How am I being a dick? She's not my wife or fiancée or—hell—even girlfriend."

"Oh yeah? Then what is she?"

He chuckles. "You're hilarious. Why are you asking? You want to be my girlfriend?"

A hearty bellow escapes me. "Hey, Vinny! Your friend over here clearly is drinking too much. Cut him off, will ya?"

Vinny shakes his head in amusement.

"Seriously, doll, I just wanted to talk to you. No harm, no foul. I'm not here to talk you out of your panties."

"Bluffing isn't a virtue," I say with disdain.

"Okay, fine. I think you're sexy, yes. I barely know you, and I can already tell you'll push my buttons."

"You're saying you barely know me, and I already annoy you?"

"I'm saying maybe I like my buttons pushed."

Okay. I won't lie. That was hot. But again, there's always a catch.

"And I'm saying it's insulting that you think I'm easy."

"Who said I thought you were easy? All I've been doing is being friendly, and you've already written me off."

I put my Manhattan down and face him. "Leif. I'm not in the market for a date."

"Never said you were, honey."

"Are you looking for a fuck?"

"I'm not gonna turn down a night of fun. So if you're offering…"

For a moment, I think about it. The bastard is ogling me, eyes already dilated. I'd be foolish to leave a bar with a man I don't know. But it's been a few years since I've been touched by a man. And one night of letting off some steam won't hurt.

In my moment of rumination, my gaze lands on a face peering at me.

It's a woman.

She looks a bit disheveled. Her dark brown hair is up in a messy bun, and she's cradling a gray knit cardigan to her. Almost as if she's protecting herself from an outside presence. My hit woman instincts tell me to canvass the bar to see who appears to be a threat to this vulnerable woman who's gazing curiously at me. Something else strikes me, though. She seems familiar. I'm not sure what it is, but something about her feels as if we've met.

But before I have time to survey what's happening and determine why I know her, the woman is gone as fast as she was seen. I look at the entrance, and the doors swivels, signaling that she left. Odd.

My gaze finds Vinny as he looks at me, seemingly waiting for me to decide what the hell I'm going to do with the brazen giant in front me, looking at me like a dog in heat. Vinny cocks an eyebrow, asking if everything is okay. I give him a reassuring nod. He looks between us again, still a bit hesitant before looking away and making a cocktail for a guest.

"You wanna get out of here?"

His cocoa eyes brightening is enough answer for me. And the next thing I know, I'm downing the rest of my Manhattan, and Leif rests his hand on the nape of my back.

It doesn't fully register that I'm fraternizing with the rival species, though, until my panties and jeans hit the floor in his apartment. But it really registers when we're rolling in his sheets. And when it's all said and done, he cuddles me against him, his soft snores a mere whisper in a sea of regrets and my trying conscience.

THREE

WILLOW

W*illow Harding and The Walk of Shame.*
I can't say I've never seen anything like it.
Desperation is tricky thing. Deprivation even more so. Of
the sexual variety, of course. In my line of work, there's
just simply no time for it. Much less a desire for it.

Leif stirs as I gently pry his arm from around me. He
goes against the movement, pulling me closer to him. If I
didn't have a meeting with Meredith in an hour, I'd find it
adorable in the most condescending way possible. But I'm
only slightly amused. The unamused part of me needs to
get the hell up and out.

"It's early," he groans against my back.

"Perfect for killing," I quip.

Sighing, he sits up, exposing his eight-pack abs. Never
in my life have I met a man with such a chiseled body, from
cheekbones, to chin, to jaw, to torso. Even his legs look
like tree trunks. But perhaps I need to stop salivating over

my one-night stand. I'm not in the market to have extended conversations with men I've slept with.

"Women are usually more clingy after sex."

I get up, looking for my bra. "I'm almost thirty. So I'll go against the grain and express the sentiment that penis isn't magical."

"You break my heart, Willow," he jokes, clutching his chest.

Rolling my eyes, I slip my bra on and look for the rest of my usual ensemble. "I have a good therapist to suggest."

"The queen of interesting conversation starters. Seriously, what's the deal? You're kind of fucking up my ego."

"I have to go."

"I can drop you off."

"I'm not going home."

"Okay, I can take you to work."

This devilishly handsome man will not let up. "The kind of work I do, you can't take me to work."

He runs a hand through his dark curls. "What are you, in the CIA or something? FBI?"

"If I tell you, I'd have to kill you."

He chuckles. "Okay, you're definitely in the FBI."

Sighing, I slip my jeans on. "Whatever helps you sleep at night." But I flinch when I feel his callused hands roam my stomach.

"What are you hiding from me?" he asks, placing a kiss on my shoulder. This feels way too intimate.

"I'm not hiding anything. I just have a meeting that I need to go to."

"I can drop you off," he repeats.

I move away from him. "Why? It's not your responsibility to drop me off."

"Um, because it's the nice thing to do? I have to be your boyfriend to do that?"

"I don't need a boyfriend or you to drop me off."

"Isn't your car still at the bar?"

Shit. I run my hand through my hair, contemplating whether I should try to pull it out of my scalp. This is why I don't do one-night stands. I can't make errors like leaving bars in the middle of the night with men without my car. This could've been a kill job, and I've already made myself susceptible to being killed. Which is a huge no-no.

"I guess I did," I grit through my teeth. "How stupid."

He chuckles, slipping a T-shirt over his huge biceps and toned pecs.

"It's not a big deal. I won't drop you off at your job if it makes you uncomfortable. But at least let me drop you off at your car. It's a long walk back to the bar. Vinny probably wouldn't like it if I made you walk back. I'm assuming he's a family friend?"

"Basically an uncle," I affirm.

He nods understandingly. "Vinny will kill me if he sees you out those windows walking up to your car, no one dropping you off in sight. He'll want to know where the hell you went."

"You probably have a busy day ahead of you," I look for any excuse to get out of this.

He scoffs. "Don't be ridiculous. I'm not doing anything today. It's my off day."

Well, now I'd just look prideful if I say no.

"Fine. You want to put on your gentleman pants? Fine."

He chuckles, shaking his head. And we leave it at that.

The drive back to the bar is a quiet one. It feels weird to be driving in this car, knowing that we just had a one-night stand. And while I've vowed to write off men for a few years now, there's something about him that's…enthralling. Why is this gorgeous man being nice to me?

We reach the bar, and I quickly get out. "Thank you for the ride."

"Wait. I had a good time last night," he stops me.

"I did, too. That was the point."

A nervous chuckle escapes him as he runs a hand through his hair yet again. "Don't make me beg, Willow. This kind of thing isn't in my wheelhouse."

"I don't get it."

"Can I have your number?"

"I told you, I don't date."

"I didn't say anything about dating. You want to be friends with benefits? Fine. We can do that. I just want an excuse to see you again. Even it means only doing the fun stuff," he says, winking.

I have no idea how we got here. Last night was only supposed to be a one-time thing. I needed to let off some steam from a kill job, and Leif is gorgeous. It seemed like the perfect opportunity. But now he's asking to make this a regular arrangement.

"If you promise not to walk up to me in the bar ever again in front of my uncle, then we have a deal. No one can know about it."

He throws his hands up in surrender. "You have my word, beautiful."

"And that," I say, pointing. "Don't do that. If this is going to be a casual arrangement, don't flirt with me. We're simply friends who…do things together."

"You can say *have sex*, honey. It's not a bad word," he chuckles.

Rolling my eyes, I hold my hand out for his phone, and he hands it to me. I put my number in his contacts. He sends me a text, and my phone beeps in my pocket. The smile he gives me is endearing…and I hate it.

"Perfect. I'll text you later?"

"Whenever you want to, dude," I say, walking off. All I hear is his deep, throaty chuckle vanish in the distance. I approach my SUV and chance a glance at Leif as he drives off. The little fucker.

I hop into my car, and my phone already pings with a message from Meredith. I text that I'm on my way and pull out of the bar lot.

"Kara Carmichael. Daughter of oil heir Lawrence Carmichael. Fiancé is Arnold Bryant, law student at Boston University."

Meredith slaps the beauty queen's profile down in front of me, and I'm immediately enamored with her platinum blond hair. She's wearing a silver sash which reads *Miss Massachusetts USA*. Her eyes are a piercing green, and the smile she sports is contagious. It seems surreal that even a stunningly happy girl like her can fall victim to the idiocy that is the male species.

"What's the damage?" I flip her photo over and look over the details of her situation.

Meredith clicks on her projector, showing a presentation.

"In the simplest terms, sexual coercion," she says, flipping to the next page, revealing a battered Kara with black eyes and busted lip. "They engage in sex without her consent. When she rejects it, he gets violent. The last time she rejected sex after a long day of final exams, he sent her to the hospital. She had to lie to authorities because of his pedigree, but it seems as if she's come to a point where she's fed up."

I flex my fingers as she flips to the next slide of the presentation, titled *Next Course of Action*.

"And what's his pedigree?"

She skips the current slide and lands on a slide titled *The Target*.

"Father is Senator Andrew Bryant. Apparently, having an oil heir for a father doesn't do much to protect you. Especially when the fucker is on track to follow in his dad's footsteps."

Kills like these are what I live for. The more advantageous the target is, the more I yearn to bathe in their golden tears.

"How'd she contact you?"

She shrugs, shutting the presentation off.

"Her sorority sister apparently used your services before on her boyfriend at the time and recommended you to her. Mitchell Moseley ring a bell to you?"

I wince in disgust. How could I forget? I get my clients through referrals, and Sarah Hensley's now-deceased boyfriend was one of the most tedious kill jobs I've ever done to date. He was a big guy, so it was difficult to apprehend him. And it didn't help that he lived in a luxury high-rise with a 24/7 bellhop and surveillance cameras everywhere in the building. Sneaking a decoy in proved harder than I had expected, so there were arrangements to be made and thought of. Thankfully, Sarah had warned me of such a huge feat.

"When does she need the job done?"

"We have some time. She wants it done by 48 hours."

"Sounds good to me. Can you draft up a mission treatment and we can meet tonight about it?"

She nods and types something into her phone.

"Will you have time to have a meeting tonight, or do you have another hot date?" she teases.

I freeze. "What?"

"Your Uncle Vinny isn't great at keeping your love life to himself, Low. He told me to come to the bar with you next time so handsome rugby players don't hit on you in front of him again."

"He really needs to mind his business," I groan. "And what do you mean by 'handsome rugby players'?"

"Yeah, he said Leif Mattson took you home for the night," she says, wiggling her eyebrows.

"You know him?"

"He's pretty big in the rugby world. He's the captain of the New England Hornets. I don't watch much rugby, but Vinny gets a lot of high profile at the bar, apparently."

"For fuck's sake," I mutter. Why wouldn't he say something if he had that information? "I already have too much on my plate to have a casual relationship with a high profile athlete."

She shrugs. "It could be fun. Maybe you need to let off some steam."

"With an athlete?"

"Yeah? So?"

"I'm supposed to be off men."

"And yet, your lady parts didn't think so."

"Mer, please, never say that shit to me again."

She stifles a laugh. "I don't think it's such a bad thing to have some fun while you're completing kills. You're obviously not marrying the dude, so let loose a little."

Meredith has been my best friend since childhood. She's always been an advocate for me living life on the edge. After my most recent trauma, she's been advocating even more so. Given her upbringing, it's the only way she can cope. Toxic parents in a toxic marriage in a toxic home makes for a toxic state of mind. And I can't say I don't love her for it. Because her insight has helped me in more ways than I can explain.

It's my safe haven. My crutch, essentially. Ever since that bastard, my life as a vigilante completes me. Entices me in ways you can't imagine. There's a rush when the first blade pierces the skin of my vicious target. A thrill when the last bullet claims the life of a brute. Euphoria when a low life takes his last breath when he asphyxiates. Day by day, kill by kill, the excitement never fails me. And once this kill is through, I'll be bathing in the tears and bloodshed, ultimately cleansing, hungry for the next one. Call me a psychopath, but I have my reasons. Reasons that would be controversial to some and viable to others. The fact of the matter is, I serve out acts of justice in an unjust world. And I wouldn't have it any other way.

"You're doing it again."

"Doing what?" I grunt.

"Your 'Willow' thing again. Your wheels are spinning, and I assume it's about that prick."

A zap of electricity shoots through my bloodstream. "I can't get the fucker out of my mind. What can I say?"

"You were glowing this morning, though. Maybe you can finally stop thinking about that asshole."

If I could show it, I'm blushing, and I hate it. "I wasn't glowing."

"Yes, you are. And it's okay. Good sex does that."

"Are we done talking about this now? I have a kill to get ready for."

But she won't let up, and a sly smile stretches across her porcelain skin.

"All right, Miss Testy. We'll talk about this when your panties aren't in a wad," she teases.

I ignore her, gather up Kara Smithson's files, and I'm on my way home, Meredith's arrogant chuckle not far behind me.

My phone beeps with a voicemail notification. I pull it out, cursing myself for forgetting my appointment. It's only 12, and I'm off my usual schedule. If I hadn't met that Leif guy, I wouldn't be this discombobulated.

I shoot her a text, and I'm on my way to her office.

FOUR

WILLOW

Bereavement leave. At the ripe old age of 20. I didn't think I'd get it approved, but I'm happy I did. Life takes you on a weird trajectory sometimes. And all you can do is adjust.

He took his last breath after a long battle. A battle I knew nothing about. Fuck cancer is a saying I've heard all too often, but it never applied more to me than now.

"How are you holding up?" is the first question my mom and dad's best friend, Vinny, asks. He's like a second father to me.

"Holding up as best I can, I guess," I say, picking at the flowers left on one of the funeral wake's tables. "Mom didn't have the decency to come?"

His silence speaks volumes. When you're Marlena Walsh nee Harding, there are other pressing issues. And going to your ex-husband's funeral just isn't one of them.

"When do you need to go back to base?" He attempts to change the subject.

"One more week" is all I add.

"If you need to, Caroline and I don't mind if you need a place to stay until it's time to go back."

"That's all right, Vinny. Meredith is letting me stay with her."

He nods his understanding, gives me a comforting hug, and leaves to join Caroline.

After a plethora of hors d'oeuvres and a scourge of hugs and comfort, I'm driving back with Meredith to her apartment.

When we get there, I set down my suitcase and jump on the bed she set up for me.

"You're always welcome here," she says. I give her a tight smile because there's not much else to say. "What are you feeling like tonight? Pizza? Chinese?"

"Chinese should be fine."

She nods and skirts off in the direction of her room.

I plop down on my back, looking up at the ceiling. My goddamn dad. He's gone forever now. And the last time I spoke to him, I told him I needed time to get over the fact that he kept it a secret from me for so long. In hindsight, I basically told him to never speak to me again. And it's fucking 20/20.

"Willow?"

I shake my head of the flashback and shift my attention to Ms. Marshall.

"Yes."

"How are you feeling, dear?"

"I'm feeling fine, Connie. I just forgot that I had a session with you today. I lost track of time."

"I don't mean that." She looks down at the scratch marks on my arms that are raised. I pull my sleeve down, trying to cover it. "How long have you been harming yourself?"

"I'm not harming myself. These are…from an accident."

Her eyebrows shoot to the roof in concern. "You were in an accident?"

"Yes, but I'm okay. These marks will go away, I promise."

Or not ever. They typically don't. Which is exactly why having one-night stands makes me feel queasy. The daunting question of where the hell I got scratch marks and a batch of abrasions on every area of skin imaginable is not one I would like to dabble in.

Ms. Marshall scribbles a few notes in her notepad as I shift my gaze to the city outside. A dense fog envelops metropolitan Boston like a crisp sheet, and the overcast skies attempt to mask a burgeoning evil that haunts the city. I've completed ten kills this week. I've yet to have a break. You'd think that humanity would get the hint after my nearly ten years of murders making the news. But expecting evil to dissipate after a slew of killings in a big city is a fantasy. Humans will always think of themselves as invincible.

"What was the accident, if you don't mind me asking?"

"What?"

She tilts her head as if to inspect me. "The marks on your arms. What caused the accident?"

"I'm not sure if I'd like to talk about that."

She looks at me in disbelief. "You can't hide forever, Willow. Our time together always ends in suspense."

"What would you like me to say?"

"I'd like to know if you're hurting yourself."

"I already told you that I'm not."

She looks at me, concerned. There's nothing to discuss. I only come to see her as a promise to Vinny, following my huge nervous breakdown ten years ago. I've told him numerous times that I don't need to see a therapist. I've been handling Dad's death and my trauma pretty well with my line of work. Is it a screwed-up way to cope?

Theoretically, yes. But it's not anyone's place to tell me how to cope. I know what I'm doing.

After our brief moment of silence, she shuts her notebook, letting out a resigned sigh. "One of these sessions, we'll have a productive talk."

"One of these days, Connie. Today just isn't that day, I guess."

She lets out a humorless chuckle. "When would you like to schedule our next session?"

My phone suddenly beeps with a text from Meredith. She wants to have a meeting for another kill job.

"I'll schedule with you when I can find some time to do it. I have an urgent meeting for work." I signal to my phone.

"And what kind of work is that?" She continues to pry.

My shoulders tense. "Contractual work."

I sense that she wants to ask more about it, but I'm already up and out of my seat, muttering a goodbye and dashing out of the door.

Vinny's bar is bustling with an energy I've never seen before. Men in rugby jerseys are sitting at the bar, yelling obscenities at the TV screen.

My gaze lands on Meredith as she drinks from a beer mug, also embracing the vulgarity that surrounds her. Vinny eyes me as I walk up to the bar, giving a look of annoyance at the enthusiastic group in front of him.

I tap Meredith on the shoulder, making her jump, and the mug she's holding spills with beer toppling over her hand.

"Dammit, Low. Try warning me next time," she grumbles, slamming her mug down and wiping her hand on a cloth.

"It's kind of hard to warn someone when the entire bar is in uproar over a game," I shout. "Why is rugby on?"

She shrugs. "New England pride. That's a silly question."

Rolling my eyes, I do my best to detach from the chaos around us. "Is there a reason you wanted to meet here? It's a little rowdy to talk about a kill job."

She gives me a sly grin before nodding her head toward the big flatscreen TV, and my stomach nearly drops to my bladder.

Leif is on the goddamn TV, running in his tightly fitted striped shirt and white shorts, ball in hand. What the hell? He told me it was his day off today.

"Fucking hell," I curse.

She giggles mischievously, ignoring my outrage. Soon, the bar starts chanting something that I can't make out because I'm staring daggers at Meredith's profile as she begins chanting with the men next to us. Traitor.

Leif sprints toward the goal, dodging other beefy men running at him, and it's quite impressive to watch. The chants grow as I feel my heart beat louder. This out-of-body experience is weird as hell. This can't be the same guy I was in bed with less than 24 hours ago. The man I met in the bar last night was sexy and confident, sure—but this man…this focused, menacing, sturdy mountain of man running across an expansive field is something I was not prepared to ever see.

It isn't until he tosses it to a teammate, and his teammate passes it back to him, that Leif slides across the ground, causing the entire bar to join in an uproar. Meredith jumps up in victory along with the men beside us. Vinny even joins in on the excitement, while I take a long sip of Meredith's beer from her mug.

It's another few moments before the crowd calms down in the bar and Meredith turns to me.

"Good game, right?"

I stare at her in disbelief. "Is this why you wanted me here?"

"Kinda," she giddily says. "Your man was kicking ass on that field, Low."

"This was a waste of time," I murmur. "I thought we were meeting tonight. I have a kill job tomorrow, and you brought me here under the pretense of an actual meeting."

"I thought it was funny," she says matter-of-factly.

"Am I laughing, Mer?"

"Maybe on the inside," she jokes. "What's got your panties in a wad, anyway?"

She's right. I shouldn't be taking my therapy session out on her. "Connie just pissed me off more than usual today. She kept prying about the scratches on my arms. It wouldn't really be a productive session if I confided in her that I'm professional killer, and marks are just part of the job. " I glance at the marks in question.

Meredith lets out a whistle that sends a message of 'that's tough.'

"So I'm assuming it was another counterproductive session with Mother Gothel?"

Her tongue-in-cheek nickname for Connie isn't new to my ears. Attempting to assume the role of mother figure, Connie has always been a nuisance. She means well, but it does get exhausting, being examined every session like a zoo animal.

"I want to put that awkwardness behind me. What's the game plan tomorrow?"

Meredith has set up a meeting time with Kara tonight in the private room upstairs to discuss the details of the kill. Vinny's bar has two floors, and the second floor essentially has the ambience of a speakeasy. Vinny knows what the meeting is about. We really didn't have to say much. Once Meredith told him that we need to meet with a man about a dog, he gave a look of understanding—though hesitant—and assured us that he would make sure no one goes upstairs between midnight and 3 a.m.

When the chaos calms down at an exponential pace, we order another round of drinks and still marvel at Leif and his entourage of Hornets winning in such a victorious fashion. Meredith tells me that it was the first game of the season. The game was so close against the Chicago team, and according to Meredith, they almost beat New York's team at the national rugby championships last season. So our team winning against them is a pretty good way to start off the season. The ironic thing about this entire situation is that I've always had a thing for athletes. Cliché? Certainly. But like any other girl, the general fascination with athletes in their trade is that they're also athletes in bed. Sue me.

It's doing me no good picturing how good in bed Leif was. I take a much-needed sip of my Manhattan and lock eyes with a familiar face.

The same woman that was staring at me yesterday. Except her dark brown hair is in a French braid, and she looks more cleaned up than she did last night. I look away for a minute to make sure I'm not hallucinating and become more puzzled when I turn to find her still staring at me.

"Meredith," I mumble. "There's a brunette woman to our right. Near the door."

She slowly turns her head in the woman's direction. My heart pumps with a weird anticipation I haven't felt in a long time.

"There's no one standing there."

I quickly look in the direction of the front door, and it's uncanny. The woman is gone.

Groaning, I cradle my head in my hands in frustration. "What the fuck is wrong with me?"

"You're not having hallucinations, are you?"

"I honestly have no idea anymore. I saw her here last night, too. When Leif was trying his lame pickup lines on me. She was staring at me as if she knew me."

Meredith snorts. "Lame pickup lines? I don't think they were that lame if you were so quick to hop into bed with him."

"Mer. I'm trying to talk to you."

Straightening her shoulders, she changes her entire demeanor. "Sorry. This woman was eyeing you, you say?"

"Mer." She thinks I'm kidding.

"Am I wrong?"

Shrugging, I toy with the straw as it sits lazily in my diluted whiskey drink. "Something about her seems odd."

"Maybe she thought you were pretty."

"Mer, stop. Staring at me once on one day, that's just a coincidence. Stare at me again the next day? Come on, that's fucking creepy."

She laughs, shaking her head in disbelief. "Paranoia is normal before a kill job. You think everyone's on to you when you're about to strangle someone in less than 48 hours." Meredith's indecency catches the attention of the drunk rugby fans at the bar. "Obviously, I'm kidding, jackasses."

They all give her a humorless laugh before going back to their scheduled program.

"It feels like I'm babysitting a hyper nine-year-old," I scold her.

She rolls her eyes. "Hey, I'm not the one freaking out and crawling out of my skin because someone was staring at me in public."

"I'm over this conversation. But if the woman shows up again and looks at me, I'm going to say something."

I'm not sure why seeing the woman freaks me out. It just does. Two nights in a row is not a coincidence. She must know me somehow. And something tells me it's a future client. Judging by how unkempt she looked last night, she could be a victim of domestic abuse. She could be a reference from a past client. Until she gets the gall to approach me, I'll keep an eye out and remain open.

It's fifteen minutes until midnight, and Meredith and I are still drowning in our drinks. I'm not even sure I'll be lucid enough to have a sustainable meeting with Kara Carmichael. I'm down to my fifth round of the night, and I'm already lying down at the bar.

"Keep your head up, Low," Meredith slurs. "We have to talk about the gig for tomorrow."

I groan, picking up my head. "Do we have to? My head feels like I'm lifting a rock."

"Rocks aren't heavy," she says, rubbing her eyes.

"Fiiine, Mer. You want me to say a boulder?"

"Seriously. Kara's going to show up soon, and we need to show that we're professionals. Not loser drunks."

This time, I snort in disbelief. I flag Vinny down, dismiss his chuckles of mockery, and we gulp down the glasses of water he sets in front of us.

"Professionals, my ass," Vinny jokes.

"Can it, Vinny," I grumble. He walks away, still laughing at our misery.

We sober up as best we can, and before we know it, Kara strolls in, an aura of uncertainty looming over her.

I share a look with Vinny as he nods in her direction. I take a few more sips of water, and Meredith does the same before she gets up and greets our client.

"Behave," Vinny warns me. "Don't use my speakeasy as a kiln if you ever decide to cremate your victims." He suddenly flinches. "Damn, I'm giving you ideas."

I shoo him away as Meredith and Kara walk up to me at the bar.

"Willow, this is Kara."

"Good to meet you, Ms. Carmichael."

She gives me a curt nod before running a nervous hand through her blond flowing locks. She looks around the bar.

"Is this a safe place to meet about this?"

"Safest place there is," I assure her. "Vinny made sure to close the bar early tonight. We're meeting upstairs."

The tension eases from her shoulders, but shades of red hit her already rosy cheeks. She hands me a folder with the words *ARNOLD DEBRIEFING.*

"I like to be prepared," she responds to the pleased grin on our faces. We like when our clients have a preliminary debriefing in addition to ours. It makes these meetings go by smoother, and it allows us to be on the same page when it comes time to kill.

And as we discuss Arnold's whereabouts tomorrow and brainstorm ways to set up for the kill, I realize that this may be my favorite kill yet.

FIVE

WILLOW

The virtual world is the prime place to escape. Your sorrows, your worries, your miseries—you leave it all behind. None of that exists in the virtual realm. No one can tell you what to do, and no one can fuck you up royally. I'd been escaping into the virtual world for the last three years, and it's a place where I've made friends and memories. Being homeschooled in my teen years didn't exactly allow me to make very many friends—outside of Meredith, who I've known since middle school.

Crazygirl225: Why were you homeschooled?

An avatar asks me in the Girls Night Out chatroom on Ritzah, an online virtual world. I type to her, explaining how my mother made me responsible for my dad's health when she decided that dealing with a healing husband was too emotionally tiring for her after Dad had his stroke. Dad had a history of health issues before he died. Whether it was due to his poor diet as an overworked attorney, being a habitual chain smoker, or dealing with the stress of Mom cheating on him *multiple times throughout their twenty-year marriage, Dad was never at his healthiest. Mentally, emotionally, or physically.*

When she left us for her boy-toy when I was in high school after a massive stroke that hospitalized him for two weeks, it was up to me to take care of him and watch over him. A tough task for a 16-year-old. When it was time for me to leave for college, I made the decision to join the infantry. It was purely a pragmatic decision, but joining the military was the best way to pay for college.

The Army Infantry…it's tough. But so am I. Nothing about my life has been glamorized. There's nothing sweet about being an infantrywoman, nothing romantic. But there's a rush. An animal inside of me that tells me to protect and save. I protected and saved my dad for nearly four years of my young life, and I didn't mind doing the same in the military. Even if it meant I got to escape my dysfunctional family life. As for leaving Dad when I finished school? Luckily, Vinny and Caroline offered to take care of him while I went away.

Crazygirl225: Wow

I'm expecting her to respond to my essay. But it's not her job to be my emotional crutch. And she seems to think the same thing, because her goth girl avatar disappears, leaving 'crazygirl225 has left the chat' in her wake. Ironic. I guess I'm the real crazy girl if I can overshare my entire life's story to a stranger online.

"How are you holding up?" Meredith appears in the doorway.

"Just chatting with some friends online," I half-lie. And she sees through me like glass.

"'Friends,' or more Ritzah online freaks?"

"We're all freaks in some way or fashion, Mer."

She laughs, putting her hair up in a ponytail. "I'm headed to the range to shoot a bit. You coming?"

Almost as if it were planned, I see a new avatar has joined the chat by the name of Kinsley_ii209.

Kinsley_ii209: Hey, beautiful.

I smile at the glancing eyes emoji he left with it.
"Raincheck on the range?"
She shakes her head, amused, as she closes the door behind her.

NewEnglandGirl423: Hey, what's up

That's all I type because I don't know how to approach the conversation. I don't normally engage with flirty guys on here because they're all trolling. But his avatar is eccentric, wearing a hoodie, sweatpants, and a horse's head. I'm instantly so amused by it that I decide engage in conversation with him.

Kinsley_ii209: I almost thought you were gonna leave me hanging. Your skin is beautiful. I love black women.

I raise an eyebrow at that.

NewEnglandGirl423: Is that your way of flirting?

Kinsley_ii209: It's my horrible way of flirting. I'm Kinsley, btw.

He seems like a quirky guy, and I can't help but to laugh.

NewEnglandGirl423: I'm Willow. My friends call me Willow

I have no idea why I gave this mere Internet stranger my real name. Maybe it's because there's something about him that makes me want to talk to him. Other than the comment on my skin, he doesn't seem like he's creepy or trolling me. At least not yet.

I wipe the residue off my knife, stashing it in my black backpack. I look back at the house where Arnold Bryant's kill took place.

"Are you sure I'm safe from…all of that?" She gestures toward the house. What an innocent girl. None of us are completely safe from the consequences of this lifestyle. But those are the risks.

"All I can say is that we can protect you from the consequences of being an accomplice. We have a decoy waiting by the river."

"A decoy?"

"Someone we hired that looks like you that can take the fall," Meredith puts in simpler terms.

"Oh" is all Kara says, gulping nervously.

She hops in the back of my Suburban as we drive down to the river. She continues asking questions throughout the ride, signaling that she's panicking. And we can't have that. Once we approach the bridge, we park in a spot that's closer to the river and in a discreet area.

"Kara, you have to calm down. Otherwise, this can't work," I warn her.

She gives me another nervous look before nodding her head. "You're right. This is just all…new to me."

Meredith chuckles ruefully, scrolling through her phone.

"If you act guilty, then someone will know. Just let this die down. Even when it hits the news that he's missing. Do not act guilty," I say.

She nods again and doesn't say anything else. Meredith helps me carry Arnold's body to the river, with Kara being the lookout. We sit back in the car, waiting for Kara's decoy to show up, and when she shows up fifteen minutes later, Kara nearly freaks out at how much she resembles herself.

"That's…her?"

"Sure is," Meredith says, bored. She hasn't been amused by Kara's childlike wonder at everything that's been happening tonight. She's acting starstruck, is what Meredith observed. I could see why that would be annoying, but we have to be patient with our clients if we want to build relationships with him and get a decent paycheck. Sometimes clients try to change the rate of pay toward the end of each kill if they notice a bad attitude or if it wasn't executed in the way they wanted. Meredith almost lost us money multiple times because of her apathetic and elitist attitude, but I've spoken to her, and she's calmed down since a recent kill where she threatened to toss a client in the river if they were unhappy with the way the kill was executed. I adore her, but she can be a loose cannon.

Kara hands me an $8,500 check and Meredith a $5,000 check, and I stash mine in my coat pocket. We drive her to a hotel where she can stay the night until our contracted cleaning crew can cleanse her house of any blood and residue.

Arnold Bryant was a somewhat tedious kill. It had to happen in two parts. Kara had to get him nice and drunk after a night out together to lower his inhibitions. She seduced him, and of course he got too aggressive. Nonetheless, she found a way to calm him down, slipping him a mickey when she made him another drink in the kitchen. Already a big guy, Kara wrestled him upstairs to their bedroom. Things turned even more sexual, and when she tied him to the bed, she put a blindfold over his eyes. It wasn't long before we pulled a switcheroo. She said she needed to go to the bathroom, only to disappear downstairs and sit in the Suburban with Meredith. I assumed her identity for the kill, jumping on top of Arnold after about five minutes. It almost became like every other kill, until Arnold started to notice something different.

"Kay, your legs feel stronger. Have…you been doing squats?" he asked, puzzled. Shit. Shit. Shit. I couldn't speak because he would've known. But when I didn't answer, he started to freak out. "Kay, what the fuck is going on? Why do you feel different? *Why won't you answer me?!*"

I quickly hopped off of him and started fishing out my gun. He started shouting across the room, but I could tell he was still drugged up because of his imprecise attempts to untie himself. I could no longer strangle him. When he finally freed himself from his restraints—lousy ribbons to restrain a mountain of a man—he charged at the dressers, but I was able to dodge him. He turned in the other direction from where he heard me, and I immediately held up my revolver, shooting him in the chest. It only stopped him, so I shot him again. In a final attempt to get rid of him, I dislodged my hunting knife and attacked him with it. He was finally subdued. His body slumped over, and it became a workout to carry him down to the Suburban. Meredith and Kara made sure to canvass the house and surrounding houses for surveillance cameras. Luckily there weren't any in view, and we made sure to park in an area that couldn't be caught on the street cameras.

Tough kill as it was, I was able to accomplish it. I need to be careful next time, though. He shouldn't have freaked out as much as he did when he was supposed to be drugged. Either the pill wasn't enough to fully incapacitate him, or it wore off in his system quickly. Something seemed faulty. I choose to chalk it up to the pill not being enough to fully incapacitate him because that is the only logical reason. I'm mulling this over in my head as I drive to drop Meredith off at home. My phone dings with a text, and my heart skips a beat as I look down at the lit-up screen.

VIKING: I wanna see you tonight ;)

"You have his name as 'Viking' in your phone?"

"He's named after a Viking," I point out.

"How broken will his heart when he finds you've reduced him to a nickname? Poor guy."

I pull up to her place. "Get out of the car, Mer."

She finds this entire thing amusing as she hops out. "Don't party too hard tonight."

"No promises," I shout after her. When she's out of sight, I pick up my phone and text Leif back.

ME: I'm pretty tired tonight.

I expect him to tap out. Especially since it's nearly 3 a.m. I'm not in the mood to be a booty call when it's past my bedtime.

VIKING: Me too. Let's be tired together

I hate that this makes me smile. No man's ever made me smile in the last nine years. And yet here I am, nearly giggling like a schoolgirl at this athlete flirting with me.

ME: No cuddling tonight.

VIKING: No promises ;D

Shaking my head, I drive in the direction of his loft. I'm so disappointed in myself. I pledged to never be at a man's beck and call. I'm a betrayal to myself. I'm a betrayal to my species. But fear not, ladies. My heart still belongs to you. It's just that tonight, my heart doesn't seem to be in sync with my brain.

"Why didn't you tell me that you play rugby?"

The devil in question flinches as if I slapped him when he opens the door.

"Hello to you, too, gorgeous."

I just stare at him before charging into his apartment. I throw my purse on his couch.

"My friend Meredith and Vinny both knew that you were the captain of the Hornets. You didn't think that was important to tell me?"

He seems unfazed by the question. "I mean, why would it matter whether or not I told you?"

Shit. It all makes sense. We're friends with benefits, so I guess it really doesn't matter whether or not I knew.

"I don't know. I just don't like being blindsided. Especially when I'm sexually involved with someone so…high profile." It's not good for my image. If we're seen together in public—or hell, even at Vinny's bar—people will begin to wonder who's the girl suddenly hanging out with the captain for a big team?

"Is it a bad thing that I play for the Hornets? Most girls would swoon at that."

"I thought we already established that I'm nearly thirty, and schoolgirl fantasies are a thing of the past for me."

He tries to stop a smile from breaking out. "Okay, Willow, I'm sorry I didn't tell you. I thought that we were keeping things casual."

"We are!" I throw my hands up in frustration. "But what if you harassed me again at Vinny's bar or paparazzi would see us in the parking lot again and begin to ask questions?"

"You have a healthy imagination."

I roll my eyes. "I'm serious. We're gonna have to lay low."

"Why does it matter? Who cares who sees us? The team's publicity team can tame any imagination that runs with journalists."

"It's still such a huge risk." My voice cracks, trying to grasp the gravity of the situation. And it doesn't help that the media is already trying to figure out who Jane Doe is. I'm currently Boston's most wanted fugitive, but they don't know it. They don't know what I look like. And I can't have any questions asked about me by the media.

"Can we please just calm down with being seen together in public?"

"Willow—"

"I'm so serious, Leif. Please at least give me *that* privacy."

I hate the confused look on his face because it says he wants me to elaborate, and I can't. I'm not even sure if I can fully trust this guy.

"Okay. We'll keep it low profile in public," he pledges, and I let out a relieved breath.

"Thank you."

He nods his understanding, approaching me for a hug. He snuggles his nose in the crook of my neck, and it feels too intimate. The old Willow would immediately pull away out of fear that he'll attack me, but the Willow as of now doesn't seem to care. Once again, my heart and brain are not in accord with each other. But I quickly forget when he starts to make short work of my clothes and I make short work of his. I can worry about the consequences of this tomorrow. Tonight is just all about staying present with the mountain of man in front of me.

SIX

WILLOW

Kinsley Focker is his name. I don't think I've heard any like it. And as I learn more about Kinsley, the more I become intrigued by him. I learn that he's in information technology, working mainly in cybersecurity.

NewEnglandGirl423: So you're a hacker.

I immediately picture a silhouette of a guy wearing a black hood, typing on three computer monitors in front of him. A feeling of unease festers inside of me. It's not a good feeling.

Kinsley_ii209: I wouldn't say that I'm the average hacker. I hack for good ;).

I can't help but smile at that. He's charming. He has been for the last two days I've been talking to him. But you can never be too careful. If there's one thing I learned from my dad about the virtual world, it's that it's not safe. A lot of creeps lurk, looking for someone to exploit. Once they manipulate them in any way they want, they're on the search for their next prey. Wash, rinse, repeat. And while there's something enticing about Kinsley, I have to be alert.

Kinsley_ii209: But I'm not on here much. Do you use Chyll?

Chyll is an instant messaging app. The appeal is that it's purely private, where users can't see your email address or home address. All the other person can see is your profile picture and your username. I give him my username, and minutes later, I get a Kin added you as a friend! *notification.*

To be able to talk to him feels like a miracle. For a second, things didn't go well between me and him. When we first met in that chat room and he was sporting his whimsical outfit with the horse's head, one of my virtual friends, Maddie, joined and couldn't read the room.

MaddieTheBaddie808: Heyyyy, Willow! Girl, what you doing in here? Kyla and Aaron are looking for you.

Her stylish avatar suddenly sat next to me, ignoring my secret admirer, who was also sitting not too far from me.

I found myself looking at Kinsley, who was patiently watching the interaction between me and my clueless friend happen.

NewEnglandGirl423: I'm just hanging out. This is my new friend, Kinsley.

MaddieTheBaddie808: Oh, cool. What's up?

Kinsley_ii209: Hey

And then Maddie just went into this tirade about a fling she's had with one of our friends on Ritzah.

MaddieTheBaddie808: He's fucking with me, Willow.

NewEnglandGirl423: Maybe you guys need a break. If it's stressing you out this much.

I didn't understand how Maddie was clueless enough to not see that I was in the middle of chatting.

MaddieTheBaddie808: Oh come on, Willow. Don't act so shy now. This can't be coming from the same girl that joked about sleeping with her ex's best friend to get back at him.

Fucking hell, Maddie. This is really not the right time.

NewEnglandGirl423: Whatever the case, Mads, I think you should cool it with Toby. We were all friends before, anyway. Don't ruin a friendship over this.

And let's fucking leave it at that. I expected her to get a clue and stop talking about it. At that point, Kinsley was already quiet. Even if he was away from the keyboard, he could still come back and simply scroll up to see the chat history in the room.

MaddieTheBaddie808: Am I talking to the same Willow?

NewEnglandGirl808: Hey, Mads? Can we talk later?

There were minutes after I sent that to her where she was silent. A speech bubble popped up above her head, signaling that she started typing.

*MaddieTheBaddie808: :O Yeah. We're all gonna
be in the Trendy Backyard chat. Let me know
when you come.*

And she disappeared as fast as she came.
*For a few minutes, Kinsley just sat there. I assumed that maybe
he left and would come back any second. But when his avatar's speech
bubble appeared above his head, my stomach dropped to my pelvis.
And it was the glancing eyes emoji again. Shit.*

Kinsley_ii209: So…that was your friend?

*NewEnglandGirl423: Yeah. She seems hyper,
huh? Haha.*

*My poor attempt to lighten up the sudden awkwardness between
us.*

*Kinsley_ii209: :/ I mean…is that who you
surround yourself with?*

*NewEnglandGirl423: She's been a friend of mine
on here for about a year.*

*Kinsley_ii209: So you're a lot like her, then? Since
you guys are so close with each other?*

He was already pulling away. Thanks a fucking lot, Maddie.

NewEnglandGirl423: I wouldn't say that…

*Kinsley_ii209: I would. I don't know, Willow.
I'm not sure if I like you a whole lot, anymore.*

*And that was when I was done. Apart from the virtual sphere,
I felt myself getting anxious. Feeling helpless, I left the chat room with
him and immediately went to the Trendy Backyard chat room with*

my friends. Clicking on the room info, I saw that everyone was in there. Including Maddie. Perfect.

NewEnglandGirl423: What the fuck, Maddie.

BazaarGirlxx111: Hello to you, too, Willow.

One of our friends, Harper, was sitting next to Maddie's avatar.

MaddieTheBaddie808: What?

NewEnglandGirl423: That guy I was talking to in the other chat room? He doesn't wanna talk to me now. Because of you.

MaddieTheBaddie808: Because of me? What did I do?

NewEnglandGirl423: You don't know how to shut your mouth!

MaddieTheBaddie808: What are you mad about? The dude with the horse's head? Are you serious?

I told her about how the guy I was sitting with was someone I was interested in and that she basically fucked it up because he lost interest in getting to know me.

MaddieTheBaddie808: Shit, Willow. I didn't know that. But...he was wearing a horse's head! I didn't think anything of it. Why didn't you send me a private message so I could get a clue?

NewEnglandGirl423: I thought you were gonna get a clue! I didn't know I needed to spell it out for you.

But she was right. I should've sent her a private message. And even so, it was hard to stay upset at Maddie. I couldn't fault her for her personality. A personality that was something I'd grown to love about her.

MaddieTheBaddie808: Let me fix this.

Before I could even stop her, her avatar disappeared, and I was left with Harper, Toby, Vik, and Caroline.

BazaarGirlxx111: Let her fix it, Willow. We'll get your man.

Harper tried to be encouraging. But it did nothing of the sort.
"Another flashback, Low?"

My gaze sets its sights on Meredith as she leans on the palm of her hand, looking at me impatiently. We're hanging out in Vinny's upstairs speakeasy, as Vinny gave us the key to lock it up for privacy.

"You know me. I ruminate."

"And you should stop."

"And if I don't?"

Connie's already given me the third degree about staying in my head and overthinking. But most thoughts deserve to stay in my psyche.

I'm not well. I'm willing to admit that. I'm not in a place to talk about wicked thoughts that would make people question my sanity. Ruminating is one of the few ways I cope with what the hell's wrong with me.

"You know, you're not as fucked up as you make yourself out to be, right? You're just another victim."

"Are we really doing this right now, Mer? Drop it."

Red rushes to her face in an episode of fury, nearly canceling out her freckles.

"I'm your best friend. Your confidant. Yes, we're doing this right fucking now," she declares in a hard voice.

"I. Am. Fine. Meredith. I don't wanna sit here and unpack why I'm having flashbacks. I reflect. That's what I do. If I can't carry out my services in the open, I sure as hell will think about it in the open."

For a second, we're stuck staring at each other, neither one of us budging. This isn't an unusual occurrence for me and Meredith. I don't love when we argue and disagree, but it's been the forefront of our friendship. Especially when I started my training as an assassin.

Simply, Meredith McKinley has always been a sadist. She loves the thrill as much as me when I carry out a kill. And while I'm deeply disturbed, Meredith has always had something brewing inside of her. She had a dark childhood. She and her older sister were kidnapped when she was eleven. After watching the death of her sister, she was never the same.

When they went missing for five days, their parents filed a missing persons report, and when she was found in the basement of the recently released sex offender at the time, next to her sister's charred corpse, the scene was unsightly. My innocent and full of life best friend had changed. She would have nightmares that would keep her awake for two days, causing her to hallucinate. She had to be admitted multiple times throughout our childhood and teenage life for having violent outbursts because of the hallucinations.

Nightmares became a recurring thing, and things escalated. We were both sophomores in high school. She and one of our classmates got into a dispute in class. Meredith assaulted the poor girl with a pencil and a pocketknife that she started carrying around after her kidnapping. It wasn't long until she was admitted into a psychiatric facility for youth. I didn't see my best friend again until we turned eighteen. She was released for behavior stabilization, and it was almost like she was a different person. Healthy, calm. But there still seemed to be a dark cloud looming over her. Over the years, she just became jaded, detached. Her violent episodes dissipated as time went on, but she started hating society. Where we had originally bonded over glitter lipstick and Barbie dolls as kids, we found a connection in something darker, wicked. It wasn't long until I got my best friend back.

And though her childhood has colored her entire world view in the same way my past has for me, she notices when I start to go off the deep end. When I start to spiral. And no doubt she sees it in me now.

She straightens her shoulders, gently grips her beer mug, and zeroes in on me.

"All I'm saying is, it happened. You met a piece of shit that amounts to nothing more than the sewer residue at the bottom of your shoe"—I snort at that—"and giving him life in your head will only lead to insanity. You're doing what you're meant to do. You help the women out there that are just like you. Recognize that. And throw that scoundrel out of your head. Because that shit manifests itself."

Easier said than fucking done. Everything about the bastard makes my skin crawl. If I could go back in time to politely roast him over a fire, I would. But Meredith is right. I shouldn't give him life in my head.

Soon after, we're talking about my next job.

"Myra McClendon, 22. This is our third heiress this month."

As my eyes scour over her file, I really pay attention to the last name. It's all too familiar.

"Let me guess. McClendon Airways?"

"Father is Victor McClendon. The target?" She puts a picture up on the projector, revealing a well-dressed frat kid. "Connor Stricken. Son of tech mogul William Stricken. It's the same old textbook domestic abuse. On-and-off recovering alcoholic. Drunken attacks against her being the main offense."

Like clockwork. We're meeting with Myra tomorrow to discuss the details of the kill, and we're going from there. From the looks of this Stricken kid, I don't expect it to be a tedious one. Benji Lockson 2.0.

When we're done with our meeting upstairs, we go back downstairs to the usual bar rush. I'm thankful for rooms like the speakeasy. The smooth jazz playing from the speakers allows for a calm atmosphere, and nothing beats the dimmed lights. It's a beautiful juxtaposition. The perfect place to meet for kills.

"Willow Harding?"

A small voice stops me as I get to the bottom of the stairs.

I turn around and lock eyes with the same woman I've been encountering here.

Each time, her appearance is different. This time, it kind of doesn't look like the same disheveled woman. Her brunette hair is down in waves, and she's wearing a black leather body con dress. Her face is done up like she's going on a night on the town. But what really makes me uneasy is the fact she knows my name. The last two times she singled me out in an entire bar full of drunks, there was an odd feeling that she knew me.

"That's me…" I tread lightly.

You'd think that, since she's dressed up for the night, she'd have an air of confidence. But her current look is juxtaposed against a nervous woman who seems to be seeking the right words to say.

"Um…you're probably wondering how the hell I know your name." Her voice is extremely small; it's hard to make it out in the sea of rugged voices shouting. "I'm not really sure how to start this."

Meredith lets out an annoyed sigh beside me. "We kind of have a long night ahead of us, hun. So if we could raincheck—"

"Wait, no." The woman freaks out, grabbing my arm. "I need your help. My boyfriend is expecting me to meet him tonight at Bristol's, but I came here instead," she says, her voice shaky.

I don't miss the terrified look in her eyes. This looks like a potential client who needs my help. If she's in this much distress, I think I owe her the space to talk about what the hell is going on.

We catch Vinny's eyes behind the bar at that moment. I gesture to him that we're going back upstairs, and he nods his understanding.

"We have a meeting room upstairs if you'd like to talk."

She stops me again. "I don't know if we have time to meet. He's on his way to the bar right now."

Her sense of urgency is really confusing. Is she wanting me to carry out a kill tonight?

"I'm not sure I understand. I think it'll do us both some good if we met upstairs." And with that, Meredith and I walk back upstairs to the speakeasy.

When I unlock the door and we walk into the intimate bar, the woman looks around, puzzled and almost shell-shocked. I put my laptop on the table, and Meredith throws her notebook back down, visibly frustrated. We all take a seat around the table. I was planning on writing up a preliminary treatment for tomorrow's meeting with Myra before heading over to Leif's place tonight. But it doesn't seem like that'll happen any time soon.

"Okay. First things first, what is your name?"

This woman has practically been stalking me, and I still don't know who she is, how the hell she found me, or what's going on.

She does her best to calm down, but there's still a burning energy radiating from her.

"My name is Veronica."

"Veronica what?" Meredith doesn't care for pleasantries.

"Veronica Canseco. From Bakersfield."

Meredith and I trade looks of confusion. "What are you doing in Port Rockwell?"

"My boyfriend and I moved here six months ago. He wanted to do his tech startup here because it's easier and cheaper than to try to take on Silicon Valley."

This is a new one for me. Future tech mogul as a target is one I've yet to tackle.

"Okay, tech guy. How long have you two been together?"

"Two and a half years. Not very long. We were friends for three years first. But it didn't take long for me to figure out that he's a fucking psychopath."

"What makes him a psychopath?"

The tension in her body manifests itself again, and red begins to color her plump cheeks.

"It's really hard to explain." Her voice begins to break. "He's into humiliation porn. Figuratively and literally."

"What do you mean?" Meredith asks. She's all ears now, and so am I.

Tears well up in her eyes as she tries to get ahold of herself.

"When we first started dating, it was on the Internet first. We were long distance. He's five years older than me, by the way. I met him in the chat rooms when I was 18. So

I was young and impressionable when we first started talking. Just graduated high school."

"How old are you now?" She looks young. Younger than me, for sure. But not as young as she most likely is.

"I'm twenty-three."

Fucking hell, she *is* young. And she's been dealing with a psychopath for five years. But the bit about her being young and impressionable gets to me. A wave of familiarity hits me like a freight train.

"Okay."

"Things were sweet. Nothing like how it is now. He was charming, striking, everything you'd want in a man."

"Of course," I reassure her. I hate that I know where this is going, though.

"But then things started to turn…sinister. Once we started getting comfortable with each other, he started asking for nudes. And I was falling in love with him, so I would do anything he would ask. But then I started to notice that he wouldn't send anything back. It was always me sending risqué photos and him getting aroused by them."

I begin to lose feeling in my hands. It's a feeling I haven't felt in a long time. Gently shaking both my hands, I continue to listen to her.

"Soon conversations surrounding his personality and what he does for work started to reveal some odd stuff. His attitude toward women started to come to the surface."

"What examples do you have for this?"

But I can tell this is hard for Veronica to broach.

"He would have a very vengeful mindset when it came to women cheating on him. At first, it was understandable. It still is understandable. He told me that he worked in cybersecurity and did casual hacking on the side for fun, so I took his word for it. But then…he would tell me stories about how men would hire him to get back at their girlfriends for cheating on them. They would hire him to hack the other guy's social media and post some humiliating shit about him."

"I fail to see how any of this affects you," Meredith says, bored.

"Mer, don't fucking do that," I grit through my teeth at her, making her flinch.

"Well, our conversations would then escalate into him joking about posting these girls' nudes to embarrass them. He said he didn't care whether or not they off themselves over it. He just wanted to ruin their lives. Soon or later…he would threaten me. If I ever cheated on him, the nudes I sent him would get posted on the Internet. If he ever got mad at me after an argument, he'd post them. If I ever broke up with him, he'd post them."

"And because you were scared, you continued dating him," I finish for her.

She gives me a look of confusion through her tear-streaked face, unsure of how I picked up on that. If only she knew…

"Yeah…so I'd continue sending him intimate stuff whenever he would ask, and he would continue to receive and not give. He has so many photos and videos of me, Willow," she whispers helplessly.

And it breaks my heart. My heart has always been with the scorned women, and that's where it'll remain.

"So what do you need us to do?"

She lets out a shaky sigh and takes a deep breath before saying, "I'd like you guys to do a stakeout at Bristol's tonight to watch us. Then, if you'd be up to it, I'd like to hire you to kill him."

SEVEN

WILLOW

MaddieTheBaddie808: I messaged him. Just wait to see what he says.

She joined the Trendy Backyard chat room a few hours later that day, and I was picturing my avatar's eyes burning into her. Abandonment was not something I was looking forward to. Not again. My mom abandoned me and Dad when I was in high school. And Dad just died. I wasn't looking for someone else that I had a potential connection with to abandon me, either.

NewEnglandGirl423: If he doesn't talk to me again, Mads, I'm gonna be so mad at you.

MaddieTheBaddie808: Don't worry, girl. We'll get it fixed. If he doesn't see that it was just a misunderstanding, that's his loss.

I considered what she said and decided she was right. She really didn't say anything that wrong for it to somehow be a reflection of who

I am. I felt really vulnerable, recently coming off my dad's funeral at the time. So dealing with rejection wasn't really something I was looking to deal with right now.

Hours passed, and I was starting to get anxious. And as each hour continued to pass, that anxious feeling didn't go away. It worsened. So I did the compulsive thing and messaged him. I basically just sent him a message, apologizing for Maddie portraying me in a somewhat negative light and explained that I'd like to get to know him more.

MaddieTheBaddie808: Did you hear back from him yet??

It was the next day, and Maddie was becoming as anxious as I was.

NewEnglandGirl423: Not yet.

And I was getting annoyed. At the time, I had just accepted that my chances were ruined with him. So I was close to letting it go. Maddie, Harper, Aaron, Toby, Kara, Vik, and I just hung in a nightclub chat room for the rest of the next day.

"How long until you go back to base?" Meredith asked after knocking on the doorframe.

I almost forgot about that. Ritzah pulled me out of reality, and I was starting to lose sight of what was happening in my world. It was truly an escape.

"I go back next week. My leave was just for two weeks."

She nodded her understanding. "How are you holding up?"

Loaded question. One I wasn't really sure I had the ability to answer.

"I've been escaping. That's really all I can do right now."

"You know you can always talk to me if you need to, right? I'm always your girl. Ten years."

The small smile on my face practically hurt because it wasn't authentic. Talking about my dad dying wasn't exactly something I wanted to do at the time. Ritzah was a place where I didn't have to worry about the heavy stuff. Everyone there was practically escaping the shit that happened in their lives. And while I loved Meredith, I just didn't want to continue making a spectacle of my life.

"Thanks, Mer. I just don't think I'm in a place yet to really talk about it."

"But you're in a place to talk about with people online?" The overall concern in her voice bothered me a bit.

"I'm not talking about anything with people online. I'd just rather have that space where I can be myself and not be judged."

This—unintentionally, might I add—made her flinch.

"You think I'd judge you for mourning your dad? Are you kidding me?"

"That's not what I meant, Mer. Look…I'm just dealing with a lot of feelings right now. And you know me, I deal with them better alone. My friends online I wouldn't really call close friends."

Meredith didn't look fully convinced, but I didn't know what else to say to ease her mind.

"The offer still stands. I'm always here if you need me, Low. Never forget that."

"I promise I won't," I reassured her.

She nodded. "Do you wanna get some pizza later?"

"Of course!"

She laughed before shutting my door. Turning my attention back to my laptop, I saw the message button highlighted with a notification. And I was instantly nervous. I opened the message. And it was from Kinsley.

From Kinsley_ü209

Hey. I got Maddie's message yesterday. I misunderstood the situation, and I'm sorry. I'm

*gonna be busy with work for a bit. So I'll talk to
you soon? xoxo*

*I couldn't contain the smile on my face. I sent a message to
Maddie, letting her know that he'd responded to our messages and
everything seemed to be good.*

"Willow, can I speak to you for a second?" Meredith asks in the speakeasy as I'm still reeling from what Veronica is asking us.

Clearing my throat, I jolt back to reality.

"Yeah," I say, my voice suddenly feeling heavy. We excuse ourselves from the table, Meredith tugging on my arm.

"Do you really wanna do this? Something about this just feels off," she whispers.

"What do you mean?"

"How the hell did she find you? From *Bakersfield?*"

"Maybe a former client referred her to me."

She looks at me in disbelief. "Even so, why would she want us to stake out tonight instead of planning an actual meeting and debriefing? All we really have is her word."

Meredith's right. She's the logic and brains between us, too. Though I'm the assassin, she's more of a cynic than I am. And I'm *severely* jaded.

"We just have to take a leap of faith. I have to assume that she's telling the truth. No one acts like that when they're lying about dealing with a sadist."

"Actors, maybe," she argues.

"Mer." I stop her. "All of these questions we have can be answered tomorrow at a meeting."

"We already have our meeting with Myra. You know, the client that's our *priority* and reached out to us the *right* way?"

I look back to Veronica, and she looks uneasy. She keeps tapping her foot impatiently and looking around the room, paranoid.

"We can squeeze her in."

Before Meredith can respond, I walk back over to Veronica.

"If we do the stakeout tonight, we'll decide if we'll move forward with the kill. If it seems like a job for me, we'll talk about a meeting tomorrow so you can answer some more questions for us. Sound good?"

Veronica nods excitedly. "That would be amazing."

"Okay, what's the plan?"

"I can't believe we're doing this," Meredith grumbles.

We're sitting in the Suburban, waiting for Veronica to drive up. Bristol's is busy tonight. It's an Irish pub outside of Boston, sitting on the water.

"If we don't like what we see tonight, we can always back out, Mer."

"This is still a waste of time. Didn't you have a date with Leif tonight?"

I flinch, having forgotten about him.

"One, it wasn't a date. Two, he knows that I had to raincheck tonight."

He doesn't know that I have to raincheck tonight. I have to text him. When Meredith gazes back at the bar, waiting on Veronica and her boyfriend to show up, I pull out my phone and turn it on. Three missed calls from Leif and two text messages.

VIKING: We still on for tonight?

VIKING: If I can't see you tonight, would you wanna come to my game tomorrow?

If there's one thing I'm learning about Leif, it's that he doesn't care. About anything. He beats to his own rhythm. It doesn't seem to faze him that I asked for privacy. And yet…

ME: Got held up at work. Sorry :) Send me the details of the game tomorrow?

I am a certified sucker.

VIKING: It's at 2 tomorrow. Don't be late ;) And sit front row.

Doing my best to contain my smile, I press a love reaction to his text, turn off silent mode, and slip the phone back into my bookbag.

"Okay, there she is," Meredith says, sitting up in the driver seat.

Veronica pulls up in a white BMW and parks across the street from where we are in the bar's small parking lot. She gets out, looking around. I call her. Fishing her phone out of her purse, she quickly picks up.

"I'm here."

"I know. We see you. We're across the street," I say, trying to wave at her. She looks around again, her gaze finding us, and she nods.

"He said he's sitting at the bar. I'll let you know when you guys can come in."

"Sounds good."

She disappears inside, hanging up. Meredith and I just sit in the car, watching the restaurant until we get the go-ahead to go in.

"I'm telling you, Low, something just feels off about this," Meredith mumbles again.

Her hesitance really is puzzling to me.

"What about this job makes you uneasy?"

"The fact that she was stalking you before reaching out to you about hiring you to kill her boyfriend. Not to mention that we're sitting here, scoping them out as a couple before we move forward with the kill. Since when do we do prescreenings before a kill job?"

I consider what she says because it does hold a lot of weight. This does happen to be an unusual way to start off a potential kill job. But I fully believe that all questions will be answered tomorrow. I can't risk walking away from this girl, only to find her dead on the news one morning. That's not something I can stomach.

"Please have a little faith, Mer. If shit starts to get weird, we can walk away whenever we want."

She gives me an annoyed sigh, thumping her head against the headrest. We sit for another fifteen minutes, awaiting Veronica's call to come in. She wants us to watch the way they interact after her boyfriend gets a few drinks in him. He's said to get violent when he's under the influence. Judging by our quick debriefing of their entire relationship, there's not much that will persuade me not to take on this job. Veronica's story is very similar to mine, and if this is the job that helps me better reconcile my baggage, then so fucking be it.

My phone dings with a text from Veronica.

VERONICA: Come in. Look for space at the far end of the bar.

I show Meredith the text. She seems to have felt restless, having to sit outside for nearly an hour.

"Let's do it" is all she says, hopping out of the car.

I grab my bookbag, and we cross the street to the bar. I canvass the bar once we're inside, my gaze landing on Veronica. She and her boyfriend are angled away from us. He's wearing a dark gray sweatshirt with his hood up, and he's leaning on the bar. The difference in their outfits is uncanny. Where she looks like she's about to go to a nightclub, he looks like he's hanging out in their living room.

We keep our heads, doing our best not to rock the boat as we walk to the far end of the bar. I make eye contact with Veronica, doing our best not to alert her boyfriend.

"What can I get you ladies to drink?" the tatted-up bartender asks once we take a seat.

"Gin and tonic, please," I order.

"Whiskey and Coke for me. Make it a double," Meredith says.

VERONICA: He's pretty out of it. He pre-gamed with his friends at another bar before coming here. So he's pretty tipsy already.

Trying not to draw attention to myself, I peek around the busy bar at them, and he's still leaned over his drink as he takes a sip. I can't make out his face too much, since his hood is pretty much covering it.

"I really don't know what this stakeout is supposed to achieve," Meredith says in a low voice.

But I just ignore her and take a sip of my drink. Instead, I start to feel an uneasy feeling that may rival Meredith's. Something about the guy's silhouette feels familiar.

"Mer? Can you peek around me super quick? Be discreet."

She gives me a confused look before slowly angling around me, looking down in Veronica's direction. I hold my breath, hoping that I'm just being dramatic and jumping to conclusions.

"I can't really see what he looks like, but he's moving around more. Not just leaned over his drink like he's gonna vomit or something."

"We're gonna have to figure out how to get a closer look. I can't see shit, sitting down here. Why'd she want us to sit down here?" We could've gotten a table and seen more.

"Maybe because this entire thing is a waste of time," she deadpans. "She probably just overheard one of our conversations once at Vinny's and heard that you're a killer."

"But why would she be just wasting our time if her boyfriend isn't abusive? What would she be benefitting from that?"

"Maybe he *is* abusive. Maybe he's not. She's probably using this opportunity to set you up. Who the fuck knows? Either way, this is a waste."

Usually Meredith's intuition is right. So I should take her word and just forfeit this entire thing. But something is telling me to see this stakeout through.

VERONICA: Can you see anything?

ME: Not really. I'm gonna try and get a closer look.

VERONICA: Okay. Be discreet!

Ignoring her lack of faith in me, I put my hoodie on, emulating her mystery boyfriend. It's a black hoodie that I use to obscure from any distractions during a kill.

I walk past them, nodding at Veronica. She makes brief eye contact as her boyfriend grabs her neck, seemingly playfully. But there's a split-second look of terror in her eyes. The look doesn't quite alarm me, though. It's the hand. It's engulfing. It's a hand that overpowers. And I have a niggling feeling that it's one I've seen before.

I'm at the edge of the bar now, and Veronica and her boyfriend are in my eyesight. I stall, waving down the bartender. I show him my half empty glass, asking for another drink, and he nods.

But I glance at Veronica. Her back is to me, and her boyfriend is turned away, as they look out the window at the tide outside. It looks like she's doing everything she can to distract him from seeing me.

I get my drink from the bartender and walk back to my seat at the end of the bar. I'm about to pass them again, but my eyes betray me.

Her boyfriend's face is in full view. And it makes me queasy.

I suddenly lose feeling in my legs; it's as if I'm walking in molasses. A familiar feeling clouds over me, and I begin to struggle with where the fuck I am.

Meredith sees me during my panic attack and grabs ahold of me.

"Low? What's wrong? Were you able to get a look?"

I'm not in the right headspace to answer her questions. A strange out-of-body experience consumes me. The world is slowly fading away, and I can't quite find my footing.

"Low, talk to me. What did you see?"

What feels like a vise slowly closes around my lungs. But I somehow find the words.

"The guy," I croak, "…with the glass fucking eye."

EIGHT

WILLOW

The guy with the glass eye. You can't mistake him for anyone else. It sticks out like a sore thumb. And while I did the damage, it still gets to me whenever I think about it. Seeing it in person is an entirely different story.

Understanding comes over Meredith's face.

"He's here?"

I nod, swallowing over the lump in my throat. The bastard…is here.

"We…need to get out of here," I croak.

Meredith nods rapidly, grabs my bag, and rushes me out of the back entrance of the restaurant, avoiding being seen. The seconds are a blur before I realize Meredith's putting me in the passenger seat of the car.

The guy with the glass eye. The guy with the glass eye. The guy with the glass eye. What the hell?

I continue to chant this in my head, trying to wrap my head around what the hell I just saw. I never thought I'd see him ever again. I was hoping he moved back to San Jose after our last run-in.

I try to communicate more with Meredith, but my throat feels too dry to say anything. She hands me what looks like a water bottle, and I struggle to open it with trembling hands. But I manage to get it open. I take multiple long sips, slowly starting to have feeling in my throat again.

"What the fuck is going on?" I groan.

"How'd you know it was him?"

"He has a fucking glass eye, Mer," I say with a shaky voice. "How can I mistake him for anyone else?"

She runs a hand through her hair, clearly frustrated.

"Shit, Willow, I-I don't know. What do you wanna do?"

I take a few more sips of water to calm my heart rate.

"The guys with the glass eye," I whisper.

She's silent for a few moments, giving me more room than I'd like to think about what I just saw.

"I told you something was off about it."

My phone dings again with a text, and I instantly turn it off, assuming it's from Veronica. I don't know what the hell is going on, but I need to go far away from whatever this is. I have a meeting with a client tomorrow for an upcoming kill that I need to get ready for.

"I should've listened to you," I nearly hesitate to admit. "I've got half a mind to book a flight out of Port Rockwell"

"Low—"

"I can't be in the same state as him, Mer. How the fuck is he still here?"

"Is there a reason you're having such a visceral reaction to seeing him?"

My gaze whips to her. "That's an honest question?"

She straightens her shoulders, releasing tension from them.

"Abuse is awful. Truly. But you had a full-on panic attack in there, Low. What is it about him?"

I didn't tell Meredith the full saga of what happened between us. And it's not really something I want to talk about tonight. So I ignore the question. I need to get home and take my mind off everything. Or…

ME: Still up to hang out tonight?

He probably won't answer. It's already after 1am, and he has a game tomorrow. I lay my head back to calm the dizziness when my phone dings with a text.

VIKING: Always ;)

Thank God. Thankfully, I already had a bag packed in the backseat for the night from our original plan, so I don't need to stop by my place. I ask Meredith to drop me off at his, and she turns around in that direction.

Minutes later, she pulls in front of his loft.

"Do you wanna meet tomorrow about it after Myra's meeting?"

The pace of my heart rate has lowered to its normal rhythm, and my insides are no longer yearning to crawl out of my body. Maybe it's the comfort in knowing that Leif is around to take my mind off the fuckery I just witnessed. Maybe it's the knowledge that I can buy my next ticket out of Port Rockwellat any moment I choose.

"I think a meeting tomorrow would be good. Somehow my cover's been blown, and I'd like to know how."

There's no fucking way that he's conveniently moved to Port Rockwell. Out of all the places he could've moved.

Meredith gives me a nod of agreement, and I hop out of the Suburban.

"In the meantime, do you think you could research this Veronica Canseco?"

"I'm already on it when I get home. Take the night off, indulge in your Leif rendezvous."

I'm glad that I'm able to chuckle after having a panic attack fifteen minutes ago. It tells me that I'm not going completely insane.

"We may wanna think about disposing of the Suburban and investing in a Tahoe," I think out loud.

"Low, seriously. I'll figure out our next game plan. Get some rest."

Before I can respond, she's already saluting me and driving off. Panic attacks are not an uncommon thing for me. I've had them consistently. My first one was when I found out Mom was cheating on Dad when I was fourteen. My beautiful, salt-of-the-earth mother could never do any wrong. And Dad…he was quiet, reserved. While I always thought of myself as a mommy's girl, I connected more with Dad soon after. We told each other everything. He was all I had when Mom left when I was in high school.

I had another panic attack when Mom decided her life would be better with a man much younger than her than it would be with me and Dad. Around the same time, Dad would get faint spells from high blood pressure episodes. I was only a sophomore in high school, and it became my responsibility to be essentially the caregiver of my father. Soon, he would need to be on medication to contain it.

Breakdowns became a thing of routine, as Dad would continue to work himself to illness. Faint spell after faint spell, it became draining to even be around him. And I hated that feeling. It wasn't resentment toward him; it was resentment toward the lady that made me. Leaving your family behind to start a new life is one thing, but to expect your teenage daughter to be the caregiver of her father while going to school is some kind of narcissism. My panic attacks wouldn't stop. And I didn't expect them to.

Then Dad had a massive stroke when I was sixteen. The experience was heartbreaking. It broke me. The strangest thing is that, while I was going through a period of resentment and distancing and alienating myself from him, the stroke is what brought us closer together. I couldn't stay in high school any longer. I immediately homeschooled myself and made sure he was taken care of throughout high school. Little did I know he was dealing with a silent death by himself. Pancreatic cancer it was. I just wish I'd had more time.

I've been on medication for my panic attacks since my very first one. As long as he was alive, I'd had them consistently. Though, it pains me to acknowledge that. After Dad died, I went off them for a bit. Surprisingly, I was okay. There was an odd moment of peace I'd felt after the funeral. It was heartbreaking, but no longer having to deal with the stress of taking care of him felt almost…peaceful. And I felt guilty for feeling that way. I missed him, I did. I was angry at him for not telling me he was terminally ill. I didn't speak to him for awhile. Until I got the call from Vinny that he died. It was surreal. I felt sad. But I didn't mourn. It was an indescribable feeling. The panic attacks calmed down, so I didn't feel like I needed to continue taking the medication.

Enter the guy with the glass fucking eye. He didn't always have it. I gave it to him. My panic attacks came back when the fucker was in my life. My anxiety became worse to the point where I needed to be hospitalized. Meredith and Vinny made me promise to get into therapy and get medicated after getting discharged. I was never the same.

I'm in therapy against my will. I'm taking medication against my will. What truly makes me happy is helping women.

The panic attacks stopped when I became a contracted killer. I was doing what brought me peace. And then tonight brought back all those demons I thought I banished.

"What's wrong?" Leif asks as he opens his door, genuinely concerned.

I walk past him, throwing my bag on the couch. "I don't wanna talk tonight."

"You never wanna talk."

"I thought that was the deal."

He swallows, his eyes never leaving me.

"Maybe that part of the deal can be eradicated for a few minutes, Willow. Can you just talk to me? I can tell you're upset."

"Don't act like you know me, Leif."

To avoid further conversation, I dispose of my top.

"Willow—"

"I don't wanna talk anymore. Please." I take off jeans, only in my bra and panties now.

His attention is now on my body, no longer looking into my eyes. His gaze briefly skirts back up to meet mine. When he sees the resolve in them, he takes his shirt off, letting out a sigh.

"I'm starting to think you only like me for my body," he tries to joke, pulling me into his arms.

"What else would I like you for?" I say before kissing him. He gives me a hungry kiss back, turning my insides into mush, and I feel it down to my ovaries.

"At some point, you'll talk to me," he whispers, kissing my forehead, confusing the fuck out of me. But I don't push back on it. There's just no point. Tomorrow, I can tackle what happened tonight. Tonight, I'll just take Meredith's advice: indulge in all that is Leif Mattson.

I stir in his bed the next morning, reaching for him. But he's not there. The smell of bacon immediately touches my nose. I reach for my phone on the side table and relax when I see that it's only 9 a.m.

I wrap his blanket around me, not feeling awake enough to get dressed. Walking into his living room, my knees nearly buckle at the sight in the kitchen. He's standing over the stove, back muscles on display. He's only in tight boxers and socks, hair in a top bun, and it's the most domestic thing I've ever seen.

I clear my throat, and he turns around, a pleased grin etching his brooding features.

"There she is," he says, gaze gliding down my body. "You look cute with my blanket around you."

Heat hits my cheeks. "What are you doing?"

"I wanted to cook us breakfast before I dropped you off and got ready for the game today. Can you still come?"

Shit. I forgot about that, in the midst of the weird direction last night went in.

"Yeah, I can still go."

He gives me a wink before turning back to the stove. "How do you like your eggs?"

My attention is immediately drawn to the TV. The news is on, with an overhead satellite camera showing a residence I'm all too familiar. I pick up the remote and turn up the volume.

"Boston University law student Arnold Bryant's body was discovered by his mother this morning in his Boston residence. His

sudden murder is the latest in a string of murders, allegedly perpetrated by the still at-large Siren Assassin, a femme fatale serial murderer that's been terrorizing the Port Rockwell community for five years. If anyone…"

I quickly turn the channel. I look to Leif, and he's looking at me with the same smirk that's he had since I've seen him this morning.

"Are you okay?"

"Yeah, why wouldn't I be?"

He looks between me and the TV before shrugging and putting eggs on two plates.

"Not much into the news?"

"It's not really something I like to watch much."

"Interesting. I pegged you as the kind of girl who's into current events."

"Maybe you should stop making assumptions about me. It doesn't seem like it gets you very far."

"Are you sure? Because I've been in your pants more than once already. Clearly, I'm doing something right," he retorts, winking at me. He's got me there.

Rolling my eyes, I begin to make haste of the eggs and bacon on my plate. I have an hour and a half before my meeting with Meredith and Myra. That meeting and the next one about last night should give me enough time to get ready for Leif's game.

"I can't wait to see you later," he says, an hour later after I'm dressed and ready to go.

I don't know how he manages to make me smile. I'm tempted to rub my chest to stop it from racing as fast as it is right now.

"Well, you won't be seeing much of me since you'll be playing, silly goose."

He rolls his eyes, leaning in for a kiss. It's not long before he drops me off at Vinny's bar, and I'm scoping around to see if Veronica is around.

I still can't believe that I fell for whatever happened last night. I don't suspect that she was screwing me over. I *do* suspect that the guy with the glass eye has been following me and is trying to fuck with me.

"We have thirty minutes until Myra gets here. How are you feeling from last night?" Meredith asks, sliding in the barstool next to me.

Sighing, I run a tired hand through my hair, drinking a glass of scotch.

"What did you find on Veronica?"

She gives me a knowing look before pulling out her laptop, showing me her notes.

"I couldn't find anything incriminating. Not even in the dark web, which is rare as hell. She seems like a good girl, comes from a good family in Bakersfield. She's from a family of lawyers, but she decided to pursue esthetics, emphasis in starting her own skincare line. Practically Miss America. She's a regular donor to charities that sponsor homeless youth."

"There's nothing incriminating about her on the dark web? How the hell is that possible?"

"She may be just a good girl that got involved with a psychopath."

"Here I thought you were skeptical of her," I point out.

"I'm not saying that I'm no longer skeptical of her. I'm just saying that there's nothing on the Internet that indicates she's a threat quite yet. It is pretty disturbing that that bastard somehow made the decision to move here. It just seems convenient. Plus, I still don't understand how she knew who you were."

There are just so many unanswered questions, and it put me in a really dangerous situation last night. I put that life far behind me, and I had no intentions of ever revisiting it.

We decide to shelve the conversation until later, because Myra is here for our meeting.

"Hey…I'm Myra," she says in a small voice.

One thing that all my clients have in common is that they're all nervous and timid when they decide to move forward with hiring me. It's not an easy decision, especially when it's your significant other.

Meredith shakes her hand. "I'm Meredith. This is Willow, the girl in charge."

I introduce myself, and we all go upstairs to the speakeasy for privacy. Myra's another organized client, with a folder labeled *CONNOR FILE*. We go over how she wants to go about executing the mission, the location of where the kill will take place, and when her deadline is.

With thirty minutes left to spare, we say our goodbyes to her, and it's just me and Meredith. The giant elephant sits quietly in his corner by the speakeasy bar. But its presence is all too consuming.

"What are we gonna do about her?"

Meredith cuts the tension. But I haven't had time to think about how to tackle this. My mind's been too busy reeling from it.

"Mer, quite frankly, I'm so fucking confused. I should've read the signs that something was off. I should've listened to you."

"I hate to say I told you so."

"Next mission, though. How the hell do I escape him?"

She sits back in the brown leather armchair, throwing her feet onto the table.

"By the looks of it, I don't think you'll be able to escape him again. He's a fucking menace."

"Okay, so how do I get rid of him?"

"I can help you," a familiar voice says behind us, making me freeze.

We turn to find Veronica staring at us, looking unsure and nervous as she comes into the room.

"What the fuck are *you* doing here?" Meredith growls.

"I think there's been a misunderstanding—"

"How'd you even get up here?"

"I asked the owner, Vinny, if you guys were here, and you guys left the door unlocked…"

"So you just walk into places you don't belong?"

"Not necessarily. I need to talk to Willow."

"Willow's busy."

"Okay, Mer? Hold on." She gives me a look of confusion. "If she needs to talk, she needs to talk."

"Preferably with privacy," Veronica adds.

"You're asking for a lot." Meredith doesn't let up.

"Just the two of us?"

Veronica nods. Meredith and I share another look before she reluctantly leaves the room.

"I'll be standing on the other side of the door," Meredith announces grimly.

We watch as she leaves before Veronica turns back to me.

"I had no idea you knew—"

"Yes, I know him," I confirm quickly.

"He's from California, though. Like me."

"I know. It's a long story. What are you doing here?" Her presence is making my skin crawl, and I need to get away. The degrees of separation are too close for comfort.

"I can see how strange this looks. That it looks like I'm setting you up."

"Precisely," I remark.

"But I really need your help." She steps closer to me conspiratorially. "My life…is in danger."

A look of fear permeates her face. I really want to help her. I do. It's my job, and I made a silent vow to myself that I would avenge the hearts of scorned women. Case in point, the women in front of me. The terrified Veronica Canseco.

And then I remember the guy with the glass eye. Kinsley fucking Focker. I'm taken back to those days. And something in me is telling me to forget it. I can't do that with my current mental state. I look at my watch, feeling impatient. I have fifteen minutes before Leif's game starts. I hate to do this.

"Ms. Canseco, I'm so sorry. But I'm simply not the woman for the job."

I dash out of the speakeasy before she can say anything. Meredith gives me a questioning look, waiting for me to update her on how the talk went. But I don't say anything. I walk past her and drop the keys to the speakeasy off with Vinny.

"There's a woman up there. When she leaves, lock up for me?"

He also gives me a questioning look that I ignore.

"Can you slow down?" Meredith asks as we approach the Suburban.

"I'm almost late for Leif's game."

"Don't avoid, Low. What did you talk about with her?"

Again, I don't answer. I simply shoot Leif a text that I'm on my way and apologize for being late. When he doesn't respond, I assume he's about to go on the field. I lay my head back against the passenger headrest and try to disassociate.

NINE

WILLOW

I was back at the base in two days. Time truly does fly by when you're having fun. So far, Kinsley had been a gem. A one in a million kind of guy. And he was just the type of escapism I was seeking. Comfort.

> Kinsley: I'm so sorry to hear that about your dad
> :/

The message from him on Chyll sent a wave of calm came over me. His death still felt surreal, and that would probably never go away. And I knew deep down there was an emotional reaction waiting to bubble to the surface. Because the sense of relief I had after he died was alarming. But…I just felt at peace.

> Willow: So what are you up to today?

Any attempt to change the subject.

> Kinsley: Some guy hired me to hack someone's social media, so I have a meeting with him later.

I knew he hacked as a hobby outside of work, but this was the first time I heard about being hired for side gigs.

> *Willow: Oh yeah? He wants you to hack it just for fun?*

> *Kinsley: Pretty much.*

I raised an eyebrow at that.

> *Willow: That's kind of an odd thing to pay someone for.*

It took him a second to respond, and it began to worry me. I hadn't realized that he offered services like that to people.

> *Kinsley: Eh, not really. His girlfriend cheated on him. So he just wants me to post something like, 'Kinda bored. Feeling like putting a dick in my mouth rn.'*

> *Willow: So it's to humiliate him.*

> *Kinsley: :D*

That specific response is very cryptic.

> *Willow: That's kinda fucked up lol.*

And I wasn't sure how to feel about it. Especially if he was a cyber defense analyst for a bank.

> *Kinsley: It's kind of a joke, babe. Besides, I'd do a whole lot worse.*

When he didn't expand on that, the wave of calm I had was suddenly replaced with slight unease.

*Willow: That's kind of an ambiguous statement
lol.*

Cheating is awful, no doubt. This may be initially funny to the guy who's social media will be saturated with polarizing responses from his followers. Maybe a slight inconvenience and minor annoyance, at most. The morality of doing this in the first place questionable, but I wouldn't press any further.

We talked for another few hours while I ate dinner and played Ritzah. Meredith joined me in the room for a bit to check out the chat rooms with me.

"These people really are freaks."

"What do you expect from people who only make friends online?"

"I don't know, Girl Who Makes Friends Online. Would you call yourself a freak?"

I just shrugged my indifference. "I think we're all freaks in one way or another. Some of us are just willing to wear our freak flags more proudly than others."

"Aww, my Willow's becoming a poet," she crooned jokingly. A bizarrely shaped avatar joined the chat room. "For fuck's sake, Low, her legs are longer than her entire torso!"

"Hey, be nice," I scolded. She rolled her eyes, clearly annoyed with me. I got a message from Kinsley on Chyll.

"Ah, the online boyfriend. How are things going with him?"

"They're going okay, I think."

She cocked an eyebrow in confusion. "You think?"

"I don't know. He works in cybersecurity."

She looked at me, clearly still confused.

"I don't get it."

"He also hacks. Like for fun."

"Hacks for fun? What, is he a nerd?"

"Mer."

"That sounds lame. What kind of shit does he hack? Like phones and shit?"

"I don't know. I have to talk to him about it. He told me earlier that he got hired to hack some guy's social media account because the guy cheated with his client's girlfriend."

"Yeah, he sounds like a loser, Low. He's taking on side gigs like that in his spare time? He doesn't have any hobbies?"

"Hacking could be a hobby, I guess."

She looked at me in disbelief before shaking her head and standing up from my bed.

"Don't get involved with people on the Internet, Low. I don't have any issues with you talking to this guy, but make sure that it stays solely on the Internet and doesn't seep into your real life. This guy could be dangerous."

Meredith has always been like my sister. I'd become accustomed to her practically mothering me.

"You have my word, Mom."

She snorted, saluting me and closing the door behind her. I looked at Kinsley's message.

Kinsley: What are you up to, beautiful?

I found myself smiling yet again.

Willow: I just finished talking to my friend. What about you?

He didn't respond. The typing bubble wasn't even appearing. Frowning, I put my phone down and just chalked it up to him being preoccupied with something else for a bit. After a few minutes of silence, he finally responded.

Kinsley: Friend?

Willow: Yeah, my friend, Meredith.

Kinsley: Oh, it's a girl. I thought you were going to say it was a guy friend you were texting :/

Willow: Lol no I don't have very many guy friends.

Kinsley: Do you have any at all?

Why was he asking about this?

Willow: None that I would call a friend lol. They're all acquaintances.

Kinsley: So I don't need to worry about cheating, then.

Willow: No babe lol. You don't need to worry about cheating.

Kinsley: Good. I want you all to myself :)

He was cute. Sometimes guys are weird about having male best friends, so I understood his concern. It wasn't really not worth it to press the conversation further. He was the first person in a while that I felt I could talk about stuff with without any judgment.

Kinsley: Send me a pic :) I wanna see you

I suddenly started freaking out. What if he thought I was ugly? I hoped he didn't expect me to look like my avatar on Ritzah.
Dispelling my out-of-character insecurities, I took a quick selfie and send it over to him.

Kinsley: You're so pretty :)

Willow: I'm alright.

Kinsley: Stop it. You're beautiful.

Something indescribable bubbled inside of me. It was hard to get a read on him. He'd taken me on a rollercoaster of emotions already.

Happiness, fear, confusion. Rinse, wash, repeat. But he didn't just stop there.

 Kinsley: I wanna see more of you.

 Willow: What do you mean? You wanna meet up?

 Kinsley: No, like…more of you.

I was struggling to understand what he meant by that. I felt like I'd shown him what I could of me.

 Willow: I don't get it, Kin lol.

 Kinsley: Do you love me?

The sudden pivot confused me.

 Willow: I mean…I don't think I know that yet. Do you know if you love me?

We'd only known each other for a few days.

 Kinsley: Of course I do. I thought you loved me, too.

 Willow: I know I like you, Kinsley. Love is just such a big word, considering we've only met five days ago.

He sent a sad face and it made me feel horrible. I didn't mean to hurt him. I just thought it was kind of a strange change in conversation.

 Willow: I didn't realize that you were falling in love so soon.

 Kinsley: And I thought you were :(

I didn't know how to move on from here. I wasn't even sure what direction the conversation was originally going in.

> *Willow: What do you mean you'd like to see more of me?*

> *Kinsley: I just wanted to get more intimate with you.*

That cleared it up pretty well. Intimate is a euphemism I can pick up on pretty easily.

> *Willow: What does that look like to you?*

> *Kinsley: It depends on if you love me or not.*

The thing was, I didn't. I didn't love him. I didn't know him. But I knew that I loved talking to him.

> *Willow: I love talking to you, Kinsley. I like you.*

> *Kinsley: Then prove it.*

He was testing the waters. I thought we'd already gotten past that phase of this online relationship, given our last interaction with Maddie. But I guess we hadn't.

I'd never sent a nude photo before. It's not something I would generally do. In fact, I used to make fun of those people who exchanged photos of that nature with people, even if it was with their significant other. How ironic. I never thought I'd become one of those girls who'd do it to keep a guy interested.

I'm not sure what it was about Kinsley. Maybe it was the fact that he thought I was beautiful. Maybe it was because, from the description he'd given me of him—six foot three, athletic, with brown hair—he sounded like just my type. Or maybe it was because for the first time in my short life, I didn't have to take on the responsible role of taking care of someone and their well-being. For the first time, I could be the one whose well-being was cared about. It wasn't the most rational state to be in. But it was my one saving grace.

I hated this for myself. It was dangerous, Meredith had a point. But I didn't get a vibe from him that he was willing to hurt me or use it against me in any manner. I thought about it for a few minutes before slowly standing up and walking to the vanity mirror.

The naked body is usually something people marvel at. It's often assumed that the woman's body is the more attractive one, between men and women. Hence why we women believe we're the prize, though not the only reason. We're told that from young that we have what men want and that we are beautiful no matter what. As such, body image isn't usually something I struggle with. When the right one comes along, however, you, too, might see uncanny imperfections that aren't there. Like how my right boob is considerably smaller than the other. Or how I have small stretch marks that line my hips. Suddenly, I became an awkward virgin that crawled into her shell when she saw herself naked in a mirror.

It took me about seven different poses before I landed on the one I thought was perfect to grab Kinsley's attention. I snapped a few photos, took a few deep breaths, and looked them over. My body image was no longer intact. But Kinsley started to message if I was okay. I doubted that he'd mock my body. There was no way of knowing if I continued with this tortured delay. I took a deeper breath than the previous ones and sent the photo I'd settled on. Then I threw my phone on the bed like it was a Molotov cocktail and quickly got dressed in my pajamas.

My entire body was brimming with a nervous energy, as I waited for him to respond. When it surpassed about five minutes, I started to overthink. Maybe he thought I was ugly. Maybe he was rethinking if he wanted to be with an ugly she-beast. Then he responded, and I stared at my phone. Rolling my shoulders back, I picked it up.

Kinsley: You're so fucking sexy.

It wasn't the most eloquent praise, but it was praise. And I might begin to love it.

Leif Mattson is killing it. As expected. Meredith and I have been marveling at the speed and ease on the field, impressed with how beefy the guys are.

"You may need to get Leif to set me up with one of his teammates," she shouts over the crowd around us.

"I'm a hit woman, not a wingwoman."

She snorts, taking a sip of her canned beer.

"In your life of work, they're one and the same, slick."

Just then, Leif is tackled by a player from the opposing team. He passes it off to a nearby teammate, who then runs down the field, passing it to another teammate. The number of tackles are a lot to follow, and it starts to give me whiplash.

"So much tackling," I mumble.

And somehow Meredith was able to hear me. "You could learn a thing or two from them."

"What's that mean?"

"You don't tackle your targets enough is what it means. You just rely on blindfolding most of them instead of taking them on headfirst."

"You realize that I'm 5'10 and 135 pounds, right? Couple that with a 195-pound man."

"You have thunder thighs, though. You don't give yourself enough credit."

"So now you're giving me advice on how to approach my kills?"

"I'm your confidant, right? Why *wouldn't* I give you constructive criticism?"

"Because you don't complete the kills."

She rolls her eyes, gaze transfixed back on the chaos in front of us.

We're twenty minutes into the second half of the game, and I'm already invested. I'm so invested that I'm agitated when nature calls.

"I need to go to the bathroom. Film the game for me?"

"Sure thing, Captain," she mocks.

I put my shades back on and walk in the direction of the concessions stands and bathrooms. Approaching the women's restroom, I come across a bounty sign with a poor sketch of a woman that looks nothing like me, offering an award of $50,000.

The sketch is of one of decoys I used a few years ago, after she was seen leaving a target's house. I was still in my beginning stages and wasn't as great with tying up loose ends. I'd missed a security camera. The only reason I wasn't caught was because I exited the target's house out of the back.

Isaac Mackenzie. Trust fund child of Stewart Mackenzie, celebrity restauranteur. He's probably my favorite kill to date. He was also my easiest to date. This was before my blindfolding methods. I was contracted by Kill Elite at the time, and Corinne Moseley handpicked me from a roster of highly trained assassins. All it took was meeting him at a nightclub, per his girlfriend's plan. I posed as an escort looking for a date and convinced him to take me back to his place for a nightcap. Our night of "fun" turned into me tying him to his bed. It made it easier to escalate from seducing him to ultimately killing him, execution style. He was cocky, aggressive, and drunk. The perfect target.

The decoy I hired was a look-alike for Corinne. She got caught on a neighbor's surveillance camera, and since then, her face has been used in these lazy sketches around Boston metro. She's yet to be caught. And there are reasons for that.

Corinne's decoy was actually a fellow contracted killer with Kill Elite, and she's since died during a failed job. And Corinne and her entire family have been living off the grid for the last three years. Her decoy isn't the only assassin that was killed during a hit job. There's a specific kind of precision and ease required for the lifestyle. While my colleagues were skilled assassins, there were certain details they may have missed that resulted in their deaths, and this can happen to anyone. Including me. In this way of living, your days are numbered. So far, I only know of two other assassins that are living off the grid. As I've said before, this life is not for the faint of heart.

And while I've found even the slightest bit of comfort in knowing that my face isn't on the radar, I'm instantly on high alert passing the bounty poster. My senses are more in tune with my surroundings, and I feel as if I'm prey, ready to fight back. The walls feel like they're closing in on me. I rush to the bathroom, doing my best to ignore the odd change in sensation.

I splash some water on my face to get ahold of myself. I don't like this feeling. The poster is nothing new. I've seen them around town and always ignore them. But something feels off. Almost as if there's a glitch in the matrix. My breathing feels shallow, and my skin is tingling. I continue to splash more water onto my face, take long, deep breaths, and slowly feel myself calming down. The odd feeling doesn't completely go away as I leave the bathroom, however.

"There she is, in all her glory."

The menacing voice makes me stop. The wind feels like it's been knocked out of me, and I'm suddenly thrown back into a state of unease.

"Seven years of having withdrawals. And it led me back to you," the voice continues.

My senses were right before. Something was off, and it freaks me the hell out that my body was able to tell.

It doesn't take more than two seconds before I come face to face with the monster, his glass eye forever etched into my memories.

TEN

WILLOW

It's like a horror film. A slasher. Except Kinsley Focker hasn't pulled out a weapon to kill me yet. He decides to go the torturous route, violently pushing me up against the brick wall underneath the bleachers, his hand tight around my neck.

"I never thought I'd see you again," he declares in a menacing voice.

I don't say anything. I don't give him the satisfaction. I promised myself I'd never be afraid of him again. Which was under the condition that I'd never see him again. I never wanted to give him the power over me that he once had. And yet here I am, in his grip, terrorized out of my mind, trying to figure out how to get the hell out of this. The only saving grace I have in this moment is the glass eye I gave him when I escaped him.

"The Siren Assassin." His nose is pressed up against my temple now, inhaling my scent. He smells of cheap whiskey and cannabis. The mixture of smells tortures my nose, nearly triggering my gag reflex. "It was too easy to figure out it was you, Low."

"Don't. Call. Me. Low," I bite out. But his grip on my neck becomes tighter.

"I call you whatever the fuck I want," he growls in the same voice he used to threaten me with years ago. I can't find it in me to speak. The longer he clenches my throat, the more I feel myself losing oxygen. My panic attack is suddenly back. "Did you really think you could just run away from me, assume an alias as an assassin, and I wouldn't find you?"

"You're…suh…posed…tuh…be…in—"

"California? Port Rockwell just seemed more…suitable for my line of work"

"Terrorizing more women? Yes, there's a very healthy market out here for that."

A hard slap across my face knocks the wind out of me, landing me on the cold concrete ground.

"You've become glib in your washed-up years. See how far that gets you with me."

I wipe the blood from my mouth.

"I'm not scared of you, Kinsley. Those days are long gone. You of all people should know that."

Which is partially a lie. His presence is a zap to my veins and a vise to my lungs.

"Oh yeah?" he challenges me.

"What's that, a kill count of 35 these days? You should really be careful, walking the mean streets of Port Rockwell. You never know what could happen."

He angrily picks me up and slams me up against the bricks walls again, feeling something crack in my side.

"You're right, you never know what could happen. So I'd watch your back. Now that I've found you, I'm not losing you again," he growls again, the stench still on his breath.

"You sure about that?"

A rueful laugh escapes him. "Have you ever known me to bluff?"

"No," I struggle to get out. "But I've never known you to be evasive."

There's only a minute of confusion that crosses his face before I finally find my HarmAlarm and sound it off, a wailing call reverberating throughout the arena.

Kinsley mutters a curse before dropping me to the ground, sprinting off, leaving his barbarian silhouette an unwanted memory in my head. Meredith appears at my side as others stand in the entranceway of the tunnel.

"What the hell happened? Are you okay?"

My bottom lip stings, I feel a sharp pain on my left side, it's hard for me to catch a breath, and I got the wind knocked out of me.

"No," I croak. "I am *not* okay."

I have a broken rib. The doctor says it'll be painful for me to even walk around. Which spells disaster.

Meredith, Vinny, and Leif are all helping me into the Suburban, and it annoys me.

"Can you guys stop? I know how to sit in a car."

"You have a broken rib, Willow. Stop trying to be superwoman. Who are you trying to impress?" Vinny asks, visibly frustrated with me.

Sighing, I just settle into the backseat of the car. Vinny sits in the passenger seat, while Leif sits in the back with me. He grabs my hand as Meredith pulls out of the ER parking lot and kisses my knuckles. If I were in my right mind, I'd pull my hand away. But I may just need comfort right now.

Minutes later, we're in front of the bar instead of my apartment, and it confuses me.

"What are we doing here?"

"We're having a meeting," Meredith says.

"Right now? I have a fucking broken rib."

"Broken rib or not, you're gonna tell us what the fuck happened."

"Mer, please, I don't wanna do this." Not when Leif is here, and he doesn't know what I do.

But she ignores me anyhow, gets out of the driver seat, and spins around to help me out of the back. When she puts her arm around me, I pull her close, so as not to be conspicuous.

"Why are you doing this now? Leif is right there," I acknowledge in a low voice.

"Don't worry. I'm gonna take him home. Vinny wants to talk to you first anyway."

Goddamn. It's been a while since I've had a serious talk with Vinny. If he wants to talk to me alone, that normally means it's about business. He comes over and carries me out of the car.

"Don't get out, Mr. Mattson. I'm taking you home."

I catch a glimpse of his understandable confusion.

"What? No, I wanna know what's going on."

"Now's not the time." She refuses to be deterred.

He looks at me, seemingly wanting me to reassure him that I'm okay.

"It's fine, Viking. I'll call you later?"

He stares at me, not budging, before nodding and getting back into the car. Vinny continues to walk me inside the bar. When we get inside, he sits me down at a dining room chair, and locks the door of the bar.

"What the hell is going on with you, Willow? How did you get assaulted?"

"I already told you."

"And it was completely random? That's what you're telling me."

"That's absolutely what it was."

"Willow," he says in an authoritative voice.

I hate talking about this. I haven't talked about it with him in a few years now.

"Do you remember my asshole of an ex?" Which is putting it nicely.

"The little hacker punk?"

I can't contain my amusement. "That's the guy."

"What about him? He did this to you? I thought he was in California."

"I thought he was, too. But he moved here with his girlfriend a while ago and found me, again."

Vinny mutters a curse before pacing in front of me.

"So this bastard has been stalking you? Is that what you're telling me?"

"I guess so."

He stalks behind the bar and grabs a bottle of Irish whiskey and three glasses. He pours all three of them off.

"Meredith is going to want a shot too." I nod as he takes a shot and slams it down on the table. "You need to get out of this business, Willow."

"What?"

"Being a hitwoman. You can't continue with this line of work."

"Vinny, you're talking crazy now."

"Willow, this kid *found* you. And he's going to keep terrorizing you."

"I don't know, either. But I made an oath to the women of Port Rockwell. I'm not giving that up."

"Stop. It's not healthy to kill men for revenge."

"So you'd rather women die at the hands of men who can't control themselves?"

"Willow," he levels with me. "This life is going to drive you insane."

"What's new? The fact that I even met this prick is enough to drive me crazy."

"So how do you think this will end?"

"With society finally catching on to the fact that, as long as they continue to hurt those most vulnerable, I'm not going anywhere. It's time you figured that out, too."

Almost on cue, Meredith knocks on the door. Vinny gets up to let her in, and she runs in, taking a seat next to me.

"Did you tell him what happened?"

"That Kinsley attacked me? Yes, we're past the pleasantries."

"So what's next?"

I look to Vinny, who looks like he's washed his hands of the conversation.

"I don't know, Vinny. What's next?"

"I've already told you my thoughts. It's up to you if you want to listen."

He then gets up and starts washing dishes behind the bar. "What's his problem?"

"He wants me to leave the lifestyle behind."

"What? Are you gonna do it?"

"I don't know what I'm gonna do, Mer. He fucking found me."

"He may be right, Low."

"What?"

"It may be time for you to hang up the sword," she jokes. "Especially now since you have a broken rib."

"I'm not letting that stop me."

"The doctor said you need to rest for at least three weeks."

The pain still stings and most likely will for a while, but there's no way I'm giving up being a hitwoman.

"Can we talk about this another time, please? I really wanna go home and get some rest. I'm tired and still a bit shaken from seeing him."

I need to be in a space by myself right now. I fucked up. I gave myself away somehow, causing Kinsley to find me. I don't know how, I don't know when. I changed my hair color and made sure to change my hairstyle. Yet, it didn't work. But I haven't felt like myself in the last two days, and I need to reclaim who I was before he came back into my life.

"Sure thing, Low," she says after a moment of hesitance. She wraps my arm around her shoulders, and we walk to the Suburban. Minutes later, she pulls up in front of my place, grabs me out of the passenger seat, and takes me up to my apartment.

I give her the key, and she walks me inside, putting me down on my bed.

"I'm gonna do some research on Kinsley, if that's okay. Gonna try to find out what brought him back out here and get more information on him."

The proposal is laughable, considering I know everything anyone ever needs to know about Kinsley Focker. But maybe there's something I missed about him. All I know is that I never wanna see him again.

"Sounds good. I'm gonna rest for the day. If Myra reaches out to the email, can you let her know that I'm taking some time for myself for a few days?"

"Do you need me to tell her when we'll be able to complete the kill?"

At this rate, I have no idea if I'll be able to complete it without fucking it up.

"See if we can move her deadline." Her deadline for the kill was originally 48 hours, but there's no way I'll be in good enough shape to do it tomorrow. I'm not physically—or mentally—in a place to complete any job.

Meredith doesn't ask any more questions. She simply sets my bookbag down on my TV stand, tells me that she'll come by within the next few days to check in on me, and then leaves, locking the door behind her.

I spend the next few hours watching Netflix to try to calm myself down and get some rest. It crosses my mind throughout the afternoon that the bastard could have my address and could show up, attempting to attack me again. But I banish the thought from my head and do my best to relax my mind.

About two hours later, I wake up to someone knocking on my door. I wipe my eyes and look at my phone to see the time, noticing a text from Leif.

VIKING: I'm coming over.

Shit. I get up slowly—basically limping—to the door. I look through the peephole and, alas, it is Leif. And judging by his brooding grimace, he definitely wants to talk about what happened today. I thought he would've spent time with his teammates after their win.

He didn't get to finish the game because of me…and I already feel bad about that. But they ended up winning. I managed to check updates after Vinny and Meredith escorted me to the hospital.

He knocks a few more times, bringing me back to reality, and I open the door to find his grimace looking back at me.

"Hey, Viking."

"I thought you said you would call me later," he points out in a dejected tone.

"I'm sorry. I fell asleep."

He lets out a sigh of relief before walking in. I close the door and follow him to the couch. When he sees me struggling to walk, he rushes back to me to assist.

"It's okay, Leif. I can walk."

"Not painlessly," he mumbles.

I roll my eyes as we sit down on the couch together. Settling in, I look up and find him looking at me skeptically.

"What?"

"You told me earlier that someone tried to rape you."

I swallow past the lump that loves to form in my throat. "Because someone did."

"I don't believe you, Willow."

It was stupid to assume that all athletes are dumb people. "I don't know what you want me to say, Leif."

"Who attacked you? And why?"

"I already told you."

"And it's bullshit. Ever since I met you, there's always been some sort of cloud looming over you. You're either really pensive or really secretive. What gives?"

I knew that this would be a discussion at some point. I just didn't know it'd be so soon in our…situationship. I technically don't owe him an explanation. I've known him for less than a month, and we've been arranging to meet up only at night. That doesn't exactly breed a deep, serious relationship.

"I meant what I said, Leif. I was attacked by an unknown assailant who tried to rape me. I sounded off my HarmAlarm, which scared him away."

But this doesn't appease him. "'Unknown assailant'? No one talks like that outside of a journalist, babe. I can't tell if you're being sarcastic or if this is who you really are."

"Maybe it's who I really am, Leif."

"Okay, if it's who you really are, who the fuck are you?"

"A personal assistant."

"Willow." He grows increasingly annoyed with me. "I'm at my wit's end with you. What's going on? Why were your friends being weird at the bar?"

"Because they're weird people."

He looks at me. Really looks at me. And the look he's giving me nearly breaks my heart. He really wants to get to know me…but I'm not in the market for a deep discussion. Let alone with a guy who has the aura of a player. It's a huge risk to let my walls down again. And with Kinsley back in my life, there's no chance in sight that I'm opening up and trusting anyone else again.

"If you're going to be so closed off with me and not going to let me help you, then at least be careful."

"I'm always careful," I whisper.

He reaches out and caresses my cheek, as I subconsciously lean into it.

"No, Willow. You're not."

I fully take in what he says, his words another soft caress on my skin. He gives me a small smile before kissing me on the head and turning to leave.

"I'm sorry, Leif," is all I can say.

He stops at the door after opening it, his back still turned to me.

"When you're ready to tell me what's going on, just give me a call."

He leaves without me responding, closing the door behind him.

I was back at base, and a sense of calm came over me. Physical training kicked my ass. Maybe it was a good thing, though. Especially since I'd been sitting in a bed for almost a week, talking to my new online boyfriend.

Shortly after showering, I checked my phone for notifications, including any messages from Kinsley.

> *Kinsley: Missing you. How come you haven't texted yet?*

I frowned, looking at what time it is. It was 8:34 a.m. Which meant, it was 5:34 a.m. back in San Jose. Why was he freaking out? I was about to message him back, but one of my comrades called for me. I'd just message him back when I had downtime.

I changed into my duty uniform and quickly scurried into the hallway to find my commanding officer standing, staring at me.

"Harding," he started.

I immediately stood at attention, saluting him.

"Sir."

"How was your leave? I'm sorry about your father."

A bit of tension left my body, but I still maintained my stance.

"It was okay, sir. My father died peacefully, sir. And that's all I wanted for him, sir."

He gave me a pleased nod.

"Good to hear, Harding. And while I'm happy that you're doing well, I've heard from CQ that you were disturbing some of your comrades last night."

Shit. I was hoping no one heard my phone call with Kinsley last night. It was the first time I'd heard his voice, and gosh, was it sexy.

He had a deep, guttural voice that melted my insides. I'd yet to see him, still. But hearing him made up for it. We did get a little loud at points during the night, so I should've expected someone to report me.

"I apologize, sir. It'll never happen again, sir."

The disapproving look on his face made my heart thump. I couldn't get punished on my first official day back in the infantry.

"It better not." His disapproving look turned into a slight grin.

"It won't, sir." I saluted him again and almost turned away to leave, but he wasn't done speaking.

"Are you still interested in sniper training? If I remember correctly, you have excellent marksmanship skills."

I'm not a smiler. So far, the only people that have been able to make me smile are Meredith and Kinsley. And yet, here I was, smiling at my commanding officer.

"Yes, sir. I'm still interested, sir."

"Very well, Harding. You'll need to take the Army Physical Fitness Test, and once you get a psych evaluation and security clearance, we'll get you started in sniper school."

I nodded, trying to stop smiling.

"Sir, yes, sir."

He nodded, and I salute him before he turned away and walked back down the hall to the exit of the barracks. I was stuck staring at him, excited with the prospect at starting training. I was knocked out of my trance when one of comrades who seemingly overheard our conversation gave me an approving fist bump.

I'm a tough girl. I like to think I am. I can handle a lot of shit. Dealing with my deadbeat mother to taking on being essentially the caretaker of my father when he was alive, I've seen some fucked-up stuff and have handled things with grace...I like to think.

But when Kinsley accused me of cheating on him…I wasn't sure if I could handle the aggression he was throwing my way.

Kinsley: YOU'VE BEEN IGNORING MY TEXTS

I couldn't say that was the most fun message I've gotten from him. I was settling into bed when he continued to spam my phone with texts. When I got back to the room an hour ago, I didn't like seeing twenty missed messages from him, freaking out.

Kinsley: ARE YOU FUCKING CHEATING ON ME OR NOT, WILLOW?

Willow: I'm NOT cheating on you, Kin. I told you, I got back to the base yesterday. And today was my first official day back.

Which was what I'd been trying to get through his head. But he wasn't getting it, or choosing not to.

Kinsley: Fuck, Willow. You could've sent me a good morning text, though :(

I was staring, dumbfounded, at my phone. What a mind-bender. From typing twenty messages in caps to me to a suddenly calm response.

Willow: I wake up at 5:00 am, here. I'm sorry if messaging you wasn't the first thing on my mind :/

Kinsley: Shit…I'm sorry, babe. It's just been such a stressful time at work for me.

Willow: What's going on?

He told me about an attempt to install software into the company's database and investigating a cyberattack that they'd recently encountered. His boss had been giving him a hard time about there being vulnerabilities caught in the system that they wanted him to investigate. So much tech talk, and I still didn't understand what any of it meant.

> *Kinsley: I'm sorry to be an asshole. You don't deserve it :/*

> *Willow: It's fine, Kin. I'll send good morning messages in the morning if it makes you feel more secure in our relationship :)*

> *Kinsley: I don't feel insecure. I just don't wanna be cheated on :)*

Yeah, I got that already. He was starting to act really weird, and I wasn't sure how I felt about it. I understood why he'd be upset if he thought I was cheating, but it was a weird thought, considering I'd told him that I was back at the base now. I wanted to tell him about how excited I was to start sniper training. But now I just felt weird, thinking about celebrating it with him.

> *Willow: Yes, babe lol. I know not to cheat on you. You don't have to scare me into not wanting to do that.*

> *Kinsley: Good. Because you know what happens if you do cheat on me ;)*

And it was that thought alone that gave me pause. I'd never doubted my relationship with Kinsley until that moment. It was a threat he joked about all too often. Especially in the last week or so. It wasn't a joke I could take lightly anymore, though.

He'd already told me about being hired to hack a random guy's social media to ruin the guy's dignity. Last night, he made an odd comment about ruining a girl's life if she ever cheated on him. "I wouldn't care if she killed herself. She asked for it."

It was a very disturbing comment. But he also already had two nudes of me. One was in front of my vanity mirror. And the other was actually a video of me masturbating because he requested it. My face being the main star. I thought I was doing something special for the guy that I was falling in love with. But...it didn't take long for me to dissociate. Willow Harding two years ago would've never done that. It was an awful feeling. But the damage had already been done. I'd disrespected Meredith's apartment, and most importantly, I'd disrespected myself. I couldn't look at myself in the mirror for the two days until I left for base.

Maybe that's why he thought I was cheating. I expressed how uncomfortable I was with him a day later, and he didn't exactly have a good response. He said that I was being a prude. That I should be happy to please him because we were in a relationship. The old Willow would've told him where to shove it. But somewhere deep inside, the old Willow was still mourning. There was an odd solace I felt, having met Kinsley. I couldn't explain it. And as disturbing as his comments regarding relationships were...I wasn't quite ready to let him go.

Veronica Canseco will not stop texting me. It has been an entire week and a half, and not a day goes by where she doesn't text me, asking me to reconsider her offer. I delete the text each time.

When she texted me the tenth time a few days ago, I just opted to block her. My senses tell me that Kinsley set her up to track me down, so I need to distance myself as much as possible. Which is what I've been doing for a bit.

I haven't been bedridden, but my rib hurts like shit. I've done light activity around the apartment to keep active, but it's been difficult.

Meredith's come by a few times to check in and bring me to the doctor to check any progress. So far, so good. It has been a while, though, since I've spoken to Leif. He texted me a few days ago, asking how I'm feeling, but I just didn't have it in me to respond. I know I'm hurting him, but I can't bring him too deep into my life until I'm certain that Kinsley and his sketchy girlfriend forget about my existence.

Three weeks in, and it's like a switch turns on. The pain isn't completely gone, but it's subsided. I can move around my apartment comfortably.

"It feels basically like new," I say to Meredith on the phone.

"That's good, Low. I was worried that it would take longer than three weeks."

"You're telling me. It wasn't easy, being out of work for almost a month. It feels like an itch I need to scratch."

"All right, you little kill junkie," she jokes. "How are you feeling about taking on more kills? I have a few inquiries that have already come through my email already."

Back to the scheduled program.

"What kind of damage are we talking with the targets?" I ask, turning on the TV. The silence in here is eerie, only hearing my voice. I need something to fill the room while I find something to cook for dinner.

"First one sounds like peak Siren Assassin era. The client, Maria Vargas, is a trust-fund baby. Her target is boyfriend, Joseph Cato…"

But I've already stopped listening. My attention is now on the news and its contents.

"Twenty-five-year-old Veronica Canseco's body was found by the Boston River after her employer reported her missing two days ago. Canseco, a recent culinary school graduate, was a promising cook..."

I turn off the TV, a wave of déjà vu suddenly hitting me. Except Leif isn't here to witness my out-of-body episode. I replay the words in my head that actually registered. *Veronica Canseco's body was found...*

The satellite camera flies over a condominium complex that looks like the exact same complex where I killed Benji Lockson. I struggle to focus on what the newswoman is saying and zero in on the exact condo where I killed him. I can spot it pretty easily in the sea of similar buildings. Why are they circling that complex? Is that how Kinsley found me out? Did he see us casing that area?

I try to piece together what could've gone wrong that night. I made sure to canvas the house and even the outside. I got rid of all the cameras and made sure there were no loose ends. What the fuck happened?

Except it finally dawns on me. The long brown hair. The petite frame. It all makes sense, even though it doesn't. Benji Lockson's fun-loving neighbor that sat across the way crosses my mind. No wonder she seemed so familiar to me.

The dancing queen.

The closer I get to his expansive window, the more I see his neighbor across the way prancing around her living room.

"Low? Low, are you there?!"

"Mer. Get here. Now."

ELEVEN

WILLOW

"Holy shit, Low" is the first thing Meredith says when she scrolls through search engine results on her computer.

"What'd you find?" I ask in a panic.

It's been an hour since I saw the news story on Veronica's death.

"'Cause of death is unknown,'" she reads from the screen.

"I don't understand." My voice cracks as I pace the room. "She texted me just a few days ago. How the hell is she dead?"

But Meredith doesn't answer. She continues typing, a focused dip in her eyebrows giving me the cue that she's no longer listening to me. I can't believe I fucked up this badly. A woman is dead because of me.

I ponder what could've happened to signal her to text so many times. Her texts didn't really indicate anything. All she kept sending me was pleas to help her. The texts alluded to her fearing for her life. And I ignored those pleas.

"Don't do that," Meredith says.

"Don't do what?"

"You didn't do anything wrong. You followed your judgment, and it ultimately turned out to be right. It led you right back to this fucker. Her death is a casualty. A tragic one, but it was not because of you."

There's nothing for me to say. A churning feeling bubbles in my stomach, and it's been nonstop since I saw that news story.

She gives me an empathetic smile and continues to scroll on her laptop.

My phone beeps with a text from Leif.

> *VIKING: Please don't make me turn into that desperate guy. Call me back. I need to know that you're okay.*

> *ME: Hey, Viking :) I'm sorry to be quiet for so long…I'm just now getting over my injury.*

> *VIKING: You're alive ;) when can I see you?*

"You were right about Kinsley. Everything I found on him I think you know already," Meredith catches my attention before I respond to Leif.

"What'd you find?"

"For starters, the startup company he supposedly started upon moving here is co-owned."

"With who?"

"You're gonna freak out."

My ears start ringing, waiting in anticipation.

"Mer. Who is it co-owned by?"

Instead of telling me, she turns my laptop around and my life flashes before my eyes.

Benji Lockson.

"I knew it," I say under my breath.

"What do you mean?"

"Remember when I was telling you how familiar Veronica seemed to me?"

"Vaguely."

"She was his neighbor. When I was canvassing Benji and Marissas home, the curtains were drawn, and there she was…dancing in the living room."

Meredith looks at me as if I've maybe lost it. "How do you know it was her? You saw her face?"

"*Yes*, Mer. It was her. She looked at me, waved, and then started watching a movie with who I know now was probably Kinsley."

It's a lot to take in. It may even be a stretch. I sense that from Meredith's silence. But it's a theory that I fully believe is true.

"So what's all this mean? It just kind of feels like it's a coincidence."

"It means one of our clients had to be a mole."

"But why would he come to Port Rockwelland conspire to fuck with you, Low? That's multiple degrees of people to go through just to get to you."

"I haven't gotten that far. You still have that hacker friend that can check out more in the dark web?"

"Yeah, I used her to help me find out more about Veronica."

I'm setting myself up to be victimized by Kinsley Focker yet again. Once we continue to find more about this prick, there's no going back. A girl is dead. And survivor's guilt is real. I ignored her cries for help. That's not something I've ever done before. Until now.

"What else did you find on him?"

"Assaulted his last two girlfriends. Obviously, you're listed, and then he had another girlfriend before Veronica Canseco. Her name was Callie Voorhees."

How does the little fucker get a girlfriend every year?

"Where's she located?"

"She's in San Jose. Also in the tech industry, too. Works for another start-up company called Rev-Up. It's a car software company."

"Any plane tickets leaving for San Jose in the morning?"

She looks at me in disbelief. "You want to leave out tomorrow?"

"That's the only way I'll get to talk to Callie Voorhees."

Meredith scrolls her phone and shows me an Instagram page on her screen.

"Here she is."

I take the phone from her and continue to scroll through the posts on her page. She's pretty. Olive skin, long brunette hair, high cheek bones, and freckles. Kinsley obviously has an attraction to women with dark features. Her entire page and persona screams aspiring influencer. It's as if she curated an image.

"What could you find on her?"

"Stanford grad with a Bachelor of Science in Data Science. Started an organization there called Pretty Girls in STEM."

"Makes sense."

"Graduated summa cum laude. Started working for one of the big tech companies as a machine learning engineer. Here's where things take a turn."

"Okay…"

"She started working there, and then a year and a half later, she got fired after a data breach of all the women working there. Across all departments."

"What did that mean for them?"

Meredith takes a long breath before continuing.

"Confidential information about each woman was leaked on social media. Many women were doxxed. A lot had crazy stalkers loiter around their homes."

I remember that. It happened last year. It was all over the news that a major tech company's women employees had their information hacked, stolen, and leaked to the public.

"Yeah, that happened not too long ago."

"Exactly. And for Callie, her nudes were leaked. You can probably guess how that happened."

I nearly shudder in disgust. That used to be an instinctual reaction to anything pertaining to humiliation and degradation. When I first started in this line of work, I was raw to my emotions toward Kinsley and the bastards of the world. Five years later, nothing surprises me anymore.

"So she was dating Kinsley at that time, I assume."

"She posted several photos with him on her social media back. And of course, he doesn't have a social media to track. I'm sure you know that."

"He didn't have one when we first started dating."

I even tried searching for his name the first time he got mad at me when Maddie embarrassed me in front of him that day. I stopped using Ritzah shortly after my relationship with Kinsley ended and I had a falling out with my virtual friends, but it would've been a blessing in disguise if I would've just moved on instead of trying to make things right with him at the time. Hindsight.

"Well, here's the straw that broke the camel's back. She was hospitalized a week later. Two days after she posted about being released from the hospital, she changed her relationship status from in a relationship to single on her social media."

"What was she hospitalized for?"

"There's no information on that. But all we know is that her nudes were leaked, she was hospitalized…and get this. She has a police record."

"What for?"

Meredith gives me a satisfied smile.

I circle the counter and look at the screen, relieving her from reading me more details about his former victim. A mugshot of a disheveled Callie appears, with a description of the charge. I need to get to San Jose.

"We need to book a flight out next thing tomorrow morning. I have to take care of a few things, so if we can leave early afternoon tomorrow, that should get us there in time to track this girl down."

Meredith gives me a nod of affirmation before researching flights. The silence in the room is ever consuming while she does, and my attention is back on the news story yet again. The satellite scan of the complex coupled with Veronica's untimely death has left a metallic taste in my mouth. The feeling comes out of nowhere, hitting me like a freight train. The room suddenly feels smaller, the vise previously squeezing my lungs slowly creeping its way back.

"Hello?"

I look up to find a semi-blurred view of Meredith. I clear my throat and straighten my shoulders.

"Yeah," I croak.

"Are you okay?"

"As good as I'll ever be. You find any flights?"

She doesn't look the least bit convinced, but she shows me the available flights, nonetheless. Searching through direct flights, we ultimately decide on one that gets to San Jose at 5:00 p.m. tomorrow.

We spend the next few hours determining a game plan when we arrive in San Jose. All we know now is that Callie works at RevUp and that she routinely works out at a local gym in San Jose every Thursday night, based on the location and mirror pictures on her social media feed. Once we come up with a preliminary plan of checking into a hotel there and scouting out where the gym Callie frequents, we agree to call it a night and regroup in the morning before our big assignment. And while I'm relieved to have a concrete plan in the works, I still feel anxious, somehow. The walls still feel as if they're closing in around me, even as we walk down the hallway of my complex.

Something is incredibly wrong. The sensation rivals the sensation at Leif's rugby game. I'd even go as far to argue it's similar to that feeling.

"Low, you promise you're okay? You look like you're about to pass out."

And I feel like I am. I don't know what's happening to me. I know that I'm nearly having a panic attack, but I'm not sure why. Something feels off. I shouldn't be feeling this anxious.

"I think I'm okay, Mer. I may just need to get some rest."

Her concerned look I've grown to know is back, but I ignore it.

"I'll let you know once I'm home," she assures me, hopping into the Suburban.

I turn around to go back inside, but the jarring noise of loud metal crashing into the pavement stops me. I skirt back around to find the Suburban capsized, and Meredith's unconscious body slumped on the ground.

She's not in a coma. Thank fucking God. She is still unconscious, though. She has a mild concussion and will be comatose for the next 48 hours. I'm no psychic. I have no supernatural powers. But sensing trouble ahead before it happens never seems to fail me when I start having panic attacks. I've learned to trust my body. And whenever something feels off, something is off.

My Suburban is totaled. I dropped it off at Vinny's home, and he promised to have someone come out to look at it tomorrow. He insisted on coming to the hospital when he heard about Meredith's "accident," but I told him I'll stop by tomorrow to let him know what happened. Even though I'm still trying to figure it out, myself. One thing is for sure: it was deliberate. And if it wasn't Kinsley that hit her, it was someone he hired. What I'm struggling to reconcile is that he found out where I live.

My suspicions were right. He followed me. It couldn't have been the night I killed Benji Lockson, though. After I killed him, I went to the bar, met Leif, and went back with him to his loft. Shit. I quickly pull out my phone and call Leif. He answers on the first ring.

"Hey, beautiful. When can I see you?"

"Hey, Viking. Um…I can come by tonight. But…I kind of ran into an emergency."

"Are you okay?"

That's a loaded question. "I'll talk to you about that later. I wanted to ask you, have you noticed anyone weird around your place?"

I'm met with an incredulous laugh before he asks, "What?"

"Have you noticed any weird cars or people near you?"

"Not that I know of, babe. What's going on?"

He probably doesn't spend a ton of time around his loft to pay attention to who's hanging out around it.

"Nothing. I can stop by in about an hour."

"Sounds good. Did you wanna stay the night?"

'No' is on the tip of my tongue, but my gaze lands on Meredith and her paced breathing, evidenced by the rhythmic EKG monitor.

"I think I may need to," I admit.

I'm met with silence, and I start to wonder if maybe it wasn't a genuine invitation. A few more seconds pass, and I hear commotion on his end, almost as if he's getting out of bed. Is he with someone?

"I'll come and get you."

"Viking, please. If you're with someone, don't bother."

"What? I'm not with anyone. I was just in bed, babe. Where are you? I'm on my way."

I let him know that I'm at the hospital, tell him the room number, and he immediately hangs up after assuring me that he'll be here soon. I feel so stupid. My paranoia will be the death of me. Or maybe it won't. It's a blessing and a curse. Assuming that Leif was with another woman and getting upset over the thought is unlike me. And yet, I almost wrote off seeing him tonight. In instances like those, it's a curse.

Watching my best friend in the hospital reminds me that staying alert and aware of my surroundings may be a blessing. If I hadn't been there when she got hit, she would've been left on the street...to die. The thought makes me shiver. This was obviously no coincidence. Everything that's happened in the last few weeks is not a coincidence. Veronica finding me, Kinsley attacking me, Veronica getting killed, Meredith being hit and put into the hospital. I wish I'd been paranoid enough to warn her that my location is somehow compromised. Veronica's death and Meredith's incident are both stark warnings. He's toying with me. The fucker is trying to get in my head. And it just might be working.

The nurse comes in minutes later and lets me know that her vitals still look good. I communicate with her that I'll be back to visit and check in tomorrow. Almost on cue, Leif texts me to let me know that he's outside. I give Meredith a kiss on the cheek, reassure her comatose state that I'll be back, and try to stop my hand from shaking. My best friend is hospitalized. My best friend who's a victim of a traumatic childhood experience. She's in this state…all because of me.

"Willow," Leif's voice says behind me.

I turn to find a concerned and freaked-out look on his face.

"Hey, Viking."

"Do you need some more time?"

Oddly enough, he seems to know exactly what I'm thinking. I'm not ready to leave her quite yet.

"Five more minutes?"

"Whatever you need, babe."

I gently rub my chest, acknowledging the warmth I feel from his understanding. I'm not good with near-death experiences. Ironic, considering my line of work. When it comes to the people close to me, it's an itch I can't scratch. Losing my dad and dealing with the aftermath is what got me to where I am. I found solace in a scoundrel. Look where that's gotten me. I can't leave her alone. I just can't bring myself to do it. But I need to.

It takes everything in me to walk hand in hand with Leif out of the hospital and into his Tesla. He doesn't probe. He doesn't judge. All he does is comfort me by holding my hand and gently caressing it.

We stop at my loft, and he walks me inside, waiting for me outside my door.

"I'll be right here," he assures me.

I pack a bag and meet him outside again.

Once we get back to his place, I grab my bag out of the back of his car, and we make our way in. The entire way up is a silent trek, and it's all too soothing as Leif alternates between holding my hand and hugging my waist against him from behind.

We make it into his place, and I drop my bag on the couch. My hand begins to feel numb, my throat becoming heavier than usual. It isn't until I slump to the ground that I begin to register that Leif is shouting my name.

I was on the verge of slitting my wrists. I'd never raised a brow at my boyfriend wanting intimate photos of me. I realized that it's par for the course in relationships. Intimate videos, even. Some couples opt in doing a sex tape to stay connected to each other. I've always been open to them all. Never have I been asked to send a fucking video of myself urinating on a toilet paper roll. And that's exactly what Kinsley was asking for.

Willow: You're kidding, right?

Kinsley: Of course not, babe. It's sexy :D

I was lying in bed in the barracks, alone in the room I shared with one of my comrades. She'd gone to the shooting range to do some nighttime live fire exercises, and I'd decided to stay back to get some rest before starting sniper school in the morning.

> *Willow: Idk if I feel comfortable sending that :/ why do you want that?*

> *Kinsley: Because I fucking said it's sexy :)*

I didn't know how to respond to this. I already felt weird about sending him a video of me masturbating in Meredith's guest bedroom. Now he was asking—no, demanding—that I send him a video that could make or break my dignity.

> *Willow: Kin…that's a weird ask. No one's ever asked me to do that before.*

> *Kinsley: If you don't love me, Willow, you can say so instead of making up excuses to not send it :/*

> *Willow: I didn't say that I don't love you.*

> *Kinsley: Then why are you making a big deal about it? Are we not in a relationship?*

> *Willow: Yes, we're in a relationship. But that doesn't mean I can keep sending these photos and videos with my face in them without fucking with my head.*

> *Kinsley: What, you think I'll post them?*

I didn't even know anymore. His moods were so sporadic, I didn't know if I'd ever fully trust him.

> *Willow: I don't think you'll post them :)*

Kinsley: Because you know I can and I will, if you want me to :)

What the fuck was his problem?

Willow: Kin, what the hell? Why would you say that?

Kinsley: Because I'm tired of women screwing me over. I thought you meant it when you said you love me.

Willow: I did mean it. I love myself, too.

Kinsley: I knew it. You're just another narcissistic bitch who leads guys on >:(Fuck you, Willow.

I was left stunned at the message. Where did all of this come from?

Willow: That's not fair for you to call me that, Kin. I'm not narcissistic and I'm not a bitch. I can't believe you'd say that to me :(

But he didn't respond. He quickly opened the message and then just left me on read. This didn't quite enrage me. But it did annoy me. I didn't get why having a humiliating video like that of me was something he desired so much. Another fifteen minutes passed by that he didn't respond. It wasn't a long time…but it was a long time for him. He was always quick to respond unless he was busy. And something told me that busyness was not the reason he was shutting me out.

I hated myself for doing it. It was stupid to do it. But if I wanted to save this relationship and convince him that I did love him, I couldn't be selfish. He had trust issues. Understandably so. He'd been cheated on and fucked over. I'd be skeptical, too. It didn't make it any less hurtful, though.

Sneaking away to the shared bathroom on the west end of the barracks, I made sure that no one was in there and positioned my camera to capture the degradation I was about to do for a man that had oddly severe trust issues. Stripping down to my underwear, I hit record on my phone and twirled around, feigning feeling sexy. I inched my panties down in a seductive shimmy and picked up the empty toilet paper roll, doing a show of presenting it to camera. As I slouched down to squat over the toilet and held the roll underneath me, I started to think about my dad. What would he think? Would he be proud of me degrading myself to please a man whose actions and behavior clearly showed that he cared nothing about my self-respect?

My mom was out of the picture, and she would damn-near celebrate me becoming a woman and living life on the edge. But as I did the most shameful thing I've ever done, I stopped recording the humiliation porn, disposed of the roll, and dressed back up in my pajamas. When I exited the stall to wash my hands, my body tensed when a fellow comrade exited a stall at the same time. My paranoia made me speculate that they knew what I'd done…even though the girl wasn't even paying attention to me. She gave me a friendly nod before washing her hands and leaving the bathroom, leaving me to question my self-respect.

TWELVE

WILLOW

I fainted. It's the next day. The sun is peering through Leif's bedroom curtains like a sign from God that I need to rise to the occasion. Feeling heat emanating from my forehead, I touch what feels like a warm washcloth.

"Rise and shine," Leif hums from the doorway. He's looking over at me, arms crossed and shirtless. "I was waiting for those eyes to open."

I sit up and take the washcloth off my forehead.

"What time is it?"

"Half past 11," he simply says, joining me on the bed.

My flight to San Francisco leaves in approximately two hours. And Leif has no idea.

"I need to start getting ready."

He looks at me, bewildered. "Get ready for what? It seemed like you had a long night. It may be best if you slept. I can make you something."

My heart pangs yet again. Why does he do this to me?

"I don't have time to rest, Viking. I need to get on my way."

He's already annoyed with me.

"Where do you need to go right now? Why can't we ever just have a some time where we can spend it together? I don't have practice or a game today. Let me take care of you."

"I can't. I have..." *to fly out to an entirely different state* "...to run some errands."

"You always have to run errands," he points out, visibly frustrated. So visibly frustrated that stressed veins pop out of his neck. "This hiding thing is getting old, Willow."

"So is this prying thing," I mutter without thinking.

"When are you going to get comfortable enough to start talking to me?"

"I talk to you all the time. I'm not really sure what much else you want."

But I do. I know exactly what he wants. He wants the assurance that I won't leave him high and dry because, even though this is a casual arrangement, this is all an ego thing for him. I know exactly what kind of guy he is. I knew it from the very beginning.

Sighing, he gets up from the bed, retrieves a T-shirt from his dresser, and walks in the direction of his living room.

"Do you need me to drop you off at these so-called 'errands'?"

"You know, being facetious doesn't look good on you, Viking."

"Yeah, well, lying's never looked as great on you either."

He leaves the way he came, and I'm left annoyed. I don't like bickering with men as if we're married. The back-

and-forth nature is grating. Even more so with Leif. He was never the kind of guy I should've entertained. I regret ever meeting him. In the best way possible. He's one of the good ones…and that's not something I'm used to. But with Kinsley back in my life, I can't let Leif in now. There's a good chance that Kinsley knows where he lives. If he's found out where I live, there's no telling where else he's followed me and found me.

I have an hour and fifteen minutes until my flight is scheduled to leave. If I can leave without any questions, that'll make things move quickly. I made sure to call a rideshare to the airport, and it's arriving in seven minutes.

Walking into the living room, I notice Leif watching some playback from his last game. I walk over to him, his body tensing, sensing that I'm in the room. I give him a kiss on the cheek.

"Are you still mad at me?" I ask, hugging his shoulders from behind.

He lets out an exasperated sigh. "I was never mad at you, Willow. I could never be mad at you. I just don't understand why there has to be secrets."

I wish there didn't have to be secrets, either. Unfortunately, it's not my call.

"It's not my decision, Viking."

"What the hell does that mean?"

"Do you trust me?"

"Should I?"

I flinch, not sure how to respond to that.

"You just have to take my word for it. Once I get back, I'll tell you everything you need to know."

If everything goes well with this trip to San Jose, that is. If I can track Callie down and get a lead on who leaked her nudes, then maybe she has more information on

Kinsley that I somehow missed in the years following our break-up.

"Just promise me that you'll be safe. Ever since that attack at my game, I've been scared for you."

I've been finding myself clutching my chest more and more lately.

"You don't need to be scared for me. I promise I'll be okay." As okay as I can manage.

With that, he gives me a peck on the lips and walks me out, giving me another kiss on the lips before closing the door.

My steps feel heavy as I begin the trek downstairs. This isn't quite an unfamiliar feeling. The anticipation and uncertainty behind it, however, is more unfamiliar for me and an ever-too-consuming feeling. I don't know what to expect from this trip. I anticipate that Callie will have an adverse reaction to a random woman investigating a traumatic experience she's had in her life. But again…it's uncertain. She could turn me away, or she could let me in. If she's anything like me, I'm banking on being turned away. But I wouldn't be Willow Harding if I didn't at least give it a chance.

I was slowly feeling jaded, dealing with Kinsley's verbal attacks. He's deranged. It was getting exhausting. The slightest thing set him off, and I didn't know how much longer I could deal with this. I thought that sending him my most humiliating video would make him happy. But nothing ever made him happy. He was initially appreciative, but then it wore off, and he became his normal aggravated self.

Kinsley: You're ignoring me again.

Willow: You're having a panic attack again.

I got the urge to throw my phone across the room. Yesterday, he was blowing up my phone about pissing him off because I didn't respond fast enough. He spam texted me, accusing me of cheating and threatening to share my intimate photos with his hacktivist buddies online. It had been nearly three weeks, and it was becoming our routine. Fast. My panic attacks were no longer a thing of the past. I was essentially—and metaphorically speaking—chained to a man that had me wrapped around his twiddling thumbs. It was exhausting. He was exhausting.

I didn't know what I would do if everything I sent him would make its presence known on the dark web. All I knew was that I might be on the verge of a psychotic break.

"Harding," my commanding officer barked behind me as I started my trek to my third week of sniper training.

Clearing my throat, I faced him head-on and stood at attention. "Sir, yes, sir."

He silently walked up to me, sizing me up, and I began to worry that maybe I'd done something wrong. An unreadable look etched his face.

"I need to speak with you, if that's all right," he requested and walked into his office. One of my comrades, Trudy, looked at me, confused. I gave her an acknowledging nod before walking into his office.

Willow: You fucking piece of shit, Kinsley

That was the first thing I messaged him once I got back to the barracks after training.

Kinsley: I told you what happens when you piss me off, Willow. You know I'm not one to bluff.

One search of the social media group with my nudes there, and I was fucking pissed. The damn bastard started it with his friends where they all share nudes of their girlfriends or girls, they were seeing whenever they got into an argument.

Willow: Why did you share the link with my boss? What the fuck is wrong with you? How did you even get his email?

My commanding officer had a very stern talk with me about it, and I was pissed. I was expecting to be placed on leave, but he was more forgiving than I expected him to be. He offered support and gave understanding about "little bastard boys that have nothing better to do than to ruin girls' lives because they can't control their emotions." The talk made me want to chuckle, but I didn't have the time to. I typically don't engage in humor when there are risqué photos of me in public domain.

Kinsley: Does it matter?

Willow: Are you fucking stupid??

Kinsley: Do you really think it's smart to talk to me like that when I've already proven I don't bluff?

I nearly crushed the phone in my hands. I was due back at marksmanship training at 5 a.m. Which was in six hours.

Willow: Why do you like to stress me out? I already have enough shit to worry about, Kinsley. My fucking dad just died, and I train long hours.

Kinsley: You think you're stressed?! I have to debug a software application that my jackass coworker engineered wrong!

Was he serious? Clearly, this had to be a joke. I hated to devalue and minimize complications people had in their lives—even though that's what he'd just done to me—but I was not sure if our two issues were comparable.

Willow: I think you're the jackass, Kinsley. I literally just said that I lost my dad and I'm training to become a sniper.

I fixed my fingers at the ready, expecting him to have another smartass remark. But it surprised me when he didn't. I looked at my phone for another five minutes before deciding that he'd gotten preoccupied with work. I should calm down, now that I felt like I'd made my case that he was being stupid. But I was still trembling from anger. My fucking nudes were on the Internet in a private group my dumbass boyfriend and his friends started to get their rocks off when they were mad at their girlfriends. How fucking fucked is that?
I was about to get in the shower when he finally responded.

Kinsley: Sniper, eh? My girlfriend's a badass.

I was left puzzled. He had to be suffering from some personality disorder. I wasn't sure what, exactly. But his behavior was not anything I'd seen before. Granted, I was twenty years old. But something seemed completely off and not canon about him.

Willow: Yes. So you're not the only one that's stressed.

I threw my phone on the bathroom counter and jumped into the shower. I'm usually relaxed after a steaming shower. It gives me the space and peace to eradicate any negative thoughts. I feel new after a shower. And it didn't fail me this time. I got out, dried my curls, and started getting ready for bed. I chanced a look at my phone and saw a message from Kinsley from fifteen minutes ago. I was surprised he hadn't spammed my phone, as he usually did when I didn't respond in ten seconds.

> *Kinsley: I'm sorry, babe…I know I'm not the only one that's stressed. Work is just a lot.*

> *Willow: I get it, Kinsley. But this has to stop. You are mad at me every other hour. Do you know how exhausting it is for me to be with someone so hotheaded?*

> *Kinsley: So now it's hard to be with me?*

Fucking hell. I had to watch what I said to him. Certain key words stuck out to him more than others.

> *Willow: When you're like this, yes, it's hard to be with you.*

> *Kinsley: I bet Isabella wouldn't think that.*

> *Willow: Who the fuck is Isabella?*

And why was he bringing her up?

> *Kinsley: She's a friend :) a friend that's much nicer to me than you are.*

> *Willow: Then go fuck her, Kinsley. I don't have time for this bullshit.*

I immediately turned off notifications to my texts, set my alarm for my early morning, and tried to get to sleep. This was something that I could deal with tomorrow, when I didn't have only five hours to sleep. Perhaps he'd freak out from my delayed responses to whatever panic attack he was having while I was asleep. The time would come when I stopped giving a fuck how he felt. That time just wasn't today.

The flight to San Francisco flew by in a whirlwind—no pun intended. My mind was on Meredith and her safety the entire way here. I made sure that Vinny and Leif checked on her, texting them while I took a rideshare to the airport.

It's Thursday, and according to her social media feed, she attends Pilates on Thursday afternoons after work. I call a rideshare to take me to my hotel in San Jose. Once my driver arrives, I throw my suitcase in his trunk, settle into his Lincoln, and ruminate more on how I let my best friend become a casualty in my life. She didn't deserve this. She has enough going on in her life, apart from her traumatic childhood. She's been my righthand woman for the bulk of my kill career. What's more, she's been my best friend for over a decade. It was a huge risk for her to be involved in my work. But it was a risk we both were willing to take.

I'm at my hotel in record time. I check in and settle in for a bit until I get a notification from my designated hacker that I contacted temporarily. Meredith was my liaison when it comes to the nitty gritty hack work. The irony of hating a hacker is making your best friend your personal hacker. But her expertise in the art of tracking and finding a vulnerable spot in software was too hard to ignore. I never thought it'd ever put her in harm's way. How naïve of me.

The hacker, Violet, calls me to let me know that her tracking of Callie puts her at the gym, 365Fitness.

Mission commenced.

I put on the tight leggings that seem to be in style, a sports bra, and sneakers. I throw my hair up in a top bun, call a rideshare to the gym, and I'm on my way. The ride is a quiet one. My driver Hugo keeps eyeing me through the rearview mirror, mentally questioning why I'm writing in my kill diary, no doubt. I catch glances from him when he thinks I don't feel his gaze, and I almost chuckle. If only he knew what I was writing about and keeping track of.

Hugo arrives in front of the gym, and I hop out, toss him a $5 dollar bill for a gratuity, and circle the side of the building. I pull out my phone, and Violet sends me a text signaling that Callie is inside. I steadily find myself falling into the trap of treating this like it's a kill. That's not what this is. And I don't want to put her in a situation where she thinks I'm here to put her life in danger.

I walk inside, taking in the air of pheromones and testosterone roaming the bustling gym. All of the platforms are occupied, in addition to the treadmills and weights racks in front of the mirrors. I canvas the gym for Callie, and my gaze lands on the woman in question.

Her brown hair is up in a messy bun. She looks in her element, wireless earphones in both ears, holding a bar on her shoulders and doing squats in front of a mirror. I canvass, looking for a free dumbbell or treadmill to busy myself with. I pull out my phone and send an update to Violet that I've spotted Callie, and she replies her confirmation. Grabbing a pair of 20-pound dumbbells, I settle in front of a mirror perpendicular to Callie's platform. That way, I can keep her in my line of sight but avoiding bringing any suspicion to myself.

I do a few dumbbell squats and watch as a stereotypical gym bro strolls up to her, mid hang snatch. He leers at her before whispering something in her ear, and she visibly tenses, angrily throwing the barbell—with 50 lb weights on each side—on the platform. She turns to him and looks to be giving him a piece of her mind, but he looks only mildly amused. The smug grin on his face as she reams into him gives me a rage that's all too familiar. A few guys who I'm assuming are his friends stalk up behind him, watching Callie speak her mind as if she's some sort of freak show attraction. It takes every ounce in me to stay to myself until I can find a way in. I continue doing my dumbbell squats, increasingly gripping them out of anger.

It isn't until I hear one of them say, "Are you on your period?" that I finally intervene.

Slamming the dumbbells down on the rack, I strut over to the scene and take in the confused gazes I get from all three of the steroid-ridden men.

"Excuse me, I think you need to apologize to her."

The brunette guy who first approached her gives me an incredulous look.

"Who the fuck are you?"

His friend next to him inserts himself into the conversation, suddenly interested. And I don't miss the type of interest that gleams in his hazel eyes.

"Yeah. Who the fuck are you?" he asks in a sexually suggestive voice. But I ignore him and zero in on the asshole scowling down at me.

"I'm her friend. And I don't appreciate you reducing women to their menstrual cycles."

He cocks an eyebrow in disbelief as his buddies chuckle behind him.

"I didn't reduce her to shit. Her reaction to me appreciating a nice ass is a bit overblown, though."

"So is your ego."

He grinds his jaw, and we commence in a stare-off. In a busy gym. But I don't back down.

Henry Cavill lookalike pipes up again and nudges his arm.

"Dude, what are you doing? Her friend is hot."

We both momentarily stop our staring contest and scoff at him.

"Hot girls aren't worth this emotional bullshit."

He glares at me with a spitfire I'm too familiar with and spins around, walking away from me, his friends following suit. Rolling my shoulders back, I turn to find a shocked Callie staring up at me.

"Hi," she says, almost absently.

"Hi."

"Who are you? I mean, that was really cool of you, but…I'm sorry, I'm really confused. Who are you?"

"I'm Willow Harding. You don't know me. But I have some questions if you don't mind me asking."

Her gaze is still transfixed on me.

"Willow Har—" she recounts to herself. "Do I know you?"

"No. But soon you will. Because I need your help."

The confused look on her face speaks volumes.

"You need my help. With what, exactly?"

It's not a good time. The novelty of not knowing who the hell I am is still fresh, and I don't think she'll fully register what I need her help with if I just out and tell her that I know Kinsley. If she's anything like me, any mention of his name and being in his presence is a sensory overload that's overstimulating. He has the power to destroy your dignity and leave weakness and despair in his wake. He's a professional sadist. One I've tried hard to avoid for years. And to see that he's tracked me down yet again and is playing a game of chicken with my life…that's something that cannot be ignored.

"Are you familiar with the boogeyman?"

She flinches. "What?"

"The boogeyman. He's found me."

She looks around as if she's being punked before looking at me again.

"I don't understand what you mean."

Taking a deep breath, I try my hardest to rid myself of the nervousness coursing through me. There's no objectively great way to address this. I suddenly lose my voice as a golf-sized lump forms in my throat. The room isn't quite spinning, but it is a close second. Callie senses my uneasiness as confusion transforms into concern on her face.

With shaky hands, I take out my phone from my workout fanny pack, pull up a photo of the glass-eyed demon, and show her.

Her reaction speaks volumes. Color vanishes from her face, as if she's seen a ghost. She rubs at her chest and clears her throat.

"You know Leif Mattson?"

THIRTEEN

WILLOW

They were there. I couldn't deny them anymore. No matter how much I wanted to. My blood ran cold when I took another look at the literal porn in front of me. And it was of myself. The number of likes continued to rise, and my anxiety followed suit.

I did this to myself. One snap of a picture, one pushed button, and my life going downhill was the result. In this case, it was multiple snaps of pictures and filming of videos. I was a fool. Why did I do this, you ask? The answer's a lot easier than what I'm about to tell you.

I met a boy. We hit it off. I fell for him…at least I thought I did. And it was clockwork from there. You'll learn to hate me. Not any more than I hate myself. And you'll learn to judge me. But not any more than I'm already judging myself. So before you pull the trigger on the judge gun too soon, allow me to tell you how things ended up this way. And why I'll never trust anyone ever again.

Kinsley Focker. A quirky hacker boy that—in the digital sense—waltzed into a chat room one day on a virtual world called Ritzah and immediately stole my heart. That's how it works, anyway.

They call it love bombing, a manipulation tactic used all too often. Kinsley was a pro. He got to know me, I got to know him. We were a somewhat slow burn of sorts. Though it didn't quite take him long to get in my good graces. It only took a few compliments and the intense mourning of my dad for me to degrade myself and send him intimate photos. I was clearly a glutton for punishment. Or I was desperate for a place of solace.

Banishing the thoughts from my head proved to be difficult as I aimed my rifle at a target during target practice. My hands were shaky, and my commanding officer noticed. It was part of my marksmanship training. I was choking. Immensely.

"What's the hold-up, soldier?"

The sweat trickling down my temple tickled me, but I couldn't wipe it away yet. I needed to focus on having steady hands.

"Just focusing, Captain."

"You've been focusing for two goddamn minutes, soldier!"

His inquisition only made me sweat more. I did everything in my power to stop thinking about my intimate pictures and videos making it to a website Kinsley and his hacker group had designed to get revenge for infidelity. And I didn't cheat on him.

"I'm doing my best, Captain," my croaky voice managed to get out.

He did a silent grunt of frustration before taking a deep breath and falling into silence behind me. I squinted harder through the rifle scope, trying my damn hardest to focus on the target. My hands were still slightly shaky, but I managed to keep the center in my line of sight. After about ten excruciating seconds of focusing and attempting to maintain precision, I took another deep breath and pulled the trigger.

He wanted me to buy him gifts on Ritzah. After not only leaking to a social media group he created, but to an amateur porn website he built. I was fully convinced he's a sociopath.

Willow: You're deluded.

Kinsley: You're ungrateful. After everything I've done for you, you can't even buy me a new shirt from the catalog?

My gaze burned through the screen, thoroughly confused.

Willow: What have you done for me, Kin? Please enlighten me.

Kinsley: Oh, being there for you mourning your dead dad isn't enough?

Willow: You're right. You deserve a fucking gold star.

Kinsley: Don't be a smartass.

I could kill him. I'd been having thoughts about it, lately. He wasn't the guy I thought he was.

Willow: You're not getting any more gifts. Not after the shit you pulled.

Kinsley: You should've never sent me anything ;)

Willow: You're a piece of shit.

Kinsley: You're too kind. Now I want two new shirts from the Ritzah catalog or I post more of your little home videos.

My heart took another leap to my stomach.

Willow: Actually, you know what? I can't spend any more money :) my mom says I can't spend anything else online like a loser.

He wanted to play games, so could I.

Kinsley: Your mom's not even in your life, dumbass.

Willow: And your mom's not in yours. Sorry.

Kinsley: Willow, I have one more video I've not posted yet. Are you sure you wanna play this game with me right now?

Willow: It's not gonna do any more damage than you've already caused. So go and fuck yourself.

With that, I blocked him and plugged my phone in, charging it. I was asking for it at this point. But I was done being scared of him. He didn't own me.

I continued to tell myself that back then, but it became no use. He did own me. He ruled over my emotions and mindset. He knew exactly the right buttons to push and when to push them. He's sinister. In the last ten years or so, everyone—including Meredith—tried to convince me that I'm exaggerating with my visceral reaction to him. But that's the thing: I'm not. Meredith doesn't know the gravity of what he did. All she knows is that he emotionally and psychologically abused me. When I was sending him those intimate photos and videos, he didn't send anything back. It was expected that I did what he asked. He waited until he was in my good graces and I could trust him before he turned. Normal Jekyll and Hyde. It wasn't something I was expecting. Or maybe I wasn't paying attention to the warning in front of me. And it seems as if my judgment hasn't changed much.

Kinsley Focker. Leif Mattson. One and the same. There had to be more to the story.

"I thought you knew" is the first thing Callie says as the waitress drops our margaritas off at the artsy, hipster restaurant she chose to meet at.

I was so taken aback by the new revelation, she thought it'd be a good idea if we met over some tacos and margaritas. I hadn't eaten dinner yet, so it wasn't an invitation I could pass up. But in the midst of the inner turmoil I was—and am currently—facing, it's still a revelation I'm struggling to wrap my head around.

"So his name is Leif Mattson. Not Kinsley Focker."

Taking a sip of her raspberry margarita, she toys with the straw before looking up at me.

"I know him as Leif. We all went to high school and college together. Kinsley's his older brother. They're half-brothers."

I remember hearing about his little brother. He told me his name was Derek, though. I remember when he would apologize for delayed responses and explain that he'd sometimes go with his brother to football practice. Or he'd tell me that he was going to his brother's graduation.

"Half-brothers," I repeat.

She nods, tucking a strand of her brown locks behind her ear.

"They have different dads. They're a unit, those two."

"What do you mean?"

She sighs and cracks her knuckles as if she's about to unveil a bombshell.

"They're kind of…porn addicts."

I wasn't expecting that. But it does make a bit of sense, considering he requested I send him borderline humiliation porn.

"That doesn't surprise me. But what makes his brother a porn addict?"

The man I formerly knew as Leif comes to mind, and it immediately breaks my heart. He fooled me. The guy with the glass eye has been Kinsley to me all along, and I've always known him as a porn addict. But hearing that Leif also is might be too much for me to absorb. The entire revelation altered my world.

My attention is back on her, though.

Callie Voorhees has olive skin. I've never seen a person with olive skin go pale. Until now. She does a sharp intake of breath, and her green eyes are like huge evergreen forests. There's a few more seconds of hesitation and mere paralysis before she sighs, holding up her drink.

"Liquid courage?"

"Do we need it?"

"For this story," she declares before downing the rest of her drink.

I stare at her, impressed. I've always seen myself as the liquid courage gal. So much to the point where Vinny created a drink in my honor called The Siren. It's my spin on a Manhattan at his bar, but it includes blue curacao and a whiskey double. Judging by her courage, Callie looks as if she can handle it well.

"Enlighten me."

She gives me a bitter laugh before adjusting in her seat.

"Oh, my pleasure. Leif and his freak of nature brother are rapists and sadists. But you didn't need me to tell you that."

"Rapists?"

"In the flesh. They used to run a scam a few years ago at the local bars out here. When he was in college, he played football, and his brother played rugby in the spring. San Jose College sports are big in this town, so they would get into exclusive eighteen-and-up clubs and bars and throw killer parties after their wins."

"What do you mean by running a scam? The parties weren't real?"

"Not real in the sense that they were any fun. The football coach was good friends with the bar owner. That should be enough said."

"Fair enough. So…what was happening at these club parties?"

The waitress suddenly walks up with our tacos and sets them down in front of us. When she walks away, Callie takes a quick bite of her shrimp taco.

"I played softball in the spring, and his brother was the same season as rugby at our school. Both teams were super close because we shared the same weight room during training. Leif was a friend of mine since freshman year, but outside of sharing the weight room, I didn't really know his brother much. Both of our teams won a lot that year. We were both number one in the state."

"Damn" is all I can say.

"Yeah…his brother was the quiet, brooding type. Didn't really speak much when he was in his element. It was kind of sexy at the beginning. I had a crush on Kinsley for much of high school and college."

The name never ceases to run a shiver up my spine.

"So he goes by his brother's name."

She runs a shaky hand through her hair again.

"He's jealous of his brother. He's always been. I had no idea that Leif had a crush on me."

"He had a crush on you?"

"Always did. I didn't know he had a crush on me until it was our college graduation. I told him I wasn't into him like that, and he didn't speak to me for a while. After Leif and I graduated, Kinsley was already working in Silicon Valley, and he was able to get me an internship at the tech company he worked at through a referral. I was a back-end engineering intern, and I started working under Kinsley. Everything seemed like it went back to normal. I always hung out with Leif, but then I started to work a lot more with Kinsley. We didn't start dating until a year later. It was after a night of drinks at a company party, and we ended sleeping together that night. I thought he would regret it…and for some time, he did. He was very short and curt with me, and it hurt. But I didn't know it would hurt Leif as much as it did. He didn't speak to me for weeks, and I finally confronted Kinsley about why he was avoiding me. He would suggest to his superior that I should transfer departments and engineer more on the front end. When I confronted him, he tried to write it off as just not feeling comfortable after sleeping together, and he didn't want to ruin our 'budding friendship.' I didn't realize how much bullshit that was, but I was twenty-two and stupid. I thought he just cared about me."

"From what it sounds like, those brothers don't care about anybody."

She gives me a slight nod, with a pained look on her face, but continuing with the story, nonetheless.

"I reassured him that he wasn't ruining anything by just talking to me. He felt bad not only for ignoring me, but for his brother because Leif had a crush on me since we first met. That was when I found out. I knew that ignoring Leif's feelings and pursuing a relationship with Kinsley was a stupid idea. But I just couldn't believe that I was finally getting a chance with the guy I fell in love from the moment I met him, you know?"

I'm all too familiar with the feeling. I immediately think back to first meeting him online. I was dumbstruck by how he made me feel. I can't fault her for being hoodwinked.

"So we started going out. It was casual at first—we went on a date later that week, and he promised me to not tell Leif. He didn't wanna hurt him. I promised, and then…we just started dating," she says with a nervous laugh. "It was everything I wanted. He was charming, handsome, athletic. Tall, dark, and handsome, I think is the better phrase for it. He's what most people would call the ideal man. It did make me feel insecure, at first. I was twenty-two, and he was twenty-six, dating me. Women were throwing themselves at him, and he's very flirty. The attention he got made me uncomfortable, and I hated when he would flirt back. I voiced this concern to him, and he promised to stop doing it, if it would make me feel more secure in the relationship. It felt like each time something came up that would damage our relationship, he would make me fall in love with him over and over again when he came up with solutions to strengthen our bond. It was the perfect manipulation. We would text and get closer and closer." She then looks down at her nails nervously. "This part…kind of gets TMI…idk if you're okay with that."

"Trust me. In my line of work, I've seen and heard it all."

She looks confused at that quip but doesn't let it stop her from telling the story.

"He got laid off from the tech company due to budget cuts, which meant that his suggestion that I intern under another test engineer actually went through. He ended up leaving, so the only time I would see him would be if I had gone over to his house or he would visit me at mine. When

I didn't see him, it would be when he got hired as a senior test engineer at a smaller tech company in San Francisco. He would travel, sometimes, off-site for testing software, and this would be in different states, if it came to it. When he was gone, he would say he missed me and wanted me to send some sexy photos and videos…"

I freeze. "What?"

"Yeah. At first, it made me uncomfortable because I had never done that before. He would laugh at me, saying that 'no girl that looked like me would be a prude.' He was shaming me. I wanted to make him happy, so I sent what he requested…and that was a picture of me, nude, in front of my mirror. I felt so humiliated…but he was happy. He said he felt closer to me, and that, in turn, made me happy. I *wanted* to make him happy. So every time he traveled or when we were apart, he would ask me to send some sexy stuff. Every time, it escalated, progressing from sultry nudes to full blown porn. He would want me to send videos of myself masturbating, me rubbing lube on my vagina, or using a hairbrush to…"

"I get it," I say, noticing her cheeks redden.

"It didn't feel like he loved me anymore. It just felt more like he was almost enjoying the fact that I would send him any and everything he wanted me to. And because I was a fucking idiot, I did."

"You're not an idiot. He's just a dipshit."

That makes her chuckle. "He was someone I loved. It came to a point, one day, when I was getting burned out from making these sex videos for his enjoyment. I made it known to him that I wasn't doing that anymore and, if that was a dealbreaker for him, he'd have to break up with me. Because I wasn't strong enough to leave him by choice; he'd have to make that choice for me. I felt good. I felt…empowered. But he didn't respond for a while after

that. I knew that he'd just be coming back from Boston—
"

"Boston?"

"Yeah…he told me that he was helping Leif get more settled at MIT, as he was planning on going to graduate school there."

"Leif has been in Boston for a while?"

She looks at me as if she has no idea why I'm inquisitive.

"He's been there since we graduated from college. I'm pretty sure he's been working on starting a small tech company, and it's been successful…from what I've…"

Sudden ringing surrounds me, slowly blocking out anything else Callie is saying. Her mouth moves, but I can't hear anything. I down a glass of water next to me, and I don't miss the concerned look that's back on her face. If this fucker's been in Port Rockwell since 've been working as a hitwoman…then that would make Veronica's claim that they'd just move to Port Rockwell a complete lie.

"Are you okay?"

I'm finally in tune with my surroundings again, the ringing gradually going away. I clear my throat and take another sip of water.

"Yeah," I croak. "It's just starting to get a bit dry in here."

"We can head to a quieter and more intimate place, if it's too much for you here—"

"No, I'm okay. I just needed a minute to myself."

She doesn't look fully convinced. "If this story is too much for you, I understand. It's kind of a lot—"

"It's okay, Callie. You were saying he was coming back from Boston, and…?"

This is enough for her to continue.

"Right. He was just coming back from Boston and he didn't respond for another two days. I remember…it was his five-year college reunion. He texted me the night before, apologized for not responding, and said that he understood why I felt weird about sending him photos and videos. He wanted to "make it up" to me by inviting me to be his date for the University of San Jose reunion the next night. I thought it was weird that he pulled a 180 and made *that* his response to me pouring my heart out about not feeling comfortable about sexting. I asked my close friend at the time, Chelsea, if I should go. She thought I should give him a chance and take some time to unwind after a long week of work. So I went. And that was the biggest mistake of my life."

"Why's that?"

"Because the invitation was their way of humiliating me."

"What do you mean? What happened that night, Callie?"

"They…*raped* me. Leif and Kinsley. It was the first time I'd seen Leif after graduation because he was so mad at me for dating his brother. And then the first time I see him after all that time…was at the college bar that we all went to after games It felt like a full-circle moment."

A new wave of emotion comes over her. Where she was more pensive telling the story, she's now overcome with fear and anxiety.

"They held the reunion at the bar?"

She shakes her head, wiping a tear from her eye.

"It was at the college stadium. But there was an after party that Kinsley wanted to go to. I was hesitant to go because I remembered the sex rooms the owner would have set up secretly on the basement floor. It was disgusting…unruly," she says with a look of horror on her face. "I never went, I'd just stay on the bar level with my teammates, but Leif and Kinsley would head down there to get their rocks off. They were my friends, so I never judged them. But…this night was different. It didn't feel like the normal after-the-game college night it was back then. Kinsley wanted me to go down there with him. I thought the basement closed down because the original owner of the bar sold it to a new one. The basement room was still alive and well, though. Now…I'm not one to kink shame—"

"You and me both. But if you did something that made you uncomfortable, there's nothing wrong with feeling that way."

She just shrugs. "I thought it was just gonna be an ordinary date night. But everyone from my class went down there because it was a night special to honor the class of 2017. It was putrid. The sex room was a display room. People would watch others having sex, and I didn't know that…Kinsley signed me up to be on display."

"Fucking hell," I mutter.

"It was awful, Willow," she says through the tears building in her eyes. "We argued about it, and I saw a side of Kinsley I'd never seen. I declined to be put on display on that. He slapped me…told me that I'd do whatever he asked me to. He cajoled, saying that he just wanted to make it up to me and help me feel more confident in myself and body if I just put it on display for an entire room of my old classmates. I was humiliated, yet again. But…I loved him. So I did it. I got naked, got into the middle of the ring, and a random classmate from college joined me in the center, eyeing me with a hungry look that nauseated me. Ben Casey. He was an old classmate that hit on me multiple times back in college, but I never entertained him because I had eyes for Kinsley. Everyone around the room shouted what sex acts to perform on each other, and I tried to get out of it. But Ben overpowered me multiple times in the ring, and the shouts of approval around us consumed me. I hated it. 'I always wanted to touch you, Callie. Dream come fucking true' is what he said. I felt so gross. I was able to get away after kneeing him in the balls and running for the stairs. But Kinsley stopped me, throwing me back down. When I got up off the ground, Leif stood over me, a sadistic smile on his face. The guy was supposedly my best friend for a little over a decade, at that point. I remember…the rank stench of cigarettes on his breath. He lifted me up, hoisting me over his shoulder, and I fought for my fucking life for him to put me down. There was a secret room in the corner of the basement, and Kinsley followed us into it, locking the door behind us. The numerous cheers outside are a mere memory. Leif threw me down on the old, yellow mattress. They both stood over me, and all I could see were their matching evil grins. Leif…he bent down and told me that he'd been waiting since freshman year to get his hands on me. I looked up at the guy that was supposed to be my boyfriend, and the evil grin turned to an emotionless stare. I no longer recognized either one of them. That night…I wish I could banish it from my head."

"Callie…"

I don't know what else to say. It's so much to take in, and a wave of uneasiness flutters underneath my flesh. It's not easy to rehash shit like that. Those bastards caused her a great fucking deal of trauma. Looking at her terrified face, I sat here and encouraged her to tap back into that trauma. And that makes me just as bad as they are.

"It's a memory that's forever etched into my brain."

"I'm so fucking sorry, Callie."

"I reported the rape. But then…they threatened to post my and many of my female coworkers' nudes to a revenge porn website. Kinsley somehow gained access to their nudes and threatened to ruin more women's lives since one was trying to 'ruin' his life. I went through with pressing the charges. And then—"

"They posted the nudes," I finish for her.

"And he said he had many more that he'd post. Said that there's too much evidence to use in court and diminish my credibility to the jury. It became too much of a risk. So to save myself the stress, I just dropped the charges. I've been trying to lay low since then. It's been years. I've been trying to get it out of my head."

All I can do is look at her. She's in distress. I had no idea the level of trauma I was expecting, but I can't say that this was it.

"Is there anything I can do for you, Callie? I feel like I reopened a traumatic wound that'd take forever to heal again."

She toys with the straw in her margarita, momentarily avoiding my gaze.

"How do you know them?"

My shoulders tense. "I don't even know where to begin."

"Try the beginning. It's only fair."

I'm not one to rehash my traumas with people that aren't those close to me. Hell, it's been an entire struggle to open up to Connie for years. But I'd be hypocritical if I didn't at least gloss over who Leif was to me…and who Kinsley is to me, now.

When I explain to her what happened with Leif who I formerly knew as Kinsley, she's left more speechless than I was at the end of her recount.

"Holy shit," she blurts. "I'm so sorry, Willow. That's awful."

"It's nowhere as awful as what happened to you, though. And you seem to be handling it way more healthily than I am."

I leave her confused yet again. "I hope you're at least in therapy. A lot of people avoid it but, with shared experiences like ours...it's a wonder we haven't harmed ourselves, already."

"Trust me. I'm in therapy." And one form of it soothes me more than the other.

After many hours of confiding in each other about our shared experiences, I decide to pay for our drinks, drive her back to her apartment for the night, and go back to my hotel. I check in with her periodically throughout the night, and each time she assures me that she's feeling okay....though I don't believe it.

I was lied to. Betrayed. I fucked up and let this guy back into my life…not realizing I did.

I hate that my chest starts to hurt, mourning whatever relationship I thought I was building with Leif…Kinsley. He fooled me.

The guy I've been repeatedly having sex with.

The guy I've been letting into my apartment.

The guy who I've brought around Vinny and Meredith.

And the guy who I was starting to fall for.

Kinsley fucking Focker.

Clearing my throat, I dial Vinny. He picks up after the third ring.

"Low?"

"Vinny. I know I promised you that I'd stop killing."

There's a moment of silence on his end before he sighs, anticipating what's to come.

"You did."

"Well, I'm sorry, but I can't promise that anymore. An extenuating circumstance has come up."

"And what's that, Low?"

"All I know…is that I'm back in business."

FOURTEEN

WILLOW

Silence is bliss. With Kinsley blocked and out of my life, I could finally be at peace again. I spent the last three weeks in PT and sniper school reveling in this fact. I spent more time with my comrades, my commanding officer has been giving me praise in my progress, and it was business as usual.

Until I got a strange message on my social media page. A spam account with no profile picture sent me a cryptic message, freaking me out.

Trade0910: You really want me to expose this truth?

Beneath the disturbing message was one of the videos that I shot for Kinsley, and my entire world nearly shattered. It was a message he'd sent to me last night, and I was only seeing it now. I don't normally check my message requests. Now I regret it. Scared out of my mind, I replied back with shaky fingers, asking whoever the person was what they wanted. My instincts told me it was definitely Kinsley or one of his fucked-up friends. I didn't get a response for a few hours.

It was the night after a long day of distance firing training. I was tired and drained.

I took a shower, still thinking about the freaky message. Why did he decide to message me three weeks later and try to blackmail me? The shower was meant to calm my nerves, but the thought of this loser bothering me again made my skin crawl.

Once I was out of the shower, I ran a comb through my wet curls, brushed my teeth, and got dressed for bed. All while wondering if the mysterious social media account had responded to me. This unnecessary stress would most likely send me into another panic attack. Bracing myself, I picked up my phone, and my heart started racing when my messages lit up with an unread one. I took a deep breath and opened it.

> *Trade0910: Lucky for you, I'm in Port Rockwell:) What I want is to see you.*

I reread the message multiple times to make sure I wasn't having a nightmare.

> *Willow: What are you doing here?*

> *Trade0910: That's not any of your business.*

> *Willow: It's my business if you're coincidentally in my hometown and asking to see me. A little weird, don't you think?*

> *Trade0910: I think it's even weirder that you blocked me and didn't tell me why :)*

I found myself wanting to strangle the damn phone and throw it across the room again. But he wasn't worth my rage. Taking another deep breath, I reined it in and thought of a carefully constructed text that showed that he no longer had any power over me.

Willow: I'm not going to engage in an argument with you, Kinsley. It's kind of lame that you created a fake account to reach out to me, instead of reaching out to me with your regular account like a normal person. But I digress :)

Okay. It was a little sassier than I intended, but he really knew how to push my buttons. I guess he still did have an uncanny power over me that I couldn't seem to shake.

Trade0910: Attitude isn't necessary, Willow. Just come and meet me. Let me buy you a drink :)

These smiley faces and the calm tone in his messages were freaking me out. He sent me a video of myself, threatening to blackmail me with it, and now he's acting apathetic toward my snideness.

Willow: When would you like to meet?

Trade0910: Are you free tonight?

I frowned, looking at the time on my phone. It was midnight, and I had to wake up at 5:30. It would be stupid to leave after a long day of training. Plus, I wouldn't feel good, getting up that early after a night out. I wasn't in the mood to entertain whatever this fucker had under his belt.

Willow: I'm not.

Trade0910: I think you are :)

And he sent me another video that I sent him, proving that he means business and that I was absolutely fucked.

He wanted to meet at a bar I'd never been to in Boston. Maybe it was because I wasn't twenty-one yet, but Meredith and I had fake IDs and had gotten into many bars with them. I've been to most bars in the city. Meridian 617 wasn't one of them.

It was a dive bar with dim, lazy lighting. It wasn't busy, but there were a few men—plus a few couples—frequenting the bar area and the pool table. The only issue? I had no idea what the fuck Kinsley looked like. The entire time we'd been Internet dating, he hadn't sent any photos of him—he'd only requested that I send photos of me. So I had no idea who I was looking for. He said he'd be there when I got there, considering the drive from Fort Wycoff was an hour and a half.

I texted Meredith to let her know that I'd be back in the metropolitan Boston area for the night, but she didn't respond. It was almost 2:30 now, so I knew she was most likely not awake. But if anything happened to me, I'd just wanted her to know where I was. I shared my location with her and made sure to tell her where I was. I did everything my dad taught me.

"Well, well, well. You can't mistake that body for anyone else's."

A deep voice spoke behind me, making my stomach turn. And it's one I've heard before.

I turned to find a tall, somewhat muscular boy with a strikingly handsome face. He had gray eyes with brown hair. He has a cowlick haircut, almost as if he'd just woken up from a nap. He was in the stereotypical hacker clothes: a dark gray sweatshirt, black sweatpants, and black Skippys. He was definitely not what I pictured as a nerdy hacker guy. He was built like a quarterback. It was an odd paradox. But this nerdy hacker violated me. Therefore, I, Willow Harding, could not give in.

"And you can't mistake that venomous voice of yours for anyone else's either."

He cocked an eyebrow, his gray eyes peering into me. "You're just as stunning in person, Willow."

I straightened my shoulders and faced him head-on. "You're too kind."

He sized me up before nodding in the direction of the bar. "Care for a drink?"

Sharing a drink with this guy was a bad idea. I didn't truly know him. His moods were extremely volatile. Saying 'no' was wise, but saying 'yes' would also ensure that my videos weren't seen by people close to me. He could send the videos to them directly, and that's humiliating.

"Sure. I don't mind a drink."

Minutes later, we were catching up and pretending as if our entire relationship didn't happen. Though, it did feel like a strained conversation. Almost as if we were expecting one or the other to bring up the elephant in the room. Then he finally stopped bullshitting.

"You wanna know why I invited you out tonight?"

"Considering that you had me drive an hour and a half knowing that I have an early wake-up time, the answer to that question would be yes."

He gave me a sly smirk.

"So you're not just quick-witted over text. It's kind of sexy."

"Why am I here, Kinsley?"

He took a long sip of his gin and tonic and wiped his mouth.

"I wanted to meet you. Really get to know Willow Harding."

"Didn't learn enough from my nudes that you requested?"

He chuckled. "You're really touchy about that."

"You posted it on the fucking Internet. How do you expect me to react?"

He rolled his eyes. "I didn't post them, Willow."

"Yeah? Then who did?"

All I got was a blank stare before he avoided eye contact, rolling his shoulders back.

"A friend."

"A friend? That's all you have for me?"

"That's all you need to know," he said quickly, giving me a pointed look. "Look, Willow. I like you. A lot. You have a mouth on you that's kind of hot. I know you're mad at me. But I didn't post your pictures and videos."

"But you still put them in the hands of someone whose eyes aren't yours."

"I'm a guy. I may have shared them with a few of my buddies and my brother, but—"

I cut him off with a rueful laugh.

"You chalk it up to you just being a guy?"

"The point is I didn't do it. Maybe it was a fucked-up friend of mine who has an equally fucked-up sense of humor."

It was hard to believe anything he said at this point. Too much had happened to just ignore and forgive. We'd gone through one drink. By the time I was finished with my second one, I throw down a $20 bill and got ready to leave.

"Well, this meet-up was a waste of time. I was hoping you invited me out to apologize for the shit you put me through in our sham of a relationship, but you never seem to disappoint."

"Don't walk away from me, Willow," he warned without looking up at me. "Don't walk away from me."

But I ignored him anyway and went to my car. King of wasting time and getting under my skin. I wished he didn't have the power. I wished I hadn't given in so much. I felt so fucking stupid. Shaking my head of this nonsense, I got in my car, put my purse in the passenger seat, and put the key in the ignition to get ready to leave.

I was on the road, thinking about finally meeting the devil himself. I squeezed the steering wheel, hating that he was just as beautiful as I'd pictured. This loser of a man had the looks of Lucifer. His incessant smirking throughout the entire night was permanently etched into my memory.

My phone beeped with a text, breaking me out of my thoughts. I looked in the passenger seat, barely making out who it was from and what it said. I did my best to maintain my eyes on the road. It beeped *again, and I reached for it with my free hand. When I finally grabbed it, a car rear-ended me. Looking in the rearview mirror, I saw that a Nissan Titan pickup truck had its high beam lights on and was tailgating me. What the fuck? I sped up, and so did the truck in question. I try to dial 911, but he bumps into me again, and my phone flies out of my hand onto the passenger seat floor.*

I come up on Neponset Valley Parkway and turned on the street to lose whoever this was. I was about a mile down the street when the truck appeared again, and I was now aware that I was being followed. It was the quiet streets of Boston in the middle of the night and I was unarmed.

The truck sped down the street, following closely behind, rear-ending me a few more times and turning up their lights again. Who the hell was this? I turned down another street, and they continued to follow me. Luckily, I found myself coming up on a few cars driving on the street. I flashed my lights, hoping to alert them of oncoming danger from behind. I pulled up next to a car, where a young blond woman gives me a look of concern. She rolled down her window.

"Are you okay?"

"There's something following me and is posing a danger to the roads tonight. Can you call the police, please?"

She nodded her head. "Of course, I can—"

The pickup truck rammed into her, sending her feet ahead. Instead of parking and confronting the perpetrator, she drove off. I had to trust that she'd alert the authorities. I put my car in drive and I was off down the street again, but the mystery truck continued to rear-end me. I rolled my window down, shouting, "Fuck you!"

They flashed their lights antagonistically. My gaze wavered between the roads and the rearview. The last time I looked through the rearview, I missed that I'd swerved into the wrong lane, and an oncoming car made me lose control of the car, making me crash into a family of trees.

The world was black for a few minutes. And the only thing that I was in tune with are my thoughts. It felt as if everything was closing in around me, and I lost the feeling in my extremities. I opened my eyes, feeling liquid dripping down my forehead, and tried to reach for my phone. A figure in black clothing slowly inched in on me as I watch them in my side view mirror. The same figure that I'd shared a drink with at the bar. Holy shit. I should've known.

When he stopped at my window, he bent down menacingly, an evil grin growing across his face.

"I told you not to walk away from me, Willow."

I tried to find my phone in the car, but Kinsley bashed my head into the steering wheel before I could. He clenched locks of my hair and inched close to my face, the stench of gin still on his breath.

"You're...psychotic," I managed to get out.

"You don't know the half of it."

He reached across my stomach and yanked me out of the car, throwing me to the ground and hitting my head on the hard pavement. I winced, trying to get up.

He walked up to me, his height making me feel like prey. It was a disturbing feeling. I backed up, using my arms, searching for a weapon to protect myself with.

"What do you want?"

"Vengeance" was all he said before rushing at me with athletic speed. He grabbed me by the throat and pulled me up from the ground. I tried to pry his hands from around my neck, but he was too strong.

"Cahn't...breathe..." I struggled to say over his hand clenched around my throat.

"You drop me and then block me like it's nothing?" he asks in disbelief. "And don't expect to pay a price?"

He dropped me to the ground and delivered a soul-sucking kick to my stomach. I coughed up blood and prayed to God that he could get me out of this deadly situation.

"You were stupid for ignoring me, Willow. No one ever ignores me and gets away with it."

I inched weakly on the pavement, looking around to see if anyone saw or heard any struggle. But everyone's lights in their homes were off.

"I hate doing this. You don't know what this shit does to me, having to teach you a lesson when you test me."

I found a fractured piece of glass from my car window. I coughed up more blood and chanced a look up at him as he continued inching on me like he was about to deliver another blow to my stomach.

"You always get ahead of yourself, Kin," I croak, reaching for the glass discreetly. "I don't know how you do it."

He chuckled another rueful laugh that chilled my bones.

"What the fuck does that mean?"

I clutched the piece in my hand. "It means that the more arrogant you are, the more likely you are to lose sight of what's in front of you."

He grunted in frustration. "Are you done with your parables?"

"Are you done being a jackass?"

He growled and lifted his leg to kick me again. But I stabbed him in his shin before he can, making him shout in agonizing pain.

"You stupid bitch!"

He swung at me, but I ducked, gave a powerful blow to his stomach, and wedged the glass shard in his eye. This disarmed him, as he flailed around trying to attack me again. I kicked him to the ground as his screaeds of agony float down the once quiet street. The lights inside homes began to turn on, signaling it's time for me to escape. I spat on him, kicking him in his groin.

"Safe travels back to San Jose, you son of a bitch."

I quickly got back in my car as he thrashes around on the ground, shouting for help and the glass shard stuck in his eye socket.

I reversed out of the street, leaving him to die. I was already a few miles down the road, eyeing his flailing body wailing out for someone to help him.

I don't know my way around San Jose. The only similarity between it and Boston is the tech industry aspect of it. Which I had no idea of in Boston. I've been too entrenched in my work as a killer that I didn't even fucking realize that, not only Leif, but Kinsley Focker could be living there.

It's not real. I've been doing my best to convince myself that it's not real. It can't be. I refuse to believe it. But I bet it's true. I don't see why Callie would lie to me. It just wouldn't make any sense.

Nothing makes sense to me anymore. Kinsley has been living in Port Rockwell. What's more, the guy that I previously knew as Leif is Kinsley, and his brother whose eye I stabbed is the actual Leif.

And if the timeline lines up correctly, he was living there even when we dated. But for some reason, he made it seem as if he was still in San Jose. I don't get it. I don't fucking get it.

An unwanted growl escapes me as I run an agitated hand through my dirty hair at the local bar in downtown San Jose.

"Are you all right?" a concerned voice asks beside me, and I look up to find an elderly man taking a sip of his lager.

"Yes, I'm okay," I groan.

"Long day, honey?"

"You don't know the half of it."

After dropping Callie off at home, I made a call to Vinny to let him know that my work is far from over. He wasn't happy, and he still isn't. But he can't stop me. He only asks that I don't involve him in my work. I'm more than welcome to use the upstairs speakeasy to have meetings, but I can't use his name or business as a company address anymore. Tough deal, but I don't have a choice.

"Care to talk about it?"

As I start to tell him that I'm not looking for a bar companion to spill all my sorrows, my phone rings with my hacker, Violet, calling. I quickly answer.

"Violet?"

"Willow, listen to me," she says with urgency. "Someone is in Callie's house."

My heart stops. "What?"

"My location pinged her at her house. But there's some other movement of someone walking into her house."

"It could just be a friend or boyfriend."

"The cameras say otherwise."

This immediately gets my attention. I throw fifteen dollars on the bar to pay for my drink and walk outside to get some privacy.

"You were able to hack into the cameras at her house?"

"Yeah…and it doesn't look good. Here's the address to her house."

In the next second, I get a text from Violet.

"What are you seeing?"

"So far, she's just walking around in the kitchen. But someone in black clothing just broke in the backdoor of her house on the first floor. It doesn't look like she's heard it."

"Shit," I curse under my breath. "I'm heading over there right now."

"Hurry, Willow."

I hang up the call, quickly call a rideshare, and I'm headed over in her direction in five minutes. I call Callie to alert her that she's in danger. She picks up on the second ring.

"Hello?"

"Callie, you're in danger. Go to a safe room on the floor you're on and lock yourself in until I get there."

"Willow? Wait, slow down. What's going on?"

"You're in danger. Someone just broke into your house."

"What?" she asks, the gravity of the situation fully dawning on her. "Wait, how do you know that?"

"Callie, get to a safe place. Now!"

"Okay, okay, um…I-let me see—who are you? What are you doing in my house?!"

"Callie!"

"No," she says, her voice choking up. "No. No! No!"

A struggle ends the phone call.

"Please step on it," I say to the driver, already feeling a cry about to come on. I can't let this girl die. I fucking can't. I've been trying to call her back, but it goes straight to voicemail the five times I do.

When he drives up to her house, I quickly get out, slam the car door, and eye the black Mercedes in the driveway next to Callie's green Volkswagen Beetle. As I come up on the front porch, the front door is intact, confirming Violet's original testimony that the perpetrator broke in through the back. I go through the back, briefly canvassing the basement and make my way up to the second floor.

Her attacker could still be in the house, so I make my steps quiet and calculated up her spiral stairs. Music continues to blare louder and louder as I reach the second floor. I pull out a pocketknife, since I was unprepared to not bring a heftier weapon. I get to the second floor, scoping out the scene. There's no evidence of a struggle. Everything seems to be neatly in its place—including a lone knife that sits on the counter next to cutting board of unfinished sliced tomatoes.

I spot the Amazon Alexa in the living room and shut the music off, silence filling the room in its place.

"Callie?"

I'm met with more silence. She has to be here, somewhere. I'm hoping and praying that this woman is still alive. She can't be another casualty. I walk up the steps to the third floor of her spacious townhouse, keeping my ears tuned for familiar voices. But there's nothing. It's completely silent. I make it to the third floor and take in the wall art, feeling a bit of déjà vu. They're not as risqué as Benji Lockson's wall art, but they definitely allude to a scorned woman. Multiple depictions of the Greek mythology siren grace her walls, including Lorelei.

When I get to a bedroom I presume to be the master, my steps slow at the gory scene in front of me.

I was too late. Callie lies in a pool of blood on her bed, wearing what looks like lingerie, her arms tied to the headboard, and her body's staged up as if she's on the cross. It's entirely too gruesome for even my eyes, so I quickly search for the nearest garbage can to vomit in. My stomach bottoms out, and it feels as if someone's beating my forehead like a drum. Almost on cue, my phone rings, agitating my oncoming migraine. I wipe my mouth with a paper towel and pick up on the fourth ring.

"Hello," I groan.

A menacing chuckle greets me, nearly turning my flesh to glass.

"Ah, there's that beautiful voice. I've missed it all too much."

"I struggle to believe that."

"Your disbelief hurts me, Willow. Truly."

"Cut the bullshit. Who am I speaking to this time? Are you Leif or Kinsley right now?"

"I'm whoever you want me to be, doll."

"Oh, forgive me, you're actually the Ghostface killer."

That chuckle that I formerly loved is back.

"If you'd like a slasher movie, Willow, I think I've proven more than once that I can create one."

The venom in his voice is none like any other. This is no longer Viking. This is the Kinsley I remember from all those years ago that texted. When I first met who I believed to be Kinsley—who I know now to be his younger half-brother, Leif—at that bar years ago, even his voice and presence were imposing. But there was something inexperienced about his presence. Like someone was pulling his strings.

The point is I didn't do it. Maybe it was a fucked-up friend of mine who has an equally fucked-up sense of humor.

It took me this fucking long to figure it out.

"I have to give it to you. You really fooled me, pretending to be the dark and mysterious guy approaching an unassuming woman in a bar. You're fucking good. You played the role well."

"I did good, huh?"

"It's almost like you're a sociopath."

He laughs his amusement. It's sickening, hearing lightness in his voice when he, no doubt, orchestrated Callie's—and definitely Veronica's—murder.

"You've always had a flair for the dramatic. It's what I loved about you."

"What the fuck do you want?"

"Other than vengeance?"

"For what?"

"The collateral damage my brother amounts to."

"He did it to himself. But I know you've been pulling his strings. But why, Kinsley? Too much of a coward to take care of your own business?"

He sighs, annoyed. "It's a long story. One I'm not going to confide with you over the phone. But there is one thing I'll confide with you."

"Yeah? And what's that?"

"The people in your life have no clue about safety. And Ghostface is always watching."

"What?"

"Vinny really shouldn't leave his front door unlocked. That's just asking for trouble."

Fucking. Hell. The phone line dies, leaving me to figure out how to get out of this mess. My nervous hands call Violet, and she picks up quickly.

"Willow?"

I try to find my words. The air in the room is thinning, and the room is closing around me again.

"Vinny. He's at Vinny's house. Send someone there, please."

"What?"

"Now, Violet! He's about to fucking die!"

I hang up quickly and try to call Vinny to alert him. His phone goes straight to voicemail each time.

Shit. Shit. Shit.

Now it's personal.

FIFTEEN

WILLOW

The ride back to base was a long one. My head was brimming with a pulsating pain that won't stop. I've had to stop multiple times just to throw up because the pain is just too much. It's an agonizing drive, trying to get ahold of the surreal situation at hand.

I met Kinsley Focker. It was a meeting I hoped to put behind me forever. The proximity I was to death was extremely jarring. For a second, my life was in his hands. That had never happened to me before. If I hadn't protected myself, I wouldn't be here. I wiped the tears falling from my eyes but winced each time I accidentally swiped the open wounds on my bottom lip and the bridge of my nose. This was the lowest I'd ever been in my life. Here, I'd thought losing my dad had that spot. But Kinsley had swiftly taken that place.

I made it back to base at 3:30 a.m. Two hours from the time I was meant to wake up. I didn't have it in me to train tomorrow. My threshold for being shouted at during training was very low, and I had an even smaller capacity to be physically present. I should have alerted the police. I really should have. But that would have opened an entire can of worms. There would be questions about what I was doing out *this time of night. Then they'd ask why an active duty soldier was meeting a stranger in the middle of the night. Then word will get back to base that I met with the guy who distributed my nudes on a revenge porn website. Then my commanding officer will argue that my personal life was intervening with my ability to train as a sniper. I would single-handedly ruin my own life. Not to say that I haven't been doing that already…but if I could avoid further intervention, then I'd just have to live with the consequences of my own actions.*

Parking my car, there was nothing else I wanted to do besides sit there and ruminate on the night I'd just had. It was surreal. I wasn't expecting anything like it. Before I realized what the hell I was doing, I repeatedly banged my head against the steering wheel. Each time, it feels like I'm closer and closer to an escape. It was an indescribable feeling. It didn't hurt any more than Kinsley Focker kicking the daylights out of me. But damn did it hurt. It hurt, but it felt so good.

I woke up the next morning to my commanding officer standing over me in my car, startling me a bit.

"Harding. What are you doing?"

I groan, lifting my head from the steering wheel I slept on for the last two hours. My head hurt more than it had last night.

"Sir, I'm sorry, sir. I had a long night, sir."

He squints at me, a sense of urgency suddenly hitting him.

"Your head is bruised, and you have open wounds all over your face. What is going on?"

"Sir…I'm sorry, I've had a long night, sir."

"Why did you have a long night, knowing that you needed to be ready for sniper training at 6:30 a.m.?"

I wasn't expecting him to find me this morning. I couldn't believe I didn't set my alarm for the morning and instead had a borderline psychotic break, banging my head against my steering wheel enough to send me to sleep.

"I can get ready quickly for training, sir. I can assure you, sir."

"If you need to take a day to yourself, Harding, that's not a problem. They'd rather you be mentally and physically present for training."

"I understand, sir. I can do it, sir."

I should really have taken him up on his offer to take a rest day. But I won't let this stop me from training. I made a promise to myself that I would make my dad proud so that he could look down on me and see that I'm the warrior that I'd always been for him.

"If you can get through today, then I suppose I cannot stop you. We cannot control what you do outside of active duty hours, but we can give you our guidance. I know with the death of your dad—"

"I'll be ready for training this morning, sir."

It was rude to cut him off, but talking about my father in casual conversation wasn't something I'd done in a while. It was territory I'd rather not entertain.

He didn't look convinced, but he nodded his understanding and backed away from my car as I fixed myself to get out.

"Your instructors know that you're late for training. Do not let this happen again, Harding."

"Sir, yes, sir."

He nodded and walked off. I needed to get ahold of myself. Last night seemed so surreal. There was no way I went to meet Kinsley. There's no way that he chased me into oblivion and caused me to crash into a car. There's absolutely no way that he assaulted me in the quiet streets of a suburb. And there's absolutely no way that I stabbed him in the eye, rendering him helpless. It all sounds like a nightmare.

At this time, I didn't have enough time to shower and get ready. I rushed to the barracks and changed into my uniform for the day. Making my way over to sniper school, I humiliated myself and got into the formation that my comrades were in at the shooting range.

"Glad you could join us," my instructor said with a hint of disapproval. I cringed, hoping that not responding would take the attention off of me. But I caught one of my comrades giving me that look of disapproval that I'd grown used to. I ignored the stares as our instructor resumed the precision training.

We were an hour into training for precision, trying to remain focused. But intrusive thoughts were on the horizon and refused to go away. I wished I could throw my brain away. I gripped my rifle tighter, thinking that would change anything. But Kinsley's cries continued to be in the forefront of my mind.

Before I knew what I was doing, I dropped the rifle and let out a frustrated grunt. I was so close to hitting rock bottom.

"Harding, let's talk," my instructor requested, and I didn't argue.

I was such an idiot. I should've stayed in last night. That would've saved me this quickly developing trauma that I couldn't seem to shake.

He took me to a secluded area away from the range to speak.

"Sir, I'm sorry, I— "

"What is going on with you? You can't keep a firm grip on your weapon, you look as if you've gotten into a fight, and I can tell you're not focused. What is happening to you?"

"It's a long story."

"If it's affecting your performance, then we need to address it. A psych evaluation is required to get into sniper school, so if we need you to retake it— "

"No, sir. I don't need to take it again. I promise I'm fine."

The look he gave me mirrored the look my commanding officer had given me. I'd disappointed them both.

"I'll let you finish training today. But we'll give you a day off tomorrow so you can regroup."

"Sir, I don't need an off day."

"Yes, you do. You offer no value if there are things weighing on you. We'll discuss after training today. Now get back into formation."

There was no sense in arguing with him. I needed to regroup. He wasn't wrong about that. But I'd never been known to show weakness. Strength is what got me through taking care of my dad. I'd only ever shown signs of weakness when Kinsley Focker came into my life.

When we were done training for the day, I was walking back to the barracks to take a shower and decompress for the night. Most of my comrades were out for the night, so I took advantage of this opportunity to have the night to myself for a bit. The shower was soothing. Though not soothing enough to stop me thinking about what had happened.

There were so many unanswered questions. Why was Kinsley in Port Rockwell Why did it seem like his in-person persona was different from his online one? Why did he attack me? And what happened after I basically left him to bleed out in the middle of the night? Nothing made sense anymore. My entire life now feels like a simulation, and I was the test subject. It was disturbing.

Drying myself off, I was running a comb through my hair, detangling my curls, when I heard a struggle in the distance. My comb dropped to the counter, my attention suddenly on the danger at hand. There was a moment of silence. And then a comrade screaming.

I ran out of the bathroom, towel still wrapped around me, and searched for a weapon. I ran to my room and quickly grabbed a pocketknife. The muffled screaming happened again, followed with a another muffled struggle coming from the room across from me. My heartbeats grew louder, my steps remained calculated, and the room started to feel smaller. But I needed to shake it off. Somehow, someone had broken into the barracks and was attacking one of my comrades. I readied my knife, cradling it.

It's now or never, Willow.

I took a deep breath and charged into the room, turning the lights on.

"Ahhh! Willow, what the fuck are you doing?!"

My comrade, Taylor, was looking at me with crazy eyes as a male hovered over her in bed, also looking at me with crazy eyes. Fucking hell.

"Shit," I whispered, dropping my knife to the ground. "Taylor, I'm sorry—"

"What are you doing with that?!" she shouts. All of a sudden, everyone turned their lights on.

Soldiers rushed out of their rooms, surrounding me as we looked at our fellow comrade and a guy in the middle of having sex. I picked up my knife and concealed it, not missing the shocked looks from everyone around me.

"I-I didn't know. I just heard a struggle, and—"

"Harding? What is this?" Our commanding officer walked up to me, looking into Taylor's room. "What the hell is going on here?"

I cleared my throat, still holding my towel up to not worsen the situation.

"I thought she was being attacked, sir. I heard struggles when I just gotten out of the shower. I—"

He walked farther into the room, stopping me. He took one look at Taylor, who looked embarrassed, and the guy she was screwing. This is a new fucking nightmare that I unwittingly caused.

"Watson. We'll talk about this fraternization in the morning." He then turned to me, a wooden look on his face.

"Harding. To my office. Now."

"Sir, I know I messed up, sir. It was a mistake, sir."

He stared at me, gaze piercing into me, seemingly trying to figure me out.

"You pull out a pocketknife on your fellow comrade in the middle of the night. Do you understand how this looks?"

"Yes, sir, I understand how it looks, sir."

"What do you expect me to do in this situation? You are considered a liability now. I will be speaking with her in the morning about sneaking another soldier onto the barracks, but this behavior is unacceptable."

I'm not well. I know I'm mentally fucked if muffled screaming, moaning, and groaning triggered me to think someone was being attacked.

"I was attacked the other night, sir," I revealed.

He flinched. "Attacked? By who? A fellow soldier?"

"No. It wasn't by a soldier. It's difficult to explain who…but that's why I have bruises and wounds all over my face."

I hated the concerned look on his face. That was precisely why I'd wanted to keep it to myself. I don't like being seen as a victim. I'm far from it. But I needed him to understand why my sanity was on the decline. I was losing my mind. I thought I could be an asset to the military, but I wasn't mentally stable enough to do this. I carried too much baggage to continue doing this. I almost attacked someone because I thought they were assaulting my comrade. At this rate, I was getting scared of myself. I couldn't do this. Not anymore.

"What can we do to help you, Harding? To support you?"

"Sir…I think I may need to start the process for a voluntary separation."

The flight back to Boston is one I struggle to sit through. After that cryptic talk with Kinsley on the phone, I called the police and let them know that there was a dead body on 2100 Halloville Lane.

When they arrived, they asked me if I happened to know who did this and, thankfully, Callie had security cameras set up on her front porch and backyard door. They also dusted for fingerprints and told me they'd let me know what they could find.

I land in Boston four hours after leaving Callie's house, after finding a last-minute flight back. I quickly checked out of the hotel and booked my next flight out. Violet confirmed that Kinsley stalking Vinny was a false alarm, not any more than an effort to intimidate me. I can't allow him to continue doing that. I won't.

Vinny calls me as soon as I make it to baggage claim.

"Low. I've been trying to call you."

"I'm back in Port Rockwell"

He hesitates before pointing out, "That was quick. Didn't you land yesterday morning?"

"He killed her, Vinny."

"What?"

"The girl I flew to San Jose to meet. He killed her."

My mind wanders back to the gory crime scene, her body sitting upright in a staged position. It's not an easy image to shake.

"How do you know he killed her?"

"Come on, Vinny."

"You said that he was living in Boston. How would he have enough time to follow you to San Jose in a day? That sounds crazy."

"He's not working alone."

"What do you mean?"

"I don't have time to explain it over the phone. How is Meredith doing?"

"Willow…" He sounds concerned for my mental well-being. I don't blame him. My mind is a jungle with vines intertwining, creating a colossal, jumbled mess.

"We can meet at the hospital and talk about it. I can't meet you at my house or yours or at the bar. They're all too isolated, in case Kinsley tries to pull a fast one. At the hospital, we'll be too surrounded for him or his brother to try to pull anything."

"Wait, wait, wait. His brother?"

"Meet me at the hospital, and I'll explain it."

Before he can say anything, I hang up and wait for my bag to circle back around. I check my watch and see that it's a little after 1:30 in the morning.

What a long day.

I need to create a gameplan to get rid of Kinsley and his freak show of a brother, once and for all. And I'm hoping Vinny and Meredith—when she's awake and lucid—can help me. I know it's only been a day since I've last seen her, but she's most likely conscious by now.

When my bag finally comes around on the baggage carousel to me, I reach for it. But not before another hand gets to it before I do.

"Let me help you with that," the icy voice says.

I lock eyes with the demon, and he has the nerve to look proud of himself. The guy with the glass eye.

"Thanks for your help…*Leif.*"

His jaw clenches, but the proud smirk remains.

"You caught on."

"It wasn't hard to. Especially when I find out the hard way."

"And what's that?"

"From one of your victims. How did you make it to San Jose so fast, by the way?"

He narrows his eyes at me. "I have no idea what you're talking about."

"Oh, I think you do."

He looks around, most likely looking for an exit.

"Talk about this in my car, shall we?"

I try to grab my bag, but he yanks it away from me, grabbing my arm in a violent manner, and walks me to an exit that leads out to ground transportation.

"You and your jackass brother have a kill count of two."

"Compared to your kill count of thirty-two?" He growls in my ear, making my blood run cold.

Once we get to his car, he opens the passenger side door and throws me in. He circles the car, putting my suitcase in the trunk. My life is in danger, yet again, with this fucking lunatic. I have to think quickly. Searching for a weapon in my purse, I feel for my mace and grip it to my side.

He hops in the driver seat and faces me.

"What the fuck does Kinsley want? He's already humiliated me by pretending to be you."

He scoffs, starting the car. "He wasn't pretending to be me, sweet Willow. He's been trying to make it up to me."

"Make what up to you? That makes no sense."

Before I know it, he punches on the brakes, sending me forward, hitting my head on the glove compartment.

"You know what makes no sense? Chicks like you."

"What the fuck is wrong with you?" I groan, cradling my head after that gnarly impact.

"It's chicks like you. Chicks that always want the same type of guy. The top ten percent."

"Fucking hell, Leif, can it with the cliché red pill bullshit."

"Am I wrong, though?! You fell awfully hard for my brother, thinking he was me."

"I didn't *think* he was you. You thought you were *him*. That's the whole thing, isn't it, you asshole? You pretend to be him, and he pretends to be you? What a fucking weird family affair."

He grinds his jaw angrily again as he grips the steering wheel.

"I'd shut the fuck up if I were you, Willow. Because your friend, the bar owner's, life is in danger."

"You already pulled this when I was in San Jose. I'm not stupid."

"That was only to get your attention, dear Willow. But his life will soon be hanging by a thread."

"What the fuck does that mean?"

The menacing grin I've had nightmares about for years is back. He pulls out his phone and shows me a livestream showing someone watching Vinny locking up the bar for the night. I start to lose feeling in my legs as a wave of disbelief envelops me.

"Does that explain enough for you?"

"What do you want from me?" I ask helplessly. A feeling I've never wanted to feel again.

"I don't want anything from you, Willow. I've done what I needed to do, as far as Callie and Veronica are concerned."

"You're a piece of shit," I growl.

But this only amuses him. "All of this…is for Kinsley. He wants something from you."

"Viking," I clarify.

"Your tall, dark, and handsome knight that you've had between your legs more times than even *you* can count."

What the fuck did I do in a past life to deserve this sort of fucked-up karma? If the answer is being a hitwoman, then the same karma should apply to these two asshats who are hellbent on ruining women's lives. What a fucking paradox. The livestream continues to inch in on Vinny as he circles the bar—presumably to make sure that all the entrance doors are locked. He starts to walk to his car, and the camera follows him.

"What does he have to do with this? Your animosity toward me has nothing to do with him!"

"The only animosity I have toward you is this." He points to his glass eye that I caused nearly ten years ago.

"You tried to kill me that night." I try to hold back my tears as the unseen person gets closer to Vinny walking to his car.

"I told you not to walk away from me, Willow. I warned you."

I don't have enough time to respond, because Vinny's muffled shouts and struggles followed by a thud and the camera cutting off gets my attention. Leif turns his phone and watches me as I process what I've just watched.

"What are you gonna do to him?" I ask, tears already assaulting my face.

"You'll find out sooner or later. For now, I want you to plan to meet me tonight."

"Why tonight?" I ask in a wooden voice, but he doesn't care to notice.

"Because we need to talk about what's happening on Friday with Kinsley."

Friday. That's my birthday. I'm turning 30.

"What's happening on Friday?"

He gives me a grim smile. "I think you know."

"Why can't he reach out to me himself? He was brave enough to do it before."

"Because that would ruin the fun," he cajoles in an odd voice.

I'm between a rock and a hard place. If I say no, then they'll kill Vinny and continue to make my life a living hell until I can get them detained. Which would most likely take a hell of a long time to accumulate evidence. But if I say yes…Vinny lives. And these assholes will get out of my life. Or they could be bluffing and kill Vinny anyway.

"Fine," I say through gritted teeth. "I'll let you know of a meeting location."

His smile is an inauthentic grin that makes me squirm. Coupled with his prosthetic eye, it's disturbing. I quickly look away, hoping that he'll let me go, now that I've agreed to meet with him. But I am optimistic.

"Go ahead with it, Kin," he suddenly says, confusing me.

I look up and watch as the livestream cam comes back up with Vinny sitting in a chair, tape over his mouth.

"Wait, what?"

He holds up a finger to quiet me as a masked assailant appears, waving at the camera.

"Leif, what the fuck is going on?!"

"Wouldn't you like to know, Low?" Before I can see what happens next, he turns his phone off and throws it in the backseat. "You're free to go now."

"That's it? You hold him hostage and then expect me to go about my life, ignoring it? At least tell me where he is!"

"Talk to you soon, Willow."

Frustrated, I get out of his car, pop the trunk, and grab my suitcase. After I shut it, he rushes off, leaving me stranded in the parking lot of the ground transportation area.

With a sense of urgency, I call Violet, and she instantly picks up.

"You never texted me that you landed."

"I need you to track Vinny's location again."

She sighs, exasperated. "Willow, he's okay. I told you that before you got on the plane."

"N-no, no. He's not, Violet. Track his location again so I can get to him."

"What's going on?"

"Just search for him!" I nearly scream. I don't have enough time for people questioning me. The man that raised me after my father's death is at risk of dying.

"Okay, okay, uh...wait, I pinged his location at...your apartment."

I instantly freeze. He's at my apartment. I knew they've been watching and following me, but...how the hell did they get into my apartment? "Willow? Willow, you there? He's at your apartment. That's a good thing, right?"

"Violet, I'll call you back, okay?"

"Wait, what's going—"

I hang up and quickly call a rideshare. *Please be okay, Vinny.*

I make it to my apartment in record time and rush upstairs. I don't know if Violet's location tracking was correct, but I wouldn't put it past these assholes to somehow break into my place.

When I get to my floor, my steps slow when I see that my door isn't kicked in. It is left ajar, as if they had a key and simply unlocked it. Walking inside, I see no evidence of a struggle.

"Vinny?"

No response. I continue to look around to see if he's maybe unconscious. I'm hoping that he's just unconscious and nothing more. I can't stomach someone else important to me leaving. Not again. The more I search without a sign of him, the more I worry and become anxious. He has to be here. Violet pinged his location to be here. That can't be wrong.

He's not in the living room. He's not in the bathroom. He's not in the guest bedroom. And he's not in my bedroom. Where the fuck could he be? Was her location placement wrong? It couldn't be. I try one last place that, if he is here, he would be. I open the closet in my bedroom, and I'm on the verge of a panic attack when his lifeless body falls out, his eyes left open and his arms tied up.

The room starts to spin, closing in on me. I suddenly feel as if I'm walking in molasses, the air feels as if it's being sucked out of the room, the walls are slowly closing in on me, and I can't feel my limbs anymore. I send Violet a quick SOS text before I completely pass out.

I fall to my knees, hovering over Vinny's body. It can't be real. I refuse to accept this as real. I don't touch his body, so as not to tamper with evidence and incriminate myself for a crime that I did not commit. It takes me a few more minutes to stare in disbelief at his body before I finally end up calling the police. I lie down on the ground, not caring if I look like I'm suffering a psychotic break. I let the waterworks flow as I feel my chest getting tight.

Vinny was all I had left, as far as someone close to my father. He warned me time and time again to leave the lifestyle behind and seek help. But I didn't listen. I didn't listen to anyone in my life. And I brought Vinny and Meredith down with me.

"Willow?" A small voice calls for me outside of my bedroom. I look up and find Violet's purple pixie cut before I see the concern on her face. Her gaze lands on Vinny, and her eyes widen in horror.

"Willow…" she says in a sad and confused voice.

"Get me the fuck out of here," I croak.

She nods, rushing to me and helping me get up off the floor. I look back down at Vinny, silently mourning.

"Do you need me to call the cops?"

"I've already called them. They're on their way."

"Would you like to wait until they get here, then?"

"I need you to take me to a church, please."

She looks at me, visibly confused.

"What?"

"A church," I repeat after clearing my throat. "I need to go to a church."

"Willow, I'm not sure I understand. It's well after midnight."

"I just need to go to a church, Violet," I reiterate for hopefully the last time. "I don't feel like explaining."

The hesitant look in her eyes is enough for me to think that she'll continue to argue. But then she nods and guides me out of the apartment. It still feels small. The walls close in the more steps I take down the hall. We make it out of the apartment without me passing out, nonetheless. When we make it outside, police sirens are the first thing we hear before the cars come speeding and parking in front of the complex.

One detective jumps out of the car and instantly escorts us away as multiple uniformed cops rush inside.

"We got a call for a dead body inside apartment 422. Don't be alarmed. We'll make sure we get you to a safe place."

"I made the call," I admit.

His demeanor softens. "Are you okay, ma'am?"

I have no idea.

"I will be. He…was a really close family friend. And I came home to find him dead," I choke up.

"We'll get you to a safe place."

"Please, Officer, I'll be fine. Just promise me you'll make sure to preserve the integrity of the body."

He gives me a curt but friendly nod and walks over to who I assume to be another detective.

Violet and I walk over to Violet's Mitsubishi, and we drive off in the direction of downtown Boston.

I'm numb. This toying that these freak of nature brothers are doing is starting to fuck with me more than I thought it would. But I like games. I *love* games. And if this is the game they'd like to play, so fucking be it.

Violet pulls in front of World Faith Church, and I just sit and stare at it. I've never been one who's into organized religion. But my father and Vinny were men of faith. The only two men who were men of value in my life. I have to honor them.

I get out and walk to the big closed doors. I kneel and begin to start a prayer.

"Father, forgive me for what it is I am about to do…"

SIXTEEN

KINSLEY

My sweet, sweet Willow. She thought she could run away from me for ten years and not pay the ultimate price. Her naïveté. It's what I loved most about her. There was something enticing about molding her into my perfect girl who listens to me. Obeys me. Trusts me. And though it was only for a short time, I loved toying with her. Seeing those breasts. Aching to touch them. Bite them. Lick them.

But I only saw them through a fucking phone screen for as long as I could remember. I wanted more. I needed it more than my last breath. I won't deny that. There's no sense in denying it. I fucking love her body, and I love her. How could I not? She's beautiful, sexy, and quick-witted. All things that reawakened ten-year-old Kinsley Focker, who watched entirely too many HBO late night specials and rubbed one out to hardcore.

I wished she hadn't been stupid enough to cross me, though. Everyone who knows me knows that I don't do well with defiance. Leif's my little brother, and he knows exactly what it was like in high school when I finally gave him the chance to sleep with one of my girlfriends.

Little Leif Mattson, my long-lost half-brother, a bastard child from my mother's fucked-up life choices, always wanted what he couldn't have. It's always been that way since middle school. It became obvious that, by the time that I got to my third girlfriend in eighth grade, he had a hard-on for every girl I liked. I originally thought it was rooted in jealousy. But it wasn't. He was just growing up. And being his older brother, I took it upon myself to mold him into the man he wanted to be.

Blaire Moriarty. My twelfth-grade girlfriend. Hot brunette, legs for days, and sugar tits like no one else's…until Willow. But she wasn't as spunky as Willow. No, she was shy and timid. It was almost a sin to have a body that luscious and a personality like a schoolgirl. At the time, I thought it was love. I loved that body like no one else. But so did Leif. My brother was in the ninth grade at the time and had a girlfriend of his own. Leif's always had a thing for huge tits, though, and his girlfriend at the time—I think her name was Lindsey—didn't fit the bill. I remember vividly that night when Blaire and I were having sex in my room after Mom and Dad went out for dinner. I snuck her into the house, and Leif was next door, toying around with some coding game he got for his birthday.

It was her first time and, damn was I a lucky son of a bitch. I'd waited three months to finally fuck this girl that I had been fantasizing about since the first date. She wanted it to be special…and so did I. I took it slow at first. Oh-so-fucking-slow. Then, it started to feel too good. *Fuck*, did it feel good. She was squeezing me like a vise, and all mental clarity went out of the window. Blaire wanted me to slow down, but I was already being sent over the edge. I was getting so close. But then she screamed. I opened my eyes, leaving my heaven for a second, to find her looking horrified at the doorway. Leif was staring, hand down his boxers, eye-crazed. His face turned a shade of red I hadn't seen since he was a little boy, when I caught him trying to take a cookie out of my cookie jar. But it was always like him. Wanting what I had.

He's my little brother, though. And I loved him. He'd never had an experience with a girl before. So this became the perfect time to include him on the fun. Who gave a fuck that Blaire wanted only me inside of her? After all, she was just a girl whose body was the main star of my dreams every single night. Blood is thicker than water and all that.

So I led him into the room, assured Blaire that everything would be okay, and watched as he inched inside my smoking hot girlfriend. She cried out many times and tried to push him off, but Leif was stronger. We've always been. She tried to kick him off of her, but I held her down as he continue to fuck her. Hearing her cries was extremely overstimulating for me, but I saw my brother happy. And when he reached his climax, he was the happiest I'd seen him in awhile. I loved seeing him happy.

Blaire, on the other hand, was disgusted. She pushed Leif off her, tears flowing down her face, searched for her clothes, and dashed out of the room. Leif was a happy camper, and Blaire never spoke to me again. I warned her that if she ever cried rape, then I'd make sure her father—who was a pastor—know that she was no longer his good little girl anymore. She kept her mouth shut, and I never saw her at school ever again. Turns out, she committed suicide the week after I threatened her. I would've felt bad. But I just didn't care. My father demanded sex from my mom all the time, and she gave it to him. She did whatever she had to do to keep him happy. He always taught us to take what we want. And that's exactly what we did.

Soon, it became a twisted game Leif and I would play. Find a new hot girl and charm her out of her panties. Perhaps even her dignity. And any girl stupid enough to fall for it and give it to us…was the one. We would take turns with girls as part of a brotherly bond. Our father was barely home, and Mom divorced him on the day of my graduation. Leif and I are all we have. I promised Leif I'd watch over him and take care of him. Give him what he wanted. Because he always wanted what he couldn't have. The dorky hacker kid and his athletic and techie older brother. A bond that no one could break.

Until Willow Harding came into the picture. Fucking hell, she turned me on my head. I'm normally not one to let a girl talk to me the way she does. But she has a mouth on her. A mouth that would look so beautiful around my dick. Better yet, it has. And it was so fucking sexy. Little did she know that I was the guy she was running from. But I know her. I'm in tune with her. The beat of her drum matches the beat of mine. No matter how many men she wants to kill to compensate for being a virtual slut for me, that will never change. Ever since I spotted her location a year ago, I was amazed. I'd just gotten traded to the New England Hornets from the San Jose Tigers, and I got the opportunity to be close to my brother.

She was as beautiful as ever. I've had visceral reactions to the female body. But I knew immediately from those wide hips, impressive rack, and toned legs that it was none other than my Willow. She had her hair cut shoulder length with bangs slightly draping over her forehead. She was wearing all black, almost as if it were her uniform. She was drinking at this rancid bar, talking to some pale redheaded girl. But my gaze was plastered on her the entire time. I had gone a year, stalking her and finding the right time to enchant her yet again. It's a compulsion I've yet to keep under wraps, but I did a good job of it until I couldn't anymore. Upon doing more research on her, I found out that she was the Siren Assassin. The mysterious hitwoman that's killed more than thirty wealthy men. The research?

Marissa Moore. The ex-girlfriend of a good friend of mine. A good friend that was killed by the Siren Assassin. Initially, I was going to stalk Willow until I could find the right time to get back into her good graces but using my brother's name. But when Leif called me one night, telling me Benji had been killed and his girlfriend, Veronica, saw her do it, I knew it was as good a time as any.

Marissa was very easy to find. Leif was able to track her down and find out more information. With enough persuasion and a bribe of $1500 to get her a nice place outside of the country, she told him that she's the Siren Assassin. It was all starting to make sense. Willow likes to wear all black, and she has this femme fatale persona about her. It's sexy. But it's also a crutch. A crutch I need to break through to look for any weaknesses. And that's exactly what I did.

As usual, she was at the bar she frequents that's owned by her father's friend. And I worked my Kinsley Focker magic. But this time…as Leif Mattson. I never thought it'd be so easy to manipulate the same person twice.

"He's dead," my little brother announces, followed by the sound of my loft door closing.

Closing my eyes with a pleased smile on my face, I start to believe that my work here is done. But my senses tell me that Willow will be out for more blood.

"Beautiful. What's next?" I ask, looking out onto the slow city of Port Rockwell It's a wonder that in the quiet streets of this city, my Willow has been creating havoc under a pseudonym. It doesn't surprise me much, but I didn't think she'd have it in her. I'm no natural-born killer myself, but there's a certain adrenaline rush, playing this little game with her. First Veronica, then her little redheaded friend, then Callie, and last but not least, the one that probably means the most to her. I'm already getting excited, planning out the next kill.

"What's her friend up to? In the hospital?"

Leif slips his sweatshirt off and throws his keys on the counter before yanking a cold beer from my fridge and shutting it aggressively.

"Who knows? I haven't even been there yet."

Leif's the killer out of the two of us. He has the hunger for blood. I just like to see it all play out, like a game of chess. Willow will play her next move soon. But I have to be one step ahead of her.

"What's going on with her mother?"

"Who knows, Kin? Can I drink my beer in peace, please?"

Confused about his sudden change in attitude, I turn to find him looking frustrated into space.

"What's up your ass?"

He grunts, slamming the bottle of beer on the table.

"I'm just…tired of having to be the puppet on the strings."

"Are you having doubts?"

"Not doubts. I just don't know if this is gonna work in our favor this time. Usually, we can terrorize these girls, and they'll get a clue and fall back. But this girl…I don't know. The fucking bitch flew to San Jose in one day to see your ex, man."

"Hey, don't call her a bitch," I warn.

He scoffs. "You mean the girl who you're playing a game of chicken with?"

"I'm not playing a game of chicken," I grit through my teeth. "I'm just waiting for her to throw in the towel."

"That's what I mean, jackass. I don't think that she'll be willing to throw in the towel. In fact, killing her uncle probably has angered her more."

And it probably will. She knows better than to mess with me, though.

"I think I can handle a 130 lb girl, Leif."

"Oh yeah? Even one who goes by the name Siren Assassin?"

Fed up with his questioning, I dash over to him, and he immediately gets up from the table.

"If you're having second thoughts, hot shot, you need to let me know. I need you to be on my side right now. If you're not, let me know and I'll handle her myself."

He swallows nervously, but his confident demeanor remains the same.

"I'm not having second thoughts. But admit it, our days are numbered. Have you forgotten what she did to my eye?" he asks, pointing at the prosthetic eye in question.

I consider where he's coming from for a moment. I expect her to go on a rampage. I know what she's capable of. But I just need to remind her of her place. She likes to play these dangerous kill games, and she has no idea that I'm the ultimate player. I have no qualms about joining her.

I grab the back of his head and cradle his forehead against mine for a heart to heart.

"Listen, Leif. You're my brother. But you're seeming to forget who the fuck I am. This"—I point to his eye—"is why I'm doing this. She deserves to pay for what she did to you."

"But you just gave me shit for calling her a bitch."

"Because you don't know her like I do. She's angry at me. So I'm taking responsibility for that. You carry out the dirty work. That's it. You don't need to form any opinion on the matter or her."

"So I don't get to voice my shit to you?"

"Not concerning her. Our problems are deeper than you know. You may have hacked her stuff way back when, but I know her. Let me deal with this in my own way without you complicating the situation with your emotions."

It's been years since I've seen my brother cry. The first time I saw him cry was when our dad beat him senseless after forcing him to participate in the sex dungeon at our family friend's bar back home and Leif didn't want to. But the last real time I ever saw him cry was when Willow gouged his eye out with a shard of glass. So when his eyes well up with tears, I can sense the fear that I haven't seen in ten years.

"Brother…this feels different," he rasps. "We've taken basically everyone away that was left in her life. There's no reconciling that."

"Let me worry about that. She's my responsibility. I'll take care of it."

At first, he doesn't seem as if he believes me. I'm not entirely sure that I believe myself. But I have to keep on a brave face for the both of us.

Before the conversation can continue any longer, my phone rings, and I immediately pick up without looking.

"Talk to me."

"Hello, Kinsley," an odd feminine voice greets me, nearly robotic. I don't even recognize who it is.

"This is Kin."

"I know. So you're into games."

I pull the phone away to see who it is that called me. But it says *No Caller ID*.

"I'm more into board games, but I'm game for riddles."

"Interesting. But what are your thoughts on mind games?"

"What?"

"I think you heard me."

"Who the hell is this?"

"The redhead you bulldozed with a Range Rover."

I look at Leif, who looks at me curiously.

"It's a wonder you're still alive, red. That was a gnarly crash."

Her raspy laugh touches my ears, almost as if she smokes a pack a day.

"It's gonna take more than an impulsive attack like that to get rid of me. You may have rendered me bedridden for a while, but trust me, I'll get my revenge."

"Get discharged from the hospital first, and then confront me."

There's a moment of silence on her end. How the hell does she have a phone anyway?

"You're right. You don't need to quite worry about me yet. I just wanted to make it known that I'm not going anywhere. Whether you die or not, I'll haunt you until the end of time, Kinsley Focker."

Before I can respond to that cryptic statement, she hangs up, leaving me to figure out what the hell that call was about.

"It was the redhead we ambushed."

"What?"

"She was saying empty threats with her goddamned smoker's voice."

"How'd she get your number?"

"I don't know. Trace the phone to the location." Something tells me that she's not in the hospital anymore.

Leif pulls out his laptop that he carries everywhere out of his bookbag and searches through various databases. He pulls up a tracking database and connects my phone to it. He types in the mysterious number, and it traces to a bar downtown.

"The redhead called you from a bar downtown. I thought she was in the hospital."

"She must've gotten discharged early or something. Can you go scope it out?"

"And risk being seen? What if Willow is there?"

"Shit," I mutter. "You're right. We have to send someone there, at least."

"Why? She's clearly baiting you. Don't fall for it."

"She wouldn't just call for fun, Leif. We need someone to go check it out."

He sighs, clearly not in the mood to further argue with me.

"Fine, I'll send Veronica." He sends a text on his phone and then quickly gets a response back. "She wants to call."

I roll my eyes. The bitch is annoying. Ever since we faked her death, she's been hassling us about paying for her time and can't get a clue. We were never going to pay her. We've already paid her to pretend to be a helpless victim that's been abused by Leif. But as I expected, she's been irritating us about it ever since.

His phone rings seconds later, and he quickly picks up.

"Why are you freaking out?" he asks after picking up. No doubt she's giving him the third degree.

"What's she saying?" I whisper.

In response, he puts the phone on speaker, and I hear Veronica's annoying voice.

"…and I still haven't gotten my $5,000 check!"

"Veronica! Chill for a second."

"Don't tell me what to do, Kinsley! I want my money now!"

"We paid you for the first job we sent you out for."

"And then Leif said he'd pay me another $5,000! I want it now. I'm not doing any more jobs until that check clears in my bank account."

I fist my hands at my side, regretting getting her involved in anything. I grab the phone from Leif, take it off speaker, and try to talk to her in a calm voice.

"Veronica, please do not give me an ultimatum."

"Or what?"

"Or I'll skin like you a frog."

She gasps in surprise. "You wouldn't dare."

"I've ordered the kills of three people. Do you really think I'm bluffing right now?"

I'm met with silence, signaling that I've gotten to her.

"Fine," she mutters. "Tell me what I need to do again."

I tell her to go to the bar that the phone number that called me traced to.

"The same girl that you've approached for hitwoman services might be there. But you need to be discreet."

"Why am I going there again?"

"Because I got a strange call from her accomplice. The redhead."

"The snarky bitch that gave me unnecessary attitude?"

I snort at the irony. "That's her. The phone number traced there. So go there and let me know what's happening."

"Whatever," she groans and hangs up, thereafter.

"She's headed there now."

We wait for the text—or call—from Veronica to let us know that she's made it to the bar. Minutes pass by, and we're sitting by the laptop, coming up with the next move to take after Willow takes hers.

It's 6:00 a.m., and the phone finally rings with a call from Veronica.

"Hello," Leif answers in a bored voice.

"I'm here at the bar…but I don't see Willow."

"Just look for a redhead that's most likely on crutches. If you see her, Willow's not far behind. You can't miss her," I shout.

Veronica grunts her frustration on the phone. It sounds as if she slams her car door closed, and a barrage of voices attacks my ears as she gets closer to the bar.

"It's so fucking busy," she complains.

"It's a bar. Now just look for the redhead."

"I don't see her."

Leif and I share a confused look. He quickly pulls up Veronica's location on his computer, using her phone number. It pinpoints her at the bar that we got the call from…but the girl's location is no longer at the bar after we refresh the tracking.

"What the fuck?"

"Where'd her location go?" I ask, confused as hell.

"I have no idea, but…I can't find her location anywhere. What the hell is happening?"

The redhead's location tracking is completely gone, but Veronica's location remains at the bar.

And just like it's out of a slasher film, my phone rings, catching me off guard. It's a number I've never seen before, but it's a Boston area code. I pick up after the fourth ring.

"This is Kinsley."

"I know."

Shit. It's Willow. I clear my throat, trying to shake it off.

"I didn't think I'd hear from you so soon. Didn't we talk an hour ago?"

She chuckles with a menace I've never heard her laugh with before.

"We did. But I think it's time we play *my* game, Kinsley Focker."

"Really? And what game is that?"

"Are you into mind games?"

"Been a player since before I could remember."

"Then this will be easy for you. I spy, with my killer eye, a young lady named Veronica that was supposed to be dead."

I freeze, locking gazes with Leif.

"Veronica," he whispers to Veronica on the phone. "You're being watched. Willow's there. Right now."

She gasps. "What?"

"She's being more than watched, Leif," Willow intervenes. "She's soon about to be abducted."

"Abducted? What does she me—ahh!"

Veronica's phone cuts out before the call ends. Leif shoots a somewhat frightened look at me.

I straighten my shoulders, trying to maintain composure as muffled screaming sounds from my phone.

"You move fast, Willow," I simply say.

"The Siren Assassin usually does."

The sound of a door closing makes me jump, and I hear women whispering and Veronica's screams.

"So what is this supposed to mean to me? Veronica is just a throwaway piece in this game of chess that we're playing. She was annoying as fuck, anyway."

"Considering she's faked her death, I'm not sure how authorities would take to finding out about that."

"And how would that lead back to me? She could just say that she faked her suicide."

"Give me some credit, Viking. I happen to think I'm more persuasive than that."

"I underestimated you, Willow."

"You always have, Kinsley. Also, tell your freak brother I know of a place we can meet on Wednesday."

Leif swallows nervously. "Oh yeah? Where's that?"

"I'll text you the details. I have business to take care of right now."

She quickly hangs up the phone, Veronica's muffled screams being cut off.

"What the fuck, Kinsley?" is all Leif can say.

"Don't freak out."

"I'm not freaking out. I'm annoyed that I let you get me involved with this mess. You didn't have the heart to tell me that this bitch is crazy?"

"That's what draws me to her, Leif. Now stop calling her a bitch."

"She stabbed me in the eye."

"And you tried to kill her."

"By your orders!" he argues.

Things are starting to get complicated. I knew killing the man closest to her would light a fire under her ass, but I didn't expect it to happen this quickly. This woman's another level of ready and avenging. It's unlike anything I'd ever think she'd be capable of. But I'm not ready to back down quite yet. I've never been one to back down. I'm an athlete, so I'm competitive by nature. I can handle it.

"Leif, don't quit on me right now, all right? I need you to help me with this. I'm not ready to lose to her now. She screwed me over ten years ago, so we're gonna keep fighting the good fight."

"What good fight? She has every right to be upset and bloodthirsty. She's killed a lot of people, Kin. Are you sure you're ready to confront someone who has a kill count in the double digits?"

It's a hard question. I'm not a killer. I'd say I'm somewhere between a sadist and masochist. Because, good

God almighty, do I love watching her squirm and stoop down to my level at the same time. It turns me on more than I'd typically admit. So I'm not ready to back down just yet. Not when I'm getting so close to getting my vengeance.

My sweet, sweet Willow. I can't wait for the day that I can finally kill her. It's an urge I've had for a while. It's a disturbing desire, but it's one that consumed me. Interacting with her ten years later is meant to be.

Or is it?

I knew she'd be here. My brother went to school here, and he knew she was here, too. But she changed her phone number after rendering him blind in one eye. So finding her alone in her element was a serendipitous happenstance. She truly is stunning. A work of art. It's scary, and it disturbs me.

When I first met her in the Internet realm, I assumed she was just this sexy avatar. Upon talking with her more—and hell, seeing her naked body on my screen—I couldn't resist her. It toyed with my psyche, my emotions. I lashed out at her numerous times. But it was never her fault. She won the genetic lottery. I've just driven myself mad at the beauty she is because I'll never understand it. Gorgeous with the right amount of crazy.

My sweet, sweet Willow. Like the graceful tree. With the feminine physique that could drive a man crazy. And that's a hill I'm willing to die on. It drives me mad. Insane. But I'm a patient man. I can play this fucked-up mind game of hers that she wants to play. I'll go through the hoops and kill whoever I need to just to see her again. It'll be brief. I've had the pleasure to appreciate her numerous times, but just one last time, I would make love to her. I'd enjoy what it feels like to be inside her one last time. And then when it's all said and done, I'll relieve myself of such madness and grace her with one last breath before her beautiful physique goes lifeless. Men do evil things when presented with a body and beauty like hers.

I'm a tortured man. Willow Harding tortures me, and she doesn't mean to. It's just an art she's learned to master in the last ten years. My little seductress. The femme fatale is alive and well inside of her, and the aura emanates from her when she's in your presence. So I'll take it upon myself to relieve all men of the distress she's bound to cause and kill her.

"It's not a matter of if I'm ready to confront her. It's a matter of if she'll let me be with her one last time before I take her last breath."

Leif looks at me with a disturbed look he's never given me before. I'm usually the more composed brother, despite my compulsion. But this level of intrigue will be the end of me if I don't get rid of her.

"You're a sick man, brother."

"I'm a *tortured* man, brother."

And I'll soon be a destroyed man if I don't come up with a gameplan. She's got Veronica in her clutches, but I'm not even the least bit worried about that. I'm more worried about whether or not Veronica will comply with whatever Willow's orders are. If she decides to comply, she'll most likely go to authorities or the news channels for a breakthrough story that she faked her death to get away from her abusive ex. But if she doesn't comply, then I'm banking on Willow doing away with her. For my sake and Leif's sake, I'm hoping that the dumb bitch doesn't comply so she can stop harassing us about a check that's nonexistent.

It's a mind game. My girl is good. I'm not sure which way her kidnapping is going to go. One way, we're royally fucked. The other way, I'm off scot-free. Well fucking played, Willow. Let the games begin.

219

SEVENTEEN

WILLOW

The process for a voluntary separation from the military takes thirty days. Until then, I was ready to go back home and settle my mind. It's better than being dishonorably discharged, and I figured the longer I stayed, the more my sanity would spiral. It was better this way.

Vinny greeted me with a warm hug the second he opened the door and found me with a suitcase. He was the first person I called when I knew I was coming back to Port Rockwell for a while. Meredith apologized for seeing my text late, but I couldn't bring myself to stay at her place. Not when I disrespected her bedroom the way that I had.

The other night was fucking with my head royally. My head had been hurting in the last day, and I felt so tired. I'd been having to wear sunglasses because even the slightest sliver of the sun fucked with my head. I didn't know what I was going to do. If my filing for voluntary separation was approved, I needed to find a job.

"Thank you for taking me in, Vinny," I said, rolling my suitcase in after me.

"Of course, honey."

"I feel like I need to take a huge nap. I'm beat."

"Before you take a nap," he started nervously, "we actually have company—"

"Hello, Willow."

Marlena Walsh sat in her usual primp and proper position, legs crossed and her perfectly manicured fingers interlocked, resting on her knee.

"Marlena" was all I said to acknowledge her.

"Do you think that's an appropriate way to acknowledge your mother?"

"You mean my mother who's been in seclusion for two months?"

She gave me a disapproving look before adjusting her wool cardigan.

"I don't believe it's any of your business where I've been, Low."

"Why are you here?"

Clearly, pleasantries weren't on the menu, and the feeling was mutual. I'd had a long morning. The last thing I wanted to do was pretend with the lady that was supposed to be my mother.

"Who is this Kinsley Focker gentleman?"

I snorted. He was far from a goddamn gentleman. And this was precisely the conversation I was trying to avoid.

"Someone I wish I would've never met."

"And he's assaulted you?" she asked with the least amount of concern she could possibly muster.

"He's more than assaulted me, Marlena."

"I understand that. Apparently, he has compromising photos and videos of you, as well. And I wonder how he would get in possession of such precious material, Willow," she said in an accusatory tone.

I looked at Vinny to get him to get me out of this mess. But he gave me the look of a disappointed father, and it didn't take me long to realize that I was being ambushed.

"Because I was a stupid girl in mourning. Any other questions?"

She tilted her head at me, confused.

"You're mourning your father, so you send inappropriate photos and videos to an Internet stranger?"

I'd been torturing myself, ruminating on my life choices leading up to this point. I hate repetition. There's something about it that bugs me, especially when it's repetition that's meant to degrade me. Questioning me about it as if I hadn't already learned from it drives me nuts.

"I don't think I need to explain myself to you, considering you didn't even show up to the funeral. Didn't you also leave your sixteen-year-old daughter to take care of her father, while you ran off with a certain young golfer?"

"What does this have to do with your vagina being on the Internet?"

"I didn't have a fucking parent figure, you dumb bitch."

"Whoa, watch it, Low," Vinny gently warned me.

She put her hand up to quiet him, gaze still on me.

"No, it's okay, Vincent. She can lash out at me all she wants. It doesn't change the fact that she let an Internet stranger get ahold of what a woman holds most precious to her."

"One could argue that precious thing would be their child," I mumbled.

Her lips lay in a flat line, visibly annoyed with my quips.

"Vincent, can you give us some space, please?"

He looked between me and Marlena before leaning down and kissing me on the cheek. Before I noticed it, he'd left me alone with Mother Gothel. She was staring me down, her self-satisfied expression still plastered on her face.

"You got me alone. Now what?"

"You're coming to live with me."

With that simple statement, it felt like the world fell out from underneath my feet. There was no goddamn way I was living with her as she robbed the cradle.

"You have terrible humor."

"You know what, believe it or not, I'm not kidding. You're coming to live with me until you can get back on your feet. If you're not going to finish out your years in the military, then you're coming to stay with me and Kevin. Because you're not going to freeload off of Vinny."

"Fuck you," I retorted. "You're out of your mind if you think I'm living with you. I'll just stay with Meredith."

"After using her guest bedroom as a private brothel?"

At this rate, I was done talking to her. This conversation wasn't going anywhere.

"We're just going in circles," I said, standing up from the couch. "I already said I'm not living with you. And I don't have the mental capacity to argue with you about this."

She sighed, rubbing her temples.

"You're just like your father. You're steadfast in doing whatever the fuck you want."

"You're damn right, Marlena."

"And that was exactly the downfall of our marriage. He couldn't keep me happy. And when I told him as much, he stayed steadfast in not giving a fuck."

"Look, I don't care to hear about you and Dad's sexual woes. I genuinely just wanna get to sleep. I'm fucking tired."

Sighing, she stood up with her purse and smoothed her long skirt.

"I can see that I'm not going to be able to get through to you today. I'll give you the space that you request. But I'm giving you until the end of this month to come to your senses."

"There are no senses to come to. I'm not moving in with you."

"So be it. Have a lovely rest of your day, Willow," she said, nearly monotone.

And with that, she nodded at me and walked out the front door, hopefully never to be seen again.

I throw my face into my hands, still reeling from the mental anguish. My nudes were on the Internet, viewed only by people who knew of them. And I had been so close to death's door less than twenty-four hours ago. I didn't know what I was going to do.

"Willow, you can't talk to your mom like that," Vinny scolded me, coming from his bedroom.

"I'm really not in the mood for a stern father figure right now."

"Well, are you in the mood for a stern uncle figure? Because that's what you're getting."

"If I can't avoid it, then lay it on me, Uncle Vinny."

A throaty chuckle escaped as he sat down on the couch across from me. In the exact same spot where Marlena was sitting. Round two.

"You know I love you, kid, but you need to stop disrespecting your mother the way you do."

"I don't acknowledge her as my mother, though."

"Your father would want you to be respectful. Me too. And it's not out of the ordinary that she's being hard on you. There are images online of you."

"I know that," I said more aggressively than I wanted to. "I already know that what I did was stupid. Why are you older people so hellbent on reliving the past as if it can be changed?"

"Because it'll affect your future now."

"In what way?"

"You were studying criminology. Do you think law firms will want to hire you with images and videos online?"

"What year are we living in?"

"The real one."

"I believe the phrase is 'the real world,' Vinny."

"I'm serious, Willow," he said in a stern voice. "I don't want this to ruin your future. We'll do whatever we can to get everything off the web, but—"

"It doesn't matter anymore. I'm not getting a job in law."

"What do you mean?"

"That's not the line of work I want to be in. Can we please talk about this another time?"

He looked at me as if the conversation was far from over, but as far as I'm concerned, this wasn't a conversation I wanted to continue. I needed to find a way to regroup and figure out where to go from here.

"I know you've had a long night. So I'll leave you to it. Tell me you've already filed a police report against this Kinsley boy."

Shit. He really wouldn't let this go.

"No, I haven't filed anything."

"What??"

"Please, Vinny—"

"So this boy is still roaming the streets because you're scared."

"I'm not scared, I'm just…I don't want any questions asked. And Kinsley comes from a rich family. There's no way anything would come of it."

"Willow. This boy tried to kill you. You're not handling this the way I thought you would."

"And what's that, Vinny? I'm not handling it like a victim? Because I'm not. I let this happen to myself. I'm not going to give him the satisfaction of showing that he's affected me. It's better this way."

There it was again. The disappointed father look. It was one I'd seen one too many times when Dad was alive. I'd grown used to it, but it was more annoying than anything right now. I didn't like lashing out at Vinny. He'd been there for me since Dad's death, and I knew he'd promised that he and Caroline would watch over me. But it was becoming a bit overkill.

"You're a strong girl. You know I know that more than anything. But Steven was my best friend. I've known since you were a little girl. I raised you like you were my own. Seeing you ride your first bike. Going to your graduations. Caroline read you bedtime stories every time your parents needed us to watch you. I've seen you grow into this beautiful young woman. Please do not let this rascal take your power away. You're precious."

Tears began to well in my ears, but I couldn't swipe them away, to not show that I was breaking. Vinny was right. I was a slave to my pride, and it was tearing me to pieces. I knew that I should report *him to the police. But I knew exactly how it was going to go. And I'd rather not subject myself to the humiliation yet again.*

"I don't know what you want me to say, Vinny," I rasped. "I'd really just like to some space to think things over."

He gave me a sad smile and another kiss on the cheek before leaving. I was left to take in the clock above their fireplace ticking and the house cat mewling and rubbing her tiny head against my ankle.

"Hi, Trixie," I silently greeted her as she briefly stopped to look up at me, only to continue rubbing against me. Leaning down to pet her head, I got up to get to sleep in their guest bedroom. But Caroline walked out of the master bedroom, giving me a gentle smile, momentarily stopping me.

"Trixie's missed you," she pointed out, walking over and pouring herself a mug of coffee.

"At least someone has."

"Don't be silly, Low. We've all missed you."

"Marlena and Vinny aren't acting like it."

"I'd have to disagree with you. They just want you to be safe. I do, too."

Here we fucking went. "Are you going to give me the third degree, too?"

She gave me a nearly humorless smile, leaning against the beautifully marbled kitchen island.

"No. You don't need me to. You know exactly what you need to do to reconcile what's happened to you. You're a smart girl."

"Am I?"

I didn't know if I was anymore. I'd let this happen to me under the guise of mourning my dad. Maybe I wasn't as smart as people— or I—made myself out to be.

"We all make mistakes. I once had a wild streak when I was around your age. We learn to grow from it."

"You weren't assaulted, though."

But perhaps that was the wrong thing to say. Her pale skin reddened as she looks down at her mug of coffee, avoiding eye contact.

"I wouldn't be so sure of that, Low."

All I did was look at her. There was so much unsaid in that statement. But I knew exactly what she meant. The tone in the room shifted to something uncomfortable. Unease.

Assault. It's all too common. I'd heard about it when I'd watch true crime dramas with my dad. He always taught me to take precautions and be alert in the world as a girl. No matter how strong you are, there will always be some guy looking to prey on you. Never let your guard down. Put on a brave face and fight back. I always listened to my dad.

Until Kinsley Focker. There was an extreme pivot when he came into my life.

I let my guard down. I trusted easily when I shouldn't have. Steven Harding was the best thing that ever happened to me, despite having to take care of him. And maybe that sounds horrible. I don't regret taking care of him. Did it make me resent him? A little bit. But did I love him more than life itself? Absolutely. He raised me. He was a shield that I wore proudly, everywhere I went. When that shield left me, somehow I let darkness in. I let a mentally fucked boy take my dignity away, and it'd be difficult for me to reconcile that. But upon hearing that Caroline was a victim herself…the proximity to it all was more than I can handle.

"I'm so sorry, Caroline."

"Don't be sorry for me," she said quickly. "It happened. All I'm saying is, we all have a wild streak at some point in our lives. And while that sort of independence is freeing, it also comes with consequences."

"So now I have to feel guilty for sharing intimate things with someone I trusted?"

"That's not what I'm saying. You just have to be careful who you share it with. And understand that, sometimes life as a woman isn't so peachy. Whether we like it or not, there are just things that we don't have the same luxuries that men have when it comes to sex. They can have sexual desires and send nudes without worrying that

it'll ruin their lives. Women don't have that luxury. Just remember that."

I was left with my mouth agape as she gave me a sympathetic smile, took a sip of her coffee, and walked back into her room.

It's an age-old debate. I think it's pretty stupid, but that doesn't change anything. I hate that I now have to fear wanting to be intimate with a man ever again. There will always be that warning voice in the back of your head telling you to abort mission. Telling you to never trust again. And maybe it's a voice that I could have ignored when the right one came into my life. But that guy wasn't coming anytime soon. For the time being, I needed to figure out where to go from here.

Opting out of taking a nap, I dropped my bags in the guest bedroom and called Meredith.

"Are you okay?! I heard you got attacked. I'm so sorry that I didn't call you. Work's been stressing me out the last few weeks."

"Don't worry about it. I have a question for you.

"Yeah, what's up?"

I take a deep breath. "What's the company you work for, again?"

Silence greeted my ears for a few seconds before she slowly said, "Willow, you know I'm not supposed to talk about that information with you."

"I know, and I'll explain why I'm asking, but I was just asking. You said it's for some high profile, confidential company. I just wanted to know which one. If it's for the CIA or FBI, then…I was curious to see if you'd be willing to put in a good word for me for a job or internship. I'm completing my criminology degree and have been in the military. Surely it wouldn't be too much of a hassle."

"Willow, take a breath." She stopped me at the end of my tirade. "It's not that simple. I don't work for the CIA or the FBI."

"But you're a hacker. Are you freelance?"

She cleared her throat. "I'm going to tell you…but you have to promise not to tell anyone what I'm about to say."

I was so confused. If she didn't work for some confidential government organization, then who did she work for?

"Okay..." I said, waiting for her to finish.

"I don't work for a...legal organization, I'll say. It's something I discovered after going to therapy for my kidnapping."

"This all sounds super cryptic. What are you hiding?"

I just wanted to see if she could potentially get me an entry-level position or at least an internship.

"The organization I work for isn't in the States, for one. I work remotely for them. And it's a criminal organization."

"Criminal?"

She sighed, clearly frustrated that I wasn't picking up on what she was talking about.

"I work for a Russian organization called Kill Elite. I don't know how to say it in Russian, but that's what it is in English. I independently contract my services out to their workers."

I found myself dumbstruck, trying to find words. The name of the organization spoke for itself, in terms of what their mission was. But my best friend working for a criminal organization? That didn't make any sense.

"I'm sorry, I'm not sure I understand. You work for a killing organization?"

"Specifically for assassins that are looking to access data they need to complete their kills."

"Meredith," I say in shock. "What the hell?"

"I wouldn't judge so quickly. It's a good job, and it's the best way I've learned to reconcile what happened."

"I understand, Mer. I do. But this is just crazy."

"Do you wanna meet up in a bit to talk about it? I'm sure there are...other things you wanna talk about, as well."

There was so much to talk about. And I really needed to rest because I sensed myself on the verge of going insane. But this new revelation about Meredith had me intrigued.

"I can meet you in about thirty minutes."

There are so many unanswered questions. But little did I know that talking about Kill Elite would change my life forever.

There's a rage burning inside of me. A rage I haven't felt in ten years. In two days, it's my thirtieth birthday, and I've spent my entire twenties devoted to giving a fucking sadistic boy my attention.

I've wasted it away, and for what? Because life has consequences. I let a stupid boy take my power away. I don't regret spending the last decade being a hitwoman. I resent the reason I do it. I resent making myself out to be a victim. I screwed up my entire life, and I didn't have to.

But hindsight is indeed 20/20. I can't back down now. I can feel bad for myself later. Right now, I'm holding Veronica Canseco hostage in Vinny's speakeasy. Shortly after speaking with the police and giving Caroline the unfortunate news, I had Violet drive me to the hospital to talk to Meredith.

She was awake right when we got there. She was happy to see us but immediately knew that I had bad news to tell her. When I told her that they killed Callie in San Jose after I met with her and that they killed Vinny, she nearly broke down. I hadn't seen her like that in awhile. My normally composed and jaded best friend cried, and that's when I knew there had to be a new game plan.

We were able to get Meredith discharged from the hospital tonight, and she decided to help me and Violet come up with a good plan.

Because it was for certain: I am killing Kinsley Focker. And it needs to be a kill so vicious, unlike anything I've ever committed before. But to commit is to be strategic. Not calculated but strategic. He likes games. Specifically, mind games. So do I. Therefore, that's what we'll play. Violet did some searching and was able to find their location, based on the phone number Kinsley's been calling me from. From there, she was able to find out that Veronica Canseco was indeed alive, that she faked her death. It wasn't a revelation I was expecting to see. It makes sense that Kinsley and Leif would set up an entire operation to take advantage of me when my senses were lowered.

But now it's my move to turn the tables back on him. He wants to use Veronica as a pawn. I'll bite.

Meredith limps into the speakeasy on crutches, nodding at me to confirm that they've got Veronica. Moments later, Violet walks in with a struggling Veronica, who tries everything in her power to fight back. Violet sits her down in front of me as she huffs her annoyance.

"This is stupid, Willow," she grits through her teeth.

"So is faking your death," I shoot back, making her flinch.

She straightens her shoulders and puts on a brave face.

"I was just doing what I was asked to do."

"I understand." I turn to look at Meredith leaning against the bar as she smokes a cigarette. "Do you have a pack?"

She nods at me, pulls out her pack of Marlboros, and hands it over.

"Here you go."

"You have a lighter?"

She pulls it out of her pocket and hands it to me.

"Why am I here, Willow? This is a waste of time. Just give it up. You won't be able to beat the brothers. Meredith's basically a cripple. And the purple-haired freak can't save you, either."

"What'd you say, bitch?" Violet readies to attack her, but Meredith holds her back.

"Let's not irritate this any more than you already have, okay?"

I light my cigarette and take a puff, causing Veronica to swipe the smoke away.

"What are you gonna do? You can't just hold me hostage. Kinsley and Leif will find a way to stop you," she argues.

I smile at her proposition. Taking another huff of my cigarette, I blow it out in her direction again to agitate her more.

"You're right, Veronica. I can't hold you hostage. I'm not gonna hurt you either."

She looks at me skeptically. "You're not?"

"No." I take another puff. "I don't believe in violence against women."

She rolls her eyes, flipping her hair away from her face.

"Is this gonna be a feminist tirade? Because I don't really care to hear about it."

"You don't have to care to hear about it. It's not a 'feminist tirade,' as you say. I'm genuinely against violence against women. You see, that's why I provide services to women who are in danger. I care about their well-being."

"Bullshit," she spews hatefully. "If you cared about my well-being, you wouldn't have kidnapped and manhandled me."

"Low, can we kill this girl already?" Meredith asks, bored, making Veronica's demeanor go from hard-ass to nervousness.

"We're not gonna kill her, Mer, don't be silly. Like I said, I don't believe in violence against women."

Veronica's demeanor eases a bit.

"Good."

She looks at me self-assured. It's a look that rivals Kinsley's and Leif's. A look I hate to see on anyone. It's a level of arrogance that's toyed with my mind for a long while.

Taking another puff of my cigarette, I'm about ready to put it out. When she swipes the smoke away, she puts her hand down, and I put the cigarette out on her wrist, watching it sizzle in her skin. She yanks her arm back, yelping in pain.

"*What the fuck?!*" she screeches.

"But I don't acknowledge you as a woman. I acknowledge you as an accomplice."

Tears well in her eyes, but they're still fiery and angry.

"*What the hell is wrong with you?!*"

I pull out another cigarette and begin to light it, watching as she watches me in fear. I let out a puff.

"I ask that you comply or I'll do it again. Now how did you meet these assholes?"

She looks at me, confused and frazzled, most likely still reeling from her skin welting from my cigarette.

"This is fucking stupid," she grits through her teeth angrily.

Right then, Meredith walks up behind her and puts out her cigarette on Veronica's shoulder.

"*Ow!* You guys are *fucking crazy!!*" she screeches again and quickly gets up from the chair and scrambles to the door. But Violet steps in front of her.

"You're not going anywhere," she says.

Veronica then turns around to look at me as I huff another cigarette. We're intimidating her. I'm essentially numb. Her screams and protests do nothing to make me sympathize. Instead, I just sit back and continue smoking my cigarette when they sit her down in front of me. Tears continue to assault her face, but she still tries to maintain a tough exterior.

"How much time do we have?" I ask Violet.

She pulls up her laptop and types for a few seconds.

"Like ten minutes."

We threw Veronica's phone out of the window, since we presumed that they were tracking her location. But Kinsley still has my phone number and is most likely tracking my location. So we're on borrowed time to elicit any necessary information out of her.

"I don't wanna keep asking because not only do I hate repetition but we're running out of time. So if I have to ask keep asking"—I pull out the lighter—"then this room goes to ashes."

She looks at me in shock and disbelief.

"And you say they're the crazy ones."

"Start talking now, Veronica," I say, lighting it up. "How did you meet them and what was their plan?"

For a second, I almost think she won't tell me. This defiant girl is entirely different from the timid, shy role that she played before. It's a jarring contrast, but the good thing about being a hitwoman is the ability to be flexible and be prepared for everything thrown my way.

"I'm an escort, okay? They hired me...well, Leif hired me as an escort. I came over to his place one night, and that's when I saw you kill Benji Lockson," she says with a resentful look on her face.

Well...I wasn't expecting to hear that.

"You were hired as an escort for one night, and that's how you were able to see Willow through the windows. Well, the timing and place is just rather convenient," Meredith says.

"It didn't occur to me until later that they had been watching you for a while. Benji was Kinsley's best friend. Marissa knows them, too. Everything she told you about Benji...was true. But she was also having an affair with Kinsley behind Benji's back."

"What the hell are you talking about?"

"Like I said, they've been watching you. Kinsley has been tracking your thirtieth birthday. He masterminded a scheme to get into your head and good graces, again. Kinsley and Benji were starting a tech business together, but Kinsley had been committing tax fraud. He didn't wanna get caught, so his original plan was to frame Benji if he got caught. So he included Marissa in the scheme. But then when he saw you at that bar one night, he did some research and found out through the grapevine that you offer killing services. So he devised another scheme where he told Marissato contact you for killing services to get rid of Benji."

This is such a fucking mind bend.

"So he was fucking Marissa and wanted to kill two birds with one stone by killing Benji and terrorizing me again."

"Something like that."

"Willow, we need to hurry this up. Kinsley's on his way here now," Violet warns.

"Shit," I mutter under my breath. "So what was the plan with you?"

"I really don't wanna talk about this," she says with fear in her voice. "I've already said too much."

"What was their plan with you? Why did they tell you to pretend to be an abuse victim?"

She swallows nervously, her gaze landing on the door as if she expects them to bust through it.

"In theory, it wasn't pretend. But it's a really long story."

"We have three minutes. Make it count."

She sighs, bouncing her leg anxiously.

"What was supposed to be an easy money night for me to entertain Kinsley turned into something sinister. I didn't know that…Leif was gonna be a part of it."

"A part of what?"

Her tears are back, and she becomes overcome with emotion.

"They raped me," she rasps.

So she is yet another victim. I'm left in shock, not sure where to go from here. I wasn't expecting her to admit to that. I wasn't sure what it was that I was expecting. But I'd be lying if I said it didn't surprise me.

"So why did you go through with their plan to trick me?"

"I have a daughter! I have a two-year-old. They threatened to take her if I reported the rape and didn't follow through with seeking you out."

It's a lot to wrap my head around. There was a lot happening in the background, and I had no idea. Everything's way too interconnected for my liking. I start to question if maybe I missed something. Or maybe I'm not as good of a hitwoman as I thought I was.

"Willow," Violet warns.

"I don't wanna have to do this, but I had to. Thank you for complying. Kinsley and Leif will be here any moment. So we need to go. So we'll get you to a safe—"

"No," Veronica stops me. "Just leave me here."

"What?"

"At this rate, they already know that I told you. There's really nothing more for me to live for."

"That's it? You're just gonna give up and let them kill you?"

She shrugs helplessly, a stark contrast to the hard-ass girl that we brought here not too long ago.

"My daughter's at my sister's house. She'll take care of her. I just don't wanna deal with these brothers anymore. Ever since I met them, my life's been going downhill. So I'll just sacrifice myself."

"Veronica—"

"Willow! If she wants to be dramatic, let her! We need to go!" Meredith shouts.

I give one last look at Veronica as she gives me a small smile.

"It was nice knowing you."

She nods at me, and it's the last thing I see before Violet yanks me away, and we dart down the stairs. Police lights shine through the stained entrance door to the bar, so we exit through the back.

We make it to the car, assisting Meredith. Watching from afar, I see Kinsley and Leif exit their car as the police charge inside.

Seeing him is a sensory overload. I almost fell in love with this guy. Viking. He charmed me yet again, and I was stupid enough to not see the signs. The insane thing is, even looking at him now, I still have an intense reaction to him. My body reacts to him in the way it did before, and I hate it.

Clearing my throat, I give Violet the go-ahead to drop Meredith off at my apartment. She's had a long night, helping us more than she probably had the energy for tonight. Since I don't trust her to be by herself tonight, I'm letting her stay at my place until everything blows over.

Once we make it back to my apartment, Violet helps me sit her down on the couch. Meredith groans in pain before saying, "That was an adventure."

I appreciate the attempt to make the situation more lighthearted, but I can't reconcile everything I've found out tonight.

"We need to find Marissa," I blurt.

"Willow—"

"I'm not done yet. We need to find her."

"Okay, we can find her tomorrow. You haven't slept in hours."

Panic is starting to set in. I can't just go about my day and night without doing something. Kinsley is working overtime to destroy me, which means I need to follow suit. I can't let him win. I can't.

EIGHTEEN

KINSLEY

I've underestimated the darling Willow Harding. She truly is a trained assassin. Her prowess is like none other. It's remarkable. But I don't feel deterred just yet. Not when she left Veronica alone with burn marks on her wrist and shoulder. She's sending us a message. A message that's been received: she's not going away anytime soon.

And that's okay. I'd hate for her to go away when her birthday is approaching. It's on Friday. That's the day I've been planning for. She's turning thirty, and I've never been more attracted to her. She was stunning then and even more stunning now. Hell, I just wish she wouldn't defy me as much as she does.

"I promise I didn't tell her anything," Veronica lies as we drag her out of the speakeasy, half an hour after police gives us the all-clear that the Siren Assassin is on the loose and they're going to put out an APB out on the mysterious man-killer. But she's not a mystery to me. What good would telling them the description of her be, though?

They'd apprehend her pretty quickly. And I'm not ready for her to be taken away from me just yet. Not again.

"I believe you, Veronica," I sigh, annoyed with her pleading.

There's nothing that she can say that will make me trust her again. Judging by the fact that they left her here alive, that tells me either one of two things: she doesn't believe in killing women, or Veronica snitched. While I'm certain that the darling Willow is a feminist at heart, I guarantee that if Veronica hadn't talked about the scheme, her body would be lying cold on the ground right now.

She lets out a sigh of relief before smiling at me, her shoulders relaxing. The police are long gone, and it's just me, her, and Leif. It's overdue that we do away with this girl. She will slowly become collateral damage to the plan, and I'm not into games of the Russian Roulette variety. As she gets up and makes a phone call, I pull Leif aside.

"We need to get rid of your escort."

He flinches, confused.

"You wanna kill her? She's been complying with the plan, though."

"She's also a pain in my ass. It shouldn't have ever gotten this far, and yet it did."

"Because of us," he says, bored. "I'm sorry, brother. I don't think it's a good idea. We need someone to keep an eye on that bitch when we can't."

"She managed to get kidnapped in public with people around. Do you really think she's capable of being flexible and thinking quickly on her feet to get out of danger?"

Leif looks back at her as she speaks animatedly to some anonymous person on the phone.

"I'll let you do the dirty work, okay? I don't feel comfortable doing it. I just wanna kill this Willow bitch for what she did to my fucking eye." He points at the prosthetic eye in question.

I don't go into how it was our fault for the attack because it doesn't matter. The original plan to kill her all those years ago went awry. This is the new plan, and I don't intend on messing it up any more than we already have.

I just simply give him a nod, pull out a long piece of wire, and whistle to grab her attention. I don't give her a second before I quickly yank the wire around her neck, closing it around her vocal cords. She violently thrashes around, trying to pull it from around her neck. Her face increasingly turns red as she struggles, trying her hardest to break free from my grip.

"Fucking hell, Kin," Leif breathes.

It's about seven minutes before she finally stops breathing and her kicks and thrashes are a thing of the past. The sweet silence warms me as I slowly loosen my grip, allowing her lax body to fall to the ground.

I stretch out my fingers to relieve them of cramping.

"See how easy that was?"

He shakes his head and darts back down the stairs of the quiet bar, and I follow him.

"I don't like this person you're making me into, Kin."

"What person is that?"

He stops at the bar on the first floor and leans over it before turning around to me with an indecisive look on his face.

"This...guy who has no remorse for human life. I'm not that guy. I'm your brother."

"Might you forget that we're in this mess because you wanted to be me?"

"*I* wanted to be *you*?!"

"You've wanted every girlfriend I've had. All I've been doing is being a big brother and letting you in on the experience of the touch of a woman," I remind him.

Anger builds in his eyes as he stares me down.

"I knew you'd rub that in my face. Blaire liked *me. You* took her from me."

"No, brother. She didn't. She was my girlfriend. I didn't take anyone from you."

He rolls his eyes and thrashes his head into his hands.

"I hate you" is all he says. "I hate you for ruining my life, getting me involved in this mess. I would've been fine just living my life, working in cybersecurity. But now you've turned me into a cybercriminal."

With that, he angrily bolts out of the bar, leaving me to look after him. Usually, I'd brush this episode off as him being angsty and stressed. That he'd get over it and forgive me. But the emotion in his eyes and voice, coupled with his sudden reluctance to follow through the plan that's in progress to kill Willow, tells me that there's something brewing inside of him. He may go rogue. My brother's always been a loose cannon. He would get violent with me throughout our high school and college years, but I'm the bigger and stronger brother that tamed his aggression. A lot of his violence was misplaced, considering both of our parents were emotionally and physically abusive. Misplaced, yes, but not misguided. I empathized with it. Our stepdad would routinely have amateur sparring matches with us in the living room to keep us tough and manly, and our mother would verbally assault us whenever we'd defy him. It was a perfectly well-oiled machine…in the most twisted sense.

I don't regret how Mother raised us. If anything, being called a loser, waste of space, and a disappointment made me become a stronger man. A smarter man. Smart enough to know that I won't let another woman fuck with my head again. And the fact that I've given the brazen Willow the power to make me lose sight of who I am guts me. But I have a few more days before her birthday. A few more days until I can do what I've set out to do.

There's still a few more loose ends to cover up before I can. Leif isn't here to help me, so I look around the speakeasy for gloves.

I find a pair of blue ones and get to work disposing of Veronica's body. Turning off all cameras in and around the bar, I throw them all in the dumpster outside and throw her body in water behind the bar.

Killing isn't easy for me. I'm not a killer. I'm a rugby player. I've been an athlete for as long as I can remember. That's what I love doing. But I can't be dishonest and say that there's a certain rush that hits me when I carry these out. Something's wrong with me. I'm well aware of that. And if anything comes out against me, that's the end of my rugby career—and life—as I know it. I've been living and breathing as Leif Mattson since my brother lost his eye.

During that time, I had just started dating Callie, and he stopped all contact with Callie because he didn't want to be seen with a missing eye. But then when we overpowered Callie that night at our college reunion, he started feeling uneasy about the cops leading it back to us when she reported it. I warned her not to because we all knew how that would end. She ended up keeping it to herself, but we still felt it necessary to exchange names for a fun exercise. We did it before so he could see what it was like to live in my shoes, but upon moving to Port Rockwell and finding Willow at the bar, we decided to see if we could fool the ever-elusive Willow Harding. When I signed with the New England Hornets after a few years of working in the tech industry, I pretended that I'd had a name change;

had Leif doctor up some false documents to prove that it was a federal name change, and voilà…I became Leif Mattson. But this time, it was more long-term…possibly even permanent. If the plan to kill Willow worked.

It has to work. I don't know what I would do if she eludes me again. I'm doing everything in my power to make sure the plan comes to fruition.

Before I know it, I'm back at my loft after cleaning up the crime scene. I'm not as immaculate as her or even Leif, but I did what I could to not compromise too much of it. I did my best to clean up the crime scene and not incriminate myself by wearing gloves and disposing of things that I touched. I did everything to the best of my ability. But there's only a matter of time before I'm linked back to past murders, if I haven't been already. The cops are looking for Willow, and they'll be looking for me, too.

The clock is ticking. Even more so with her birthday coming up. My gaze lands on the stove. I'm hitting rock bottom. It's becoming clearer and clearer. But I have no other choice. I've gone this long without getting caught. I won't let that streak go now. Before I take action in what I'm about to do, I pull out my phone to make a quick call to Leif, hoping that he's cooled down from our spat back at the bar. Surprisingly, he picks up on the second ring, and an irritated groan greets my ears.

"Hello?"

"Leif, it's me."

Another groan tortures my ears. "Uh…I'm kind of busy right now, Kin."

I suspected it from when he first picked up the phone, but if the feminine giggle in the background is anything to go by, it's to confirm that he's entertaining someone tonight.

"Aren't you supposed to be meeting Willow tonight?"

The mysterious girl in the background whispers, "You guys are still terrorizing that crazy bitch?"

I pull back, gazing confused at my phone. Whoever this girl is knows who I'm talking about.

"Leif, who the fuck is there with you?"

He tries to quiet her, and all I hear is her voicing annoyance.

"Don't freak out, you know her."

"Who is she? We killed Veronica."

There's a struggle between them before the girl in question speaks on the line.

"My name starts with an M, you asshole, and for the record, it's probably not best to voice that admission on a line where someone else can hear it."

Oh, fuck me. "Marissa?" Benji's girlfriend he left behind that helped us find Willow.

"The one and only. Now can you talk to him later? I'm kind of wearing him out."

He takes the phone from her, causing her to protest.

"Think twice before you take the phone from me again. I'm meeting her tonight, yeah. It's 2:30pm right now, though, and she hasn't called me about a meeting place. What's your point?"

Having to explain what doesn't need to be said is counterproductive. I can tell he's still in a shitty mood, so I won't bother him.

"I just wanted to call you to let you know that I'm about to burn off fingerprints so nothing tracks back to me. We need to talk about how we can pin the murders on Willow."

He chuckles menacingly. "Just tell me what you wanna do, and I can make it work."

I smile, feeling at ease. "Great. We'll talk later about the plan tomorrow."

"Yeah, yeah, whatever. Marissa's getting handsy, so I'm gonna get off the phone."

Rolling my eyes, I manage to keep the disgust out of my voice.

"Just call me back when you're able to put it back in your pants."

He gives me a sarcastic laugh before hanging up. That response is a really good sign. Sarcasm is our preferred language as brothers, so I take that as a win. My attention is back on the stove. I turn it on and brace myself for a sensation that'll rival the one I get when I kill the darling Willow.

NINETEEN

LEIF

The urge to drive my head through into a brick wall consumes me every day. Ever since my near-death experience that night on a quiet suburban street, relieving myself of the never-ending torment has never looked sweeter. This life is not one I pictured for myself. I never thought I'd be the guy my brother goes to for risky business. Alas, here I am.

But I don't ruminate on my life any longer. I have a mission to complete tonight. My brother wants to kill her tomorrow night, and there are certain rules to this game of chess that we want to set forth. I am aware of the elusive Willow Harding's rebellion. It's crystal clear that blind obedience is not her forte. Perhaps there's a bit of training in the books where she's concerned. Otherwise, I can't promise Kinsley that she'll live long enough to see her birthday. By no means am I a killer. But the damn bitch stabbed me in the eye, so I'm not particularly forgiving and patient about any defiance.

Marissa kissing me on the cheek as I cradle her to my side is the only thing that pulls me back to reality. She cuddles against me, but the action repulses me. I immediately pull away and get up, leaving her to cradle a pillow.

"What's wrong?" she asks in a small voice.

Her incessant questioning about everything tonight has been bothering me to no end. Involving her in this entire scheme was probably a bad idea, reflecting on it. She and Veronica were basically the same person the entire time. They became, in a sense, clingy. It's exhausting. Though I don't have intrusive thoughts about getting rid of Marissa like Kinsley did about Veronica fatally, I do need to get her out of here so I can rest up for the big night. I don't know if I quite have a plan yet.

Willow is coming up the place to meet. But the ultimate objective is to lure her to Kinsley's house from the meeting place she chooses and keep her captive until the morning of her birthday. But if there's anything that the transient Willow Harding taught us, it's that she's always one step ahead. It's the hardest game we've ever had to play when it came to schemes. Luckily, it's not my job to come up with a gameplan.

I'm the executer. Kinsley's the mastermind. And since he's devoted to devising a plan to eradicate the siren, he's yet to send me a plan of how it will actually come to fruition. If he doesn't send me at least a treatment by this afternoon, then I'll have no choice but to take the plan into my own hands. I have no qualms with doing so. The dumb bitch rendered me blind in one eye, and I've been hanging on a thread, letting her escape. Kinsley has been more patient with her because he's fucking attracted to her and nearly in love with her. So in love that he wants to kill her. My method of killing will most likely be more barbaric than

Kinsley's thoughtful and calculated plan. But that's always been my brother. He's the purposeful, calculated son of a bitch. The master manipulator. I learned from the best but not well. I'm not as calculated. I'm driven by rage, anger. I hate Willow Harding. My brother loves her in the most twisted sense.

We're the dynamic duo. It's why we work. I've never been able to control myself. But control is not who I am, and I will never claim that. I will claim the We're the dynamic duo. It's why we work. I've never been able to control myself. But control is not who I am, and I will never claim that. I will claim the life of Willow Harding if my brother continues to prolong this plan.

"Marissa, we'll have to catch up another time. I have shit to do today," I say, putting on a T-shirt.

She rubs her hand over my arm tattoo to calm me down. But I'm not in the mood.

"But I thought we were doing brunch."

"No," I groan. "We can do brunch another day. In case you didn't notice, my brother wants to start working on a plan to get rid of this bitch."

She rolls her eyes and cradles my comforter to her nude chest.

"You and your brother are deluded if you think you're gonna kill her. She's cuckoo."

"So am I," I reassure her. "Besides, we'll have a plan in place. But I need you to lay low. Because she doesn't know you never left Port Rockwell."

She flips her brunette locks over her shoulders and stands up. No argument, no eye contact. Even before she started cheating on Benji with me, I picked up that this is her way of being mad at someone. She gives you the silent treatment and avoids you in any way she can. Any other time, I would try to ease her mind and reach a level of understanding with her. But time is of the essence, and I don't have the energy to coddle the feelings of an adult woman who knows what arrangement is in place. So I let her change, grab her things, and walk her out of my apartment.

As I walk back to the bedroom, I hear a loud thud and a muffled scream in the outside of my apartment. I'm back at the door in a matter of seconds, peeking into the hallway. As I suspected, there's no one there or a sign of a struggle. My alarm bells are ringing, as the transient the Siren Assassin comes to mind.

I close the door and pull out my phone, looking for my text thread with Marissa. I send a text, asking if she made it to her car. Nervous that she hasn't responded after nearly five minutes, I feel a sense of relief when she responds, telling me that she ran into an old friend she knows in the apartment complex and is catching up with them right now a few doors down from me.

Willow is messing with my head.

But I don't worry about it too much longer. I'm already drafting up an outline of how I'm kidnapping her tonight. She's not easy to apprehend. A force to be reckoned with, you might say. I think it's just that she's experienced. I was almost amazed at how easy it was to get ahold of her at my brother's rugby game. She has cracks in her armor, and I excel in taking advantage of those. She's not anyone I would ever be afraid of. When I have her where I want her, she's so easy to intimidate. For a second, I even understood Kinsley's fascination with her. When she's vulnerable, she has this fear in her eyes, as if she's willing to surrender herself in exchange for her safety. But when she's this badass femme fatale, it's domineering, sexy. The duality to the shrew is so captivating that I almost fell for it.

I refuse to be stupid like my brother, though. I want to execute a clean plan. A plan that will eradicate her for good.

So the plan as follows is: meet the elusive siren at her choice meeting place.

Get there before she does.

Build comradery with the bartender before she arrives.

Pay him to slip a mickey into her drink.

Once she arrives begins the plan. It should be smooth sailing from there.

Bring her unconscious body to Kinsley's apartment—but not before we strip her of her phone and weapons.

Happy birthday to the darling Willow Harding.

In theory, it's an easy plan. With any other woman, it'd be an easy plan. It takes one slip-up for this particular woman to catch on, however. And I can't allow that to happen.

It's now 3:00pm, and I get a text message from an unknown number.

Meet me at Manila 203 at 8.

I've never heard of it. And I've yet to hear from Kinsley about the plan. A few more hours pass, and I've still yet to receive anything from Kinsley. My patience is wearing thin.

Fuck it. I decide to head to the gym on the first floor to get pumped up for tonight. I throw on some gym clothes and I'm on my way. As I lock my door, I notice a woman leaving her apartment a few doors down. She doesn't look like the type of girl Marissa would be friends with—much less old friends—and I start to get suspicious. She looks like a loner—large black-rimmed bifocals, thick sweater, and jeans. Her blond hair is up in a messy bun, and she looks skittish when she sees me gazing at her.

"Hey," I bark. She looks at me, her cheeks turning a tomato shade of red. "Ah—"

"Rebecca," she croaks but looks as if she instantly regrets saying it the moment it leaves her mouth.

"Right, Rebecca. Are you friends with a brunette named Marissa?"

The crazed look she gives me tells me everything I need to know; she has no idea who the hell I'm talking about.

"I…don't know a Marissa. What makes you ask?"

I stare at her for a few seconds, making her more nervous. Maybe Marissa was talking about another neighbor a few doors down.

"Nothing. Thanks." I keep it short, put in my wireless earphones, and make the trek down the hallway to the first floor.

Something feels completely off for some reason. I think back to the muffled screaming I heard earlier, and I can't remember if it sounded like two old friends celebrating reconnecting again. Especially after the moody persona Marissa had when she left, I don't imagine her being in high spirits enough to be excited to see an old friend. But in reality…I genuinely don't know. I don't know what I heard. This goddamn bitch has me in my head.

I'm not even on the treadmill yet when Kinsley finally gives me a call. I answer quickly.

"It took you long enough," I greet him.

"Sorry for not wanting to interrupt your sexy time with one of our freelancers," he deadpans.

"She left a while ago, bro. That's not even the point, though. Why'd it take you so long to send over an outline? Are you fucking someone, too?"

"Shut up. I was watching tapes to prepare for the game tomorrow. But I think I have everything set."

He gives me a plan that's similar to mine about tonight. Though, instead of drugging her, he thinks we should just stick with the plan of apologizing for harassing her and surrendering. I'll even admit that I'll turn myself in to the police and admit to the murders of Veronica, Callie, and Vinny. Hopefully, this will ease her mind and lower her guard. When she leaves is when the plan will be executed. As she reaches her car, I'll knock her unconscious and then take her to Kinsley's apartment. Everything should be all said and done in time for his game in the early afternoon. No more Willow Harding, no more Siren Assassin to worry about.

"Sounds solid, Kin," I approve.

"Great. What time are you meeting her?"

"She wants to meet at 8 p.m."

"Perfect. Get ready to go by 7 p.m."

I can't help but roll my eyes. He's always telling me what to do.

"Yeah, yeah, whatever. I'm just gonna get this workout in and then I'll be ready to go by then. Don't worry your little head."

"See you later, then, brother." He quickly ends the call, allowing my music to continue playing.

I have a some time before I make this plan come to life. It's nerve-wracking. If I were her, I'd be brimming with a taste for vengeance after someone close to me was killed. I don't know how this is going to go. This is risky. I could be signing a death wish right now and not even know it. But I can't reconcile that I'm essentially blind in one eye. So I'll take the chance and do it.

The afternoon flew by, and I'm sitting in my car, parked across from the dive bar I've never been to. The lights inside look like some sort of rave, as purple and red illuminate the club chock full of dancing bodies. It doesn't look like a dive bar. In fact, it resembles just that: a rave.

I have no idea how she found this place. It looks very close to the vibe of the college bar back in San Jose.

Kinsley calls me, and I quickly pick up.

"Are you there yet?"

"Yeah, I'm here. But it doesn't look like the type of dive bar we're used to."

"What does that mean?"

"It kind of…looks like the bar back home. In San Jose."

He's silent for a few moments, and I begin to think he hung up by mistake.

"What's it called?"

"Manila 203."

I hear typing on his end, signaling that he's probably researching the place. When he chuckles, that's when I know something's wrong.

"Ah, she's playing chess…while we're playing checkers."

"What?"

"It's a nightclub. But there's also a basement that moonlights as a sex party and fantasy room."

"Shit," I curse.

"Don't worry, brother. You guys aren't going to the basement, anyway. So don't freak out. She's trying to send a message, though."

I gulp nervously, wishing I hadn't gotten myself into this.

"And what's that?"

He doesn't say anything for a few seconds. "Just follow through with the plan and everything should be fine. Don't let it bother you."

"Kinsley—"

"I have to go. A teammate wants to catch up tonight before I see you later. Just keep me posted."

He ends the call with a swiftness that drives me nuts. I don't understand how my own brother can't tell that I'm scared out of my mind right now. He put me in this situation, and now he's leaving me to basically fend for myself. Circumstances of this plan have clearly changed, but he won't acknowledge that honestly.

I can't give up now, though. We've come this far to try to attempt to take her down, so I'm not letting this opportunity go to waste. I'm so close. So close to reclaiming myself. I'm not this evil person that my brother has turned me into. I know I need to take accountability for who I am now, but I would've been fine just wallowing in the shadows of the charming Kinsley Focker. My older half-brother I always looked up to…until recently. He wasn't wrong; I wanted what he had. Has. But everything that he's involved me in is not out of love. It's out of malice. I don't know who this guy is anymore. He's not my brother, and he's already shown he doesn't care if anything happens to me. So now I just have to fly on my own.

I hop out of my car and begrudgingly walk in the direction of the bustling bar. I don't know what the hell to expect. In an odd way, this changes the plan. I was expecting the old run-of-the-mill dive bar. But this is the perfect mind game the elusive Willow Harding is setting forth. I can't back down now, though.

I let out a shaky breath as the electronic music blasts the room. I search for Willow, but I don't see a familiar silhouette. She doesn't seem to be here yet. Looking down at my watch, I clock that it's fifty minutes before eight.

I find a free seat at the bar after jostling through the sweaty bodies and order a scotch on the rocks. One of the first steps of the plan is talk up the bartender, so I have some time to spare. I wave him over, and he gives me a friendly nod, signaling that he'll be over in a second.

Minutes later, I'm drinking an Old Fashioned and updating Kinsley on what's happening...even though he's not responding.

"Hello, handsome," a sultry voice says beside me.

I turn to find a platinum blond, bodacious woman with smoky eyes giving me the sexiest grin I've ever seen, and it nearly stops me in my tracks.

"Hey," I say, clearing my throat. Her grin grows slightly wider as I take a moment to admire her get-up. She's wearing a white bustier that pushes her tits up. The white garter belt that's holding up her denim leg warmers looks marvelous against her tan skin. She looks like every walking fantasy I've ever had.

"I don't think I've ever seen you here before. You come here often?"

"This is my first time. What about you?"

A baby dimple pops out as she smiles bigger, catching my attention.

"I'm the resident dancer here at Manila. So I come more often that I'd probably like," she jokes.

"Ah, I see. So this is a strip club." I look around the club for poles, and I don't see any.

"Something like that," she says mischievously, leaving me puzzled. "We sometimes have Gentlemen's Night in our basement. I call it the dungeon," she whispers.

I swallow past the lump that loves to form in my throat. "The dungeon, eh?"

"It's just kind of hidden. No one really knows about it other than the fact that there's a bar down there." She then looks around to seemingly make sure no one's listening before turning back to me. "But there's also a secret steam room and arena down there," she whispers.

"Ah, so there *is* a sex room down there," I say without thinking.

And she notices. It doesn't say it on their website. Kinsley most likely accessed my database to find whatever he could in the dark web and saw evidence that there's a secret room.

"Only if you keep it between us," she makes me promise.

"What are you talking about?"

She grins at me, and her friendly demeanor turns more friendly.

"Exactly. So…you don't seem like the type of guy to come to a scandalous club like this. What gives?"

Oh, nothing. I'm just here to execute the kidnapping of my brother's psycho ex-girlfriend. No biggie.

"Just wanted to check it out. I have a friend I'm supposed to be meeting tonight that frequents here a lot. Seems pretty chill."

"Oh, it's more than chill, my friend. It's paradise. You're waiting on a friend?"

I find myself looking at the clock again, but then something else hits me hard. I steady myself, confused about what the hell that was.

"Yeah," I confirm, clearing my throat. "Sh-she was supposed to be here at eight."

Her eyebrows shoot up in surprise. "Oh, a girlfriend. I didn't know that—"

"It's okay. She's not someone I'm dating. It's just a friend. She'll be here around 8 p.m., so there's no rush."

The once beautiful girl in front of me now has three heads, and the room starts to spin a bit. I'm able to keep myself upright, but my equilibrium seems very off. The three-headed beauty in front of me looks concerned for me.

"Are you all right?" she asks in an echo.

I don't know anymore. I can't find the words to speak, and my fingers feel tingly. My arms begin to lose their feeling. I open my mouth to speak, but nothing can come out. I don't understand what's happening to me right now. I reach for the girl's hand, and she takes it, cradling it in hers. She says one last thing to me, but I can't make it out. Her likeness becomes less and less apparent as I slowly feel myself slip to unconsciousness.

Sweat beads on my forehead, and I feel it tickling my temples as well. Hell would feel a lot sweeter than whatever heat is emanating from the room I'm in. Slowly waking up, I look around and flinch at the purple-red-magenta lighting. In fact, it's the only thing I can make out because steam clouds my vision. I try to stand up, but I'm restrained to the pole behind the bench I'm sitting on. What the fuck is going on?

"Ah, lovely. You're awake," the platinum blonde's voice echoes through the steam room.

I look around to see where she might be, but there's no one around in sight.

"Where are you?!"

Before I know it, she stalks out of the steam as if she's taking human form, and her demeanor is nothing like it was at the bar. This new girl is something of a menacing temptress. She stalks towards me like a predator and squats down in front of me.

"You look hot with sweat dripping down your face and your hair slick," she says in a throaty voice.

"Why the hell am I tied up?"

"The firecracker siren sent me your way."

"What? What the fuck are you talking about?"

But she doesn't respond. She winks at me, places a kiss on my lips, and struts away from me, leaving to watch me admire her plump ass disappear into the steam yet again. I struggle to detach myself, but whoever tied me up got me good. Fucking hell, what did I get myself into? What is this? If fucking Willow has something to do with this…shit.

The firecracker siren is indeed playing chess.

Suddenly, the main lights turn off, but the side lights built into the walls stay on. The steam intensifies, making my vision more impaired and it hard to breathe. I repeatedly yank on the rope tied around my wrists, but to no luck. I try a few more times and launch myself forward with force, falling with a jolting impact to the slippery floor. I look at the pool and the rope—which appears to have been cut—slumping on the bench. Someone cut the rope and dashed away into the steam.

It's only slightly lit around the walls, so I can only see silhouettes in the colored steam. But there's no one around. I quickly search for my pocketknife, disappointed to find that it's been confiscated. And it takes me a second to register as much while, at the same time, music begins playing on a loud stereo.

"Willow," I sing-song. "Come out and play."

No response…as expected. The bitch is a master player. I'll admit, she had me for a little bit. But I won't let my guard down and show she's gotten to me. She has the experience and intellect to pick up on fear. She can detect cracks in your armor. It's rather impressive.

"You called?" a voice—that no doubt belongs to her—echoes. I turn in the direction of where it came from, but a gunshot fires from the steam, and I dodge it pretty quickly. Goddamn. I look around the room for an exit, but I can't quite see one in the cloudy room. Shit. I dart around, trying my hardest not to cough or pass out. The steam intensifies as each second passes, and it's starting to become suffocating. How the hell did I let this happen?

I don't have enough time to think about it. Pulling out my phone, I notice that I only have one bar of service. I try to text Kinsley, but I get a *Message Not Delivered* notification. Calling then becomes my last resort, but it doesn't go through. Fuck.

A piercing whip strike jolts me, and I jump back in surprise. What the fuck?

I look down at my arm, feeling a sharp twinge of pain, and find blood slowly pouring from a slash mark. I look around to find the source, but no one's around. I need to get the hell out of here. I run in one direction, feeling some sort of relief when I find a door with an EXIT sign above it. But the feeling soon goes away when it registers that it's locked. I scope out the room for another door, but it's way too hard to see in this condition.

"Leaving so soon?" Willow's voice echoes through the steamy room, and this time marks the first time I've ever been terrified of the bitch.

Following it is another whip slashing my skin, but I can finally see that it's not a whip. It looks as if she's armed herself with a knife of sorts. The cut pierces my skin so deep that tears begin to sting my eyes from the pain.

"You're fucking crazy!"

I run in another direction to find an unlocked door. When I pull on the closest door, I find that it's also locked.

"Don't leave. We're just getting started," she mocks in a deep, sultry voice.

And before I know it, the siren herself nearly glides out of the steam, her hair this time platinum blond and inches longer. It's slick as the strands stick together, and her eyes rival a raccoon's, with what I assume to be black mascara dripping down. She's wearing a white bra and panties combo with white heels and is armed with a long pickaxe. I've never seen her in this image, and it frightens the fuck out of me. It's something out of a horror movie. She slowly struts up to me, but I back away.

"You look fucking insane," I say in an accidentally shaky voice. I can't let her know that she's affecting me. This new woman is not like the Willow that I've seen in the last decade.

Her stone face slowly transforms into a grim smile. The scene is disturbing yet enchanting. What a hellish paradox.

She forcefully pushes me to the ground, causing me to yelp in horror. I fight to stand back up, but the ground is too slippery to properly find my footing. I'm fucked. It's the last few moments of my life, but at least I can go out with the legacy that I fought to survive. Clearly not hard enough, as evidenced by me getting into this situation in the first place. But I won't die in vain. I won't. I did this for my brother and for reconciliation with being left partially blind.

I don't cry. I've not been a crier since I was in middle school. And yet I find myself crying more often as of late than I'd like to acknowledge.

"You're a force to be reckoned with, Willow Harding." I choke up, fully acknowledging this is it for me.

With the satisfaction of a robber breaking into an expensive jewelry store, she sports the most cunning smile that rivals Kinsley's mischievous one and leans toward me, steam enclosing around her face, the stench of tequila on her breath.

She lifts her pickaxe in cinematic fashion and declares, "Willow Harding is not here."

TWENTY

WILLOW

I kill with a vengeance I can't describe. As I've noted before, I kill with my bare hands. Usually murder by asphyxiation or gunfire. There's something freeing about piercing Leif's skin. Liberating, essentially. And while I had a moment of regret, witnessing tears building in his eyes, I reclaimed who Willow Harding was in that moment, slashing that pickaxe through his flesh: a cold blood killer.

Maybe something is wrong with me. I could indeed be crazy. Perhaps I'm going mad. I'm fully aware that I'm not well. But just as he and Kinsley didn't feel any regret for their attacks on me and other women, I don't feel any either.

I stand over Leif's lifeless body as steam continues to cloud around me. I run a hand through my slick blond extensions and straighten my shoulders. Violet is currently my getaway girl, as she's waiting for me on a hidden side street adjacent to the club. It won't take much to drag him out. The club is inundated with pheromone-infested bodies, and they won't notice anything that happens around them. They didn't even notice my mission accomplice, Ingrid, walking a lifeless body out of the club and down into the club's basement.

As always, there's a risk with carrying out kills in a public setting. An audience is not ideal, but I don't completely rule it out. Desperate times call for desperate measures. But then it occurs to me that maybe it's not worth it to risk it right now. I'm numb. But I still have my wits about me.

I make the trek back upstairs and make a quick call to Ingrid to dispose of his body. She shows up in seconds and drags him out of the room as I turn off the steam.

It was a tribute to their depraved sex room they tortured Callie in, and that's what made this kill more fulfilling. These boys can't take what they dish out. And that's okay. I'm more than happy to make them comfortable getting used to me not going anywhere.

Besides, it's almost my birthday. I'm the birthday girl. And the ultimate birthday present is just on the tips of my fingers. I have twenty-four hours to get rid of Kinsley Focker. The man, the myth, the legend. The man who stole my youth away from me and bullied me into no longer being the innocent, impressionable girl I once was. Judgment day is almost here, and he's the last one to kill on my to-do list.

"How are you feeling?" Violet asks as I slip into the passenger seat, fresh from paying Ingrid her stipend for the night and now changed into my normal ensemble of black turtleneck, black jeans, and black combat boots. I still sport the blond extensions, slicked back and away from my face.

"Rejuvenated" is all I say, earning a pleased grin from her.

I sit back into my seat as we pull out of the adjacent parking lot to the club.

Violet pulls up in front of the bar, and I jump out. While I'm still basking in taking down one half of the disturbed duo, there's one extraneous piece that I didn't want to be included.

Marissa Moore. Violet kidnapped her from Leif's apartment complex after tracking his phone. She was a fighter. And I didn't mean to kill her. All we wanted to do was ask her questions about her involvement with Leif and Kinsley. She tried to trick us into letting her go, and when we didn't, she attacked Violet. That was when I had to incapacitate her. She was as noncompliant as Veronica, if not more.

I stalk toward the river behind Vinny's bar and look out onto it. Her body's no longer floating on the surface, as it was earlier before killing Leif. It's the one kill I wish I didn't need to commit and will loom over me until the end of my days.

"Willow." Violet appears behind me. "Come on, we need to go. We need to get you back home before Kinsley sees you."

I get back to my apartment in record time, double-locking the door after Violet leaves. I don't foresee Kinsley coming here in the middle of the night. Not if he knows what's good for him. Once he finds out that his precious little brother is dead, I'd like to speculate that he wouldn't step foot near my place.

First thing in the morning, I'm having an alarm system installed. Safety is my first priority on my birthday tomorrow.

Hours pass by, and I'm staying secluded in my apartment the entire day. As I draft up a plan for tomorrow's killing, Meredith immediately comes to mind.

She wanted to dropped off at her Mom's home because she didn't want to interrupt my space. I tried to explain to her that she wasn't intruding, but she's an independent soul. It's hard to convince.

I'm about to check in on her via text when an email comes through. From Kill Elite. The company I no longer work for, after they fucked me over on one of my last kills with them. With the email being in Russian, I translate it to English. And the kind of email that can change your life forever.

It's my birthday morning, and I wake up to a security installation specialist knocking on my door. It's a lovely birthday present As he finishes installing it, I notice happy birthday texts from my therapist, Meredith, Violet, and Caroline.

"All you have to do is put in the code," the worker points out to me, "and it'll arm the apartment. Press this button to disarm when you get back inside. If you need to make emergency calls, this button will ping the local police station."

It's not smart to arm my apartment when I'm considered a danger to society and I'm wanted across the entire state of Massachusetts. But I'm banking on Kinsley not risking coming here and knowing what's good for him.

I thank him for installing it and send him on his way. I'm making breakfast when Violet calls me.

"Good morning, birthday girl. How are you feeling now that it's the big day?"

It's a loaded question. I'm feeling excited, but there's also a degree of anxious energy. Ironically, they go hand in hand.

"I'm not sure yet. I still have so much to do before tonight."

If there's anything I've learned about the diabolical Kinsley Focker, it's that he's a plotter. It's been hours, and I'm sure he'll catch on to the fact that his brother is dead. Neither one of us has any idea where we're meeting each other. It's up in the air. But we both know we're meeting on the basis that one of us is bound to die tonight. And that's something I've never had to worry about before. Until now.

"Don't waste your birthday. You know what you need to do tonight. If you fixate on the plan too much, you'll psyche yourself out."

I know in my head that she's right. That I could recycle an original plan from a past kill to get rid of him once and for all. But it's not ideal. Something tells me he knows exactly what my past kills entailed, and I can't risk the kill being compromised. If he were an idiot, this would be much easier.

I can't think about it anymore, though, because the TV grabs my attention.

It's the national news.

A picture of Callie is plastered on the screen, with a headline saying MISSING SAN JOSE WOMAN FOUND DEAD IN HER APARTMENT. The clock is ticking.

"Shit. They found Callie," I blurt out.

"What? How do you know that?"

"The news story is on my fucking TV. I'm losing time. Soon everything will lead back to Leif back to Kinsley back to me. I'll talk to you later, okay?"

I quit the call before she can answer and turn off the TV. That lit a fire under my ass like I don't know what. Veronica's 'death' was labeled as foul play. Callie's on the other side of the country, so not much can make them lead it back to me. But I can't risk it.

I quickly get dressed to go see Meredith and update her on everything as it happens. As I'm running a comb through my hair, my phone pings with the text. Assuming that it's Violet texting me, I prepare myself to reassure her that I won't fixate on the plan for tonight.

But I'm surprised when I see it's from my therapist, Ms. Marshall.

> *CONNIE: Good morning, Willow. Happy birthday again! I just wanted to remind you that we have a 1:30pm appointment today. See you soon!*

Shit. I really need to start putting these meetings in my calendar. I've been losing track of the times I'm supposed to see her. The thing is, I really don't have time to. But if I cancel within twenty-four hours, then she's going to charge me for the price of the entire appointment, out of pocket.

I'm between a rock and a hard place. I sift through my brain, trying to figure out why she didn't send me a reminder yesterday or, hell, even a few days ago. I would've been able to account for the time it would take up. Now I have to plan my day around this fucking appointment. Damn.

"It's good to see you, Willow. I was starting to think you died," she says, chuckling.

If it weren't for the irony within that statement, I would laugh along with her. But it hits too close to home.

"Yeah, I've…just been busy. It's been a busy month for me," I say truthfully.

"I can only imagine. How are you holding up? How's your, uh, contractual work going?"

The way she asks raises a red flag for me because it's telling. Almost as if she knows something. It makes my skin crawl again, and I don't like the feeling.

"It's going fine, Connie. Not much else to say."

Her demeanor turns into something I've never seen before. She doesn't look as happy to see me and appears as if she's hiding something. I suddenly feel out of my element, quickly planning my escape.

"I'm glad to hear that it went well. I hope that everything's been going well for you."

"It has," I say, nearly cutting her off. "No complaints, Connie."

She only stares at me with a concerned grin, and I begin to suspect that she has a hidden camera in here somewhere, waiting for a confession.

"Good."

Something's weird. Either this life is making me more paranoid than I already am, or she knows something. I grab my purse and get ready to leave.

"Actually, Connie, I think I have a dentist appointment in a little bit. So can we reschedule this appointment when my schedule opens up again?"

"So soon? We were just getting started."

"Yeah, I, uh, got a reminder text on the way here that I have a cleaning."

"Surely you can reschedule that appointment—"

"I'm six months overdue." Why is she arguing this?

"And I think it can wait, Low," a voice says that I've avoided for years.

I close my eyes in defeat and realize what the hell is going on. This was a set-up. There was no appointment with Connie. I turn to find the judgmental woman glaring at me with daggers, and I start to think that this intervention has nothing to do with going without contact for the last ten years.

"Hello, Mother."

She gives me her signature tight-lipped smile before sitting down, crossing her legs, and patting the spot next to her. The damn bitch wants me to sit next to her after not seeing her for years. The last time I spoke to her, she tried to get me to move in with her so she didn't have to live with the fact that her daughter was an Internet whore who flashed her tits, ass, and vagina to the lowest bidder. Her words exactly.

"Connie, why the hell did you set this up?"

"Because I haven't been able to get through to you. And I'm concerned about you walking the streets, if I'm being frank," she says in her stern, authoritative voice.

I gulp, feeling my stomach bubble with a nervousness that I've never felt before. Kills make me nervous. Kinsley Focker makes me nervous. But the prospect of getting caught and reported to the police before I've even taken him down makes me a bit hysterical.

"There's nothing to talk about. I've already told you this."

"You're right." She switches gears. "Maybe there is nothing to talk about. But if what I heard from your mother is true, then I have no choice but to report you to the police."

There it is. I've officially reached the end of my days. It came a lot sooner than I thought it would, considering I was banking on Kinsley being the one to die tonight. While I'm not dying anytime soon, spending the rest of my days being holed up in a jail cell is the end as I know it.

I turn to the lady that's supposed to be my mother and am instantly repulsed by her satisfied smirk.

"You really are the devil."

"No, darling Willow, I'm just your mother. I did what I had to do to get your attention. You didn't take my opportunity to be sheltered and get back on your feet. You instead find solace in killing men for money."

I cover my face in horror, my brain suddenly not able to stop my hands from shaking.

"How the hell did you find that out?"

"Caroline is a family friend and is mourning her husband, whose death you caused. His phone was retrieved and so were messages between you and him, asking him to keep your second identity a secret. Siren Assassin?"

This is a nightmare of the torture variety. I'm paralyzed, and my limbs start tingling. I don't know where I am anymore. I open my mouth to speak, but it doesn't even sound like my voice anymore.

"I don't know what to say," I croak.

"How about you'll comply with whatever we say and we don't report you for the heinous crimes you've committed," Marlena offers.

Blackmail. I never thought I'd be on the receiving end of it. Again. Life truly is a full circle moment.

"I don't need to comply with shit. I didn't do anything that warrants an intervention."

"I'd think murder is something that warrants more than an intervention. Perhaps rehabilitation?"

This entire scene is fucked up. Connie is looking at me like I'm deranged, and Marlena is looking at me like she's disappointed in me.

"I don't need rehabilitation, Marlena."

"You need to stop," she whispers. "It's tearing you apart. Look at you, you can barely look at me without crippling anxiety. You have to let this go, Willow. And continue therapy with Connie."

"Maybe killing is my therapy, Marlena."

She flinches, looking at me as if she doesn't recognize who I am. And maybe she doesn't. *I* barely recognize who I am.

"Let me be the voice of reason," Connie intervenes. "There are ways we can help you. I can't promise that I won't get the authorities involved, but—"

"Then I can't promise that I'll comply with anything you say. Look, this is bigger than the both of you. I'm standing up for women that are victims."

"By killing their abusers?"

"Someone has to!"

"Okay, Willow—"

Pulling out my pocketknife stops them in their tracks. It's stupid of me to do it, but I have no other choice. I can't stop now. Not when I'm so close.

"Willow," Connie says slowly to calm me down, "put the weapon down."

"I won't let you stop me. Either one of you. This is who I am. Accept it or fuck off."

I grab my purse as both my mother and Connie hold up their hands in surrender. Tears build in my mother's eyes, while Connie looks horrified.

"We can get you help," Connie whispers.

But I inch out of the room, closing the door behind me. Once I feel comfortable, I dart out of the office and head to my car. The clock is ticking faster. I need to figure something out. I wasn't expecting this to happen today. It's all too soon, and it puts a damper on the plan for the day.

I drive in the direction of Meredith and her mom's house and let her know what the hell is going on. I call her first, and she picks up quickly.

"Low, are you okay?"

"Is your mom home?"

"No, she works the morning shift at the hospital. Have you seen the news?"

"Yes, I've seen it, Mer. But there's more."

"What?"

"I've been compromised."

She gasps. "What? How?!"

"Caroline found text messages between me and Vinny about the Siren Assassin alias, and she told my mom about it. It's a long story. But things are about to change."

"Like what? I don't understand what the hell is going on."

My attention is temporarily taken away from the issue at hand and focuses in on the horror in front of me. My stomach drops at the sight of my apartment complex.

The building is up in smoke as fire emanates from it. All of my neighbors are out in the parking lot and across the street, watching the mass casualty ensue.

"Willow? Hello??"

"Mer...I'm gonna need to call you back."

I cut the line as she tries to argue and draw my attention back to the fire. I park my car across the street and get out, watching the building collapse along with everyone else.

The fucking bastard. He has to be responsible for this. Maybe I'm being paranoid, but this happening is rather convenient on my birthday and the night after I killed Leif.

"I know," a neighbor says, walking up beside me. "It's a mess. How could this have happened?"

I turn to look at the person in question, and they wipe their face of tears. This is starting to become a pattern. And it'll be never-ending. Here I thought I was the master player at mind games. Kinsley Focker is in his own league.

Right as I walk closer to the apartment complex, a firefighter jumping out of the red van spots me, squinting his eyes as if he knows me. Fuck.

"Ma'am?"

I shake my head. No. No, this can't be happening. How the hell did this day turn into this? The firefighter grabs the attention of a detective walking by and points in my direction. The man with salt and pepper hair looks confused before his gaze lands on me. Then it's as if something clicks in his head. His eyes widen in horror, and he starts to walk toward me.

"Can we speak with you, ma'am?"

But I don't stay around long enough for a conversation. I dart back to my car, feeling the detective hot on my heels.

"Hey! Stop!"

I start the engine of my car and quickly back out of the lot, dashing into the street haphazardly.

I need to find a safe haven. A few seconds later, two police cars chase after me with sirens blaring. Fucking hell, this is not how this was supposed to go. My assassin instincts aren't kicking in like they should be as I try to figure out what the fuck to do. I can't go to Meredith. I can't go to Violet's place because they're following me. I need a plan B.

A few turns and rough U-turns later, I decide that this must be my fate. I knew last night felt too good to be true. Kinsley is too cunning. He figured out a way to ruin my life while also exposing who the hell I am. His level of expertise is not something I was prepared for. I'm in a fucking high-speed chase with cops on my tail, and Kinsley gets to stay still alive and healthy. This is the end of the road for me.

Tears assault my eyes, my throat becoming too heavy to bear. I hate this. As I approach downtown, I come across the bridge where I dropped Benji Lockson's body. The police are still gunning for me to stop. But I don't. Instead, I step on the gas and drive into the river. If this is how it ends, I'll go out with a fucking bang.

TWENTY-ONE

KINSLEY

"*The Siren Assassin, a long-time menace to the Port Rockwell community of Boston, has died after she drove her car into Majestic River.*"

I mute the news story, fully captivated by the beautiful image of the hitwoman on the screen. Darling Willow. She reached her demise. I wasn't planning on it to happen so soon. But I let my emotions get the best of me.

Leif stopped texting me. The last text I got from him was that he was waiting at the bar for Willow to show up. It soon turned into radio silence. I was never an anxious person. That's not me. But if the bitch killed my brother, then I made a pledge that all bets were off and it would be time to kill her with no remorse.

It wasn't until this morning when I called him for nearly the fifteenth time and a raspy feminine voice picked up. My heart stopped because it wasn't Marissa's voice. I know my brother has become something of a smooth operator, but this woman had the aura that she was hiding something. Something conniving was brewing in her voice, and it didn't take me long to figure it out: my brother is dead.

I failed him. I didn't protect him like I promised him I would. I never thought it would come to this. I would've rather sacrificed myself and not my little brother. I fucked up.

Getting ahold of Marissa proved to be hard, too. So not only did she get rid of my brother, but she killed one of our call girls. I didn't want to believe that she did. I assumed that the Siren Assassin's heart belongs to women. Until I see Marissa alive, I'll live with the narrative that she's dead.

There's one other problem; I'm no hacker. I know the basics to search the dark web and uncover information that Leif previously has. But I don't have the skillset to hack into the databases he had the ability to. Not only am I without my brother and confidant, but I'm also without my teammate. Though, with Willow gone, there's no need for a hacker anymore. I should feel relief. Calm. But I don't. I feel unfulfilled. Like something's missing.

Fuck, it was definitely a bad idea to make a rash decision, setting her apartment on fire. I didn't think she'd escape the police. After concluding that my brother was dead, I did the impulsive thing and reported it to the cops. I even told them I might know who the Siren Assassin is. The city of Port Rockwell now has a new sketch of Siren Assassin, and it is the darling Willow.

Though she partakes in illegality, I thought she would at least be compliant with an arrest. Boy, was I wrong. And here we are.

I have a game in about thirty minutes. I'm sitting in the locker room watching the news story go viral on social media, while my teammates are pumping themselves up.

"Mattson! You good?" My co-captain, Dillon, gets my attention.

I chuck my phone in my gym bag and jump up from the bench to focus on the game at hand. We're three games away from the MLR Championship game, and we've been moving up the bracket with ease. We can't break that streak because I'm fixating on a dead woman. Now that she's out of my life, I should be focused on living my life. She can't try to ruin my life anymore, and I don't have to come up with some abstract plan to kill her.

The coach pulls us in for a huddle and further encourages us to play the game of our lives. When we break from the huddle and my teammates run out to do the arena introductions, Coach pulls me aside.

"Your girl doing better?"

It feels as if something squeezes my lungs at the mention of her.

I clear my throat and affirm, "Yeah, she's doing all right."

"Good. It's been a while since we've spoken about her—"

"And she's good, Coach. Can we get to the game now?"

My sudden change of topic seems to raise flags as his gaze grows suspicious.

"Okay, Captain." He shakes it off. "Let's get to playing."

I nod and jog out of the room onto the cheering arena. I can live life as I wanted to. As long as she is no more, then I can breathe again.

Once again, we're victorious. We've advanced on the bracket, and now we're well on our way on the road to the championships.

The team decides to go and celebrate at a bar downtown. It's a good way to clear my head and truly celebrate with my teammates. I haven't had the privilege to do so with everything going on. I should be mourning my brother and the darling Willow. But I just can't bring myself to do it. I'm the final person in this mind game. The mind game that is no more. It doesn't seem real. It feels like I'm missing something. It's an incessant feeling that's been on my mind even during the game.

"You've been so quiet, man. What's on your mind?"

Dillon seems concerned about my silence today, and I'm starting to become paranoid that he knows something. Survivor's guilt is a fairly recent thing for me, so I don't know how to navigate living in the after.

"Nothing. Nothing at all. Great game today, guys," I say, patting him on the back.

He accepts willingly and goes back to chatting with the rest of the teammates. And I go back to my quiet corner, nursing a lager. As the night goes on, Coach does a toast to celebrate our prospect of making it to the championship, and we trickle out of the bar hours later. Dillon and a forward, Patrick, are belligerently drunk. I call them both a rideshare before I go on my way back home.

Then I get a wacky idea. On the way home, I pass the club where Leif was supposed to meet Willow last night. On a whim, I park across the street and watch as people trickle in and out. It looks like your everyday, run-of-the-mill club.

But it's not just another nightclub to me. It'll forever be the place where my brother met his demise. I let him loose into the wild and abandoned him with no regard for what might happen to him. I got spoiled. He'd overpowered her in numerous run-ins, so I thought nothing of it. I knew she'd be out for blood. I just didn't think it'd be so sudden.

I have half a mind to go inside and scope it out. See what this place has to offer. But it's probably best if I head back home and lounge for the rest of the day. I have to come to terms with it, some way, somehow. Taking a deep breath, I hop out of the car and make my way inside.

It's a slow afternoon as far as business goes, as bargoers are spaced out around the quiet club. It doesn't look or sound anything like Leif described it. I walk up to the bar and flag down the bartender.

He meets me at the bar, throwing a towel on the bar top.

"What can I get started for ya?"

"What are your scotch options?"

He lists off what's on the shelves, and I decide to settle on a top shelf brand. I look around as he pours it on the rocks and puts it in front of me.

"Great game today, man."

"Thanks. You happen to serve a guy with a prosthetic eye last night?"

Something dubious flashes in the previously relaxed man's eyes, as if he wasn't expecting me to ask.

"Who's asking?"

I only stare at him because he seems as if he's hiding something. What could he be hiding?

"I am. Did you serve him last night?"

He gulps and runs a veiny hand through his hair.

"I mean, yeah…but the blond girl told me to. She said some smoking hot brunette told her to."

"Blond? What blond girl?"

He looks around, seemingly to make sure that no one can hear our conversation.

"I'm not really sure if I can talk about this, dude."

"Look, that guy was my brother. And I have reason to think he was killed last night."

He cocks an eyebrow. "Shit, man. I—I had no idea."

"So I think I deserve an explanation of what the hell happened."

He sighs and looks around again.

"The blond girl said she was a hitwoman with some European organization and works regularly with the girl. I told her that I don't engage in illegal shit, but she promised to pay me $50,000—"

"So you took her money and unwittingly became a fucking chess piece in their sick game."

Willow, Willow, Willow. Taking a page from my handbook and hiring accomplices to her crimes.

He nods, ashamed. "So I slipped some shit into his drink, and they paid me after everything was all said and done. Listen, I'm sorry, man. I didn't know they were gonna kill him. I just thought they were gonna rough him up a bit."

But I'm already tuning him out. His mouth is moving, but words are registering for me. The blond woman.

"What did she sound like? This blond woman?"

He shrugs. "Bombshell. Big tits, smoky eyes, legs for days. Smoker's voice in the sense that it was raspy. We get hot girls in here all the time, but she looked like she stepped out of the Playboy mansion."

How he describes her voice is what stands out to me the most. That sounds like the woman I spoke on the phone with last night. But something tells me that she's already on her way back to Europe, if she's not already there. I don't have Leif's expertise to track her location, and I don't think this fuckrag has her information.

"You wouldn't happen to have this woman's phone number or anything?"

He shakes his head. "She only gave me a check, written from Kill Elite Inc. That's it."

I frown at the name. What the fucking hell is Kill Elite?

"That's the organization she works for?"

"Supposedly. We didn't really get into specifics. She came in early yesterday and propositioned me because she was hired by someone else."

"Did you see this other brunette?" I already know that he's most likely talking about Willow. I'd like to make sure I'm not mistaking anything.

"No. She never showed her face. She just said she was smoking hot and used to be a master assassin with the same organization."

Indeed, he is talking about Willow. This is the first time I'm hearing of an underground criminal organization, however. If this woman that kidnapped my brother works with them, how did Willow find out about them and get in contact with her?

"Thank you, uh—"

"Just call me Marty."

Pseudonym. I can spot it anywhere. And with the intel he just told me, I understand why he's using it. I finish up what's left of my drink, throw a $100 bill on the bar, watching as his eyes go wide.

"Marty. You've been a lot of help."

He gives me a nervous nod as his cheeks turn a dramatic shade of tomato.

Walking out of the club, I pull out my phone and hit STOP RECORDING. I never thought it would be so easy to help an accomplice incriminate themselves so quickly.

This should be enough to give to the police. This will not only incriminate him, but it could help in tracking this blond woman down.

I'm at the police station in minutes and quickly assume the role of distressed older brother. I hop out of the car, my heart thumping growing exponentially louder in my ears as I take each step.

I walk into the bustling station, looking around as if I'm stuck and not sure what to do—which is partially true, especially since I have no idea where my brother's body is. A male detective holding a folder notices my anguish and rushes over to me.

"Hi. How can we help you?"

I look around as all the other detectives are gazing at me curiously.

"My brother's been missing since last night. And I think I have proof that the Siren Assassin is involved."

The man's eyebrows shoot to the roof in surprise as he pulls me aside to an interrogation room.

The moment we sit down in the room, he offers me a cup of coffee, and I invent. Everything false, everything true, and everything in between. Willow may be dead, but the other temptress is still alive and on the streets. Until I'm confident she's detained, I'm not letting this go.

When everything's all said and done, he stands up and walks me out the room. He lets me know that they have to do more investigating before they can make an arrest on Marty and the mysterious blond bombshell.

For now, I'm put even more at ease than I was this morning upon learning that Willow's dead. But only time will tell.

EIGHT MONTHS LATER

It's my birthday. Thirty-one has never looked sweeter. We won the championships, I just signed a $20 million dollar extension deal with the Hornets, and even better news…my brother's killers are off the street. Two out of the three.

Marty got arrested a month after I turned him into the police for being an accomplice to murder. The blond girl is still on the loose, unfortunately. Authorities think she fled back to Europe, and I happen to think she did, too. There's technically no way to tie her to the crimes or even get any information on her. According to the police, the database for Kill Elite shows over thirty different blondes, and no one from the organization is willing to speak on the death of my brother.

So there's no way to make an arrest. And since the organization is underground and on foreign soil, they can't make a case. They've even tried to get Russian authorities to dissolve the organization, but Kill Elite masquerades as a ballet academy on the Internet. The only way to access it is through the dark web, and they don't have the desire to put a stop to the organization. All of this tells me one thing: Willow Harding had to have worked for the organization.

It doesn't matter anymore, though. I'm just coming back from spending the day with my team at a driving range for my birthday. With the rugby season being over, I can finally relax. That is, until I drive up on the apartment complex I burnt down months ago. They rebuilt them, and something indescribable stings at my chest. The new complex looks new, almost as if nothing happened to damage the integrity of the architecture. It feels surreal.

It's 7:00 in the evening, and I have no plans for the rest of the day. Something is telling me to take a trek down memory lane, but there's another part of me saying that it's a bad idea. It may not be as much as a bad idea as it just me being weird. There is also the chance that Willow's old apartment looks how it did, minus everything that made it hers.

Fuck it. It won't hurt anyone if I just bask in the memory of her one last time. Even if the memory of her brings back intense emotions that I can't control. I'm entirely too compulsive—and impulsive—for my own good. It's what drives me. No woman's ever driven me to insanity like Willow had. I've always gotten my fix when it came to women. It was easy to get them to listen and obey me. But the elusive Willow Harding wasn't so easy to tame.

I make it to her old floor, and it's an eerie feeling. You can tell that the complex is new, but they manage to keep the exact same construction as the old building. Almost as if my attempt didn't even make a dent in the building's integrity. The symbolism starts to raise some alarm bells in my head.

Coming up on her old apartment, all the emotions hit me at once. Confusion. Excitement. Fear. I have no idea what to expect or even what I think I'll find. I'd just like to remember her one last time. The first thing I notice is…the door is unlocked. I'm initially hesitant to walk in. But there's limited furniture. A couch, chair, knife set, and a mirror. An apartment that looks as if someone's just moved in. But the unlocked door gives me pause. Is this just irresponsibility by the tenant? Or is something else at play here? Something has got to give.

I take a slow step into the apartment, turn on the light in the living area, and notice that the layout is the same. Nothing seems to have changed, as I expected. The island in the kitchen seems as if it never left. The fridge looks like the old fridge that she used to have. Everything brings back old memories. Willow never let me spend time at her apartment back when she knew me as Leif, but I've seen inside this place when I was stalking her behind the scenes. It feels good to be back.

"Hello, Kinsley."

I pause, feeling as if my matrix is glitching. It doesn't make sense. It's only been a second, and I still feel her poisonous voice floating through my veins. I turn around to find her sitting in the folding chair, posing like Sharon Stone. Her black hair is slicked back, and she's sporting her usual black turtleneck, black jeans, and black combat boots. Holy hell, she looks like a fantasy. A fantasy I'd like to live again and again and again.

"I bet you never thought you'd see me again."

Clearing my throat, I say, "Hello, Willow. You're right. I didn't think I'd see you again."

A menacing grin etches her face, and it makes my stomach queasy.

"I could say the same to you."

She doesn't sound or look the same. The old Willow was indeed a seductress. But right now, her smoky eyes match her deep, soothing voice. This feels like a fucking fever dream.

"My darling Willow Harding. You're supposed to be dead."

Her beguiling chuckle enchants me more than it ever has. Fuck, it's demented to partially enjoy being near her again.

"And yet, here I am. What are you doing in my apartment, Kinsley?"

I straighten my shoulders and face her with a bravery I've used to get me through uncomfortable situations.

"Reliving a time when you were more obedient."

"That's never happened. What are you doing in my apartment, Kinsley?"

"I'm sorry, come again?" I tease.

But she's not amused. With an ease of a masterful siren, she leans forward, her silhouette now shaping her body, the shape of her face in the light.

She enunciates, "What are you doing in my apartment?"

It's a great question. One I don't think she's quite ready for me to answer. My gaze goes down her body, taking in how her turtleneck hugs her breasts and jeans showing how shapely she is. Just like that, the original plan from eight months ago seems to come back to me.

"I wanted to relive a fantasy that you took away from me. But now that I see you're alive, it doesn't have to be a fantasy anymore."

She tilts her head at me, as if she's trying to understand what the hell that means.

"And what exactly does that mean?"

"In the simplest terms, I have to kill you."

She cocks an eyebrow humorously, and it's not a reaction I expect. It appears she thinks I'm bluffing.

"Killing isn't for the faint of heart, Kinsley. I think you and I both know that more than anybody," she teases.

I can't help but smirk at her. Her wits are so fucking sexy. I inch on her, leaning in and gripping my hands on the armrest.

"You didn't let me finish, darling Willow. I have to kill you. But first, I have to feel you against my skin one last time," I whisper, a mere inch from her plump lips.

She meets my smirk and leans up to softly meet my lips. We're now less than an inch away from each other. I believe I definitely met my match when Willow Harding came into my life. All of this was a fucking mind game. Faking her death to dressing like sex on legs. I've never been more in love.

I let out a sigh, gently rubbing my lips against hers. She smells and tastes like strawberries and honey. A lethal mix. I struggle to suppress the groan of pleasure that comes out.

A humorless laugh is juxtaposed against her previous humorous smile.

"I've wanted to kill you for a long time, Kinsley Focker. I never thought I'd see the day when I would."

TWENTY-TWO

WILLOW

Kinsley Focker is going to die today. Eight months, and I've had it on my mind the entire time. The only way to get out of the public sphere was to fake my death. Too many eyes were on me as the Siren Assassin, and it just became too much to handle. Even I, Willow Harding, can get too overwhelmed with being under a microscope. The only people who know I am alive are Meredith and Violet. And now…the man of the hour.

The man who has a depraved obsession with my body. He hasn't stopped looking at me in a predatory way. His gaze lasts than maybe five seconds on my eyes, and then it goes back to my chest and hips. I knew it'd take a bit of a ruse to encounter him again. Once I saw that the complex was rebuilt, I took shelter here for a while. I waited it out to see if he'd show up. A month and a half and counting. I hunkered down here, swiftly sneaking my way past the landlord. A squatter, in a sense. It was a longshot to assume he'd show up here in my old domain.

He's becoming predictable. I've learned to pick up on his instincts. It seems as if I've got him where I want him.

"You want inside me, Kinsley?"

He lets out a guttural growl before lifting me up off the chair I was sitting in. I wrap my arms around his neck, feeling his trap muscles contract from my touch. He's easy to please. If this is what he wants, this is what he'll get. Which brings me to step one: set the scene.

I reach down, grabbing his boner that's poking me from his jeans. Another growl emits from him, and he looks for access to my neck, roughly biting down on my flesh. So primal.

"I want inside you like my next breath, Willow."

He lifts me up as I wrap my legs around his waist. But there's nowhere to go. There's no furniture besides the chair and couch. So he slams me up against the wall, lifting my turtleneck over my head and tossing it to the floor. He pulls back, admires my boobs, and squeezes them.

"How are you so fucking sexy, my darling Willow?"

It's demented, but it feels so good. It's a sensation that only he has the power to cause within me. And he's the sadist I've been trying to kill.

When I don't respond, he continues paying special attention to my neck, inhaling my scent. I reach for the hem of his long-sleeve tee and pull it over his head. He quickly disposes of it and thrusts it across the room as I run my hands over his perfectly sculpted pecs and abs. It should be illegal to have a body like this on a sinister mastermind.

"Get it in while you still can. It'll be the last time you'll ever get it do it," I warn, throwing my head back against the wall when he grinds against me.

"I wouldn't be so sure, babe. Whether you face reality or not, you're dying tonight."

Fear is a transient feeling, and it's soon replaced with amusement. This is all just another mind game we're playing. And I'm loving it.

"Unlike you, Kinsley, I'm not scared to die. You can slap me, shank me, strangle me. Do whatever the fuck you want to me. I'm not scared to die."

He makes eye contact with me and holds it before unbuckling his jeans and dropping them to the floor.

"Then we're looking at a painless kill, are we, honey?"

I swallow, disgusted at how wicked this man is. I can't believe I ever got myself involved with him. Trying to just get through this, I pull him closer as he positions himself in front of me. He moves inside with ease, and I let my head thud against the wall. He's so big and so barbaric, it's a fucking crime.

"I hate you so much," I groan as he slowly glides in and out of me.

"That fucking sucks to hear you say that, Willow. Because I love you so much."

With that, he slams inside of me, catching me off guard.

"Oh, *fuck.*"

He lets out of a mischievous laugh, going back to slowly gliding in and out. Such a fucking Casanova. I have to remember that all of this isn't coming from a place of love, no matter how many times he says it is.

When I arch my back, he growls yet again and yanks my jeans down, letting me kick them off. We're both completely naked, bare, and exposed. It's the most vulnerable you could possibly get with someone. He was the first person I've ever gotten vulnerable with.

And this will have to end. I can tell he's close to an orgasm. His eyes are rolled back, and his body goes stiff. I'm also close. It's as if we're one person. Our bodies have always been in tune with each other. Each time, better than the last time. And today is not any different.

He does a few more thrusts inside of me, and then I finally feel it. Both of us, as if we're one tune, cry out in euphoria. His head falls into the crook of my neck, shivering as he goes limp. I run a shaky hand through my hair that's not a bit curly from sweating. His hot breath on my neck warms me, and I start to remember what we're both here to do.

"All right, birthday boy—"

Before I can finish, his hand tightly clasps around my neck, rendering me breathless. I reach for his hand, but he's a meaty guy. His strength is nothing like his brother's. This is something like bionic strength.

His gaze of arousal is now an expressionless one. Almost like he's in a trance.

"I hear you're into mind games, love. Checkmate," he declares, his blank face turning into an insidious grin.

Turning to my side, I force his hands off me and knee him in the balls. He yelps, jumping back and cradling his groin. As he jumps around, I spit on him.

"You fucking bitch, Willow," he grunts, laughing ruefully. He lunges for me, but I don't let him capture me again. I sprint to the kitchen and grab a butcher knife.

He catches up with me, and when he sees the knife at my side, he stops in his tracks.

"Crafty Willow. You never fail to surprise," he teases.

"Got to keep you on your toes," I remark.

This big, burly man stands in front of me, everything out in its glory. He stands like a Greek statue in front of me, it's a very odd scene.

"I didn't know we'd be wielding weapons for this."

"Everything's fair game. Right, Kinsley?"

He grinds his jaw in anger. "You don't know who you're fucking with."

"Ditto."

He straightens his shoulders and faces me off before charging at me. I get out of the way, but he's extremely agile. He charges at me again and tackles me to the ground, causing me to drop the knife. He puts me in a chokehold yet again.

"Wow, babe. I thought you'd put up more of a fight."

I reach for the knife that's a few feet away from me. When he sees me reaching for it, he holds my arm down. Fuck. He sees my inner dilemma and leans down, licking the side of my face, making my stomach turn.

Before he can saying anything else, I headbutt him with a gut-wrenching blow, sending him back. He wipes a sliver of blood from lips.

"Cute."

He rushes at me again, but I sprint out of the kitchen. He grabs my hair and knocks me into the wall. I elbow him in the face and kick him away from me. It barely sends him back, barely deterring him. I grab the mirror hung up on the wall and slam it against his head. He falls to the ground, a gnarly gash mark on his face.

I give him a second to get his wits about him. He stands up and wipes the blood from the cut, wincing.

"I thought you'd put up more of a fight," I repeat back to him.

Something dark flashes in his eyes. He charges me again and launches a punch, but I duck, as he makes contact with the wall. I deliver a blow to his stomach, and he only winces. He pushes me up against the wall and tries to choke me again. I use one hand to pull his hand from around my neck and jab my finger into his right eye, causing him to scream and mirroring the same injury I caused for his brother.

"Round fucking 2."

I jab it farther into his eye, and he loosens his grip. I headbutt him, and he takes a moment to try to mend his eye. He punches me in the face, and I fall to the ground. Hopping on top of me, he strikes my face, stomach, and neck.

"Fucking die," he growls angrily.

I reach up and stab him in the eye again with my finger, causing him to jump off me. He jumps around in agony, cradling his eye. Again, I spot the knife a few feet away and grab it while he's freaking out. When he turns to me, I deliver one lethal blow to his stomach, incapacitating him.

He's stunned for a few moments, and we share a moment. Tears brim in my eyes as he gives me a pleading look.

"Willow," he rasps.

I pull his head against mine with the blade still jutting from his stomach.

"I know, I know."

He slowly falls to the ground, and I try to stay with him. I pull the knife out and lie with him on the floor. Blood starts pouring out of the wound, and I do nothing to stop the bleeding. He puts his hand over it, and I just lie beside him.

"Checkmate." I repeat his word back to him.

He gives me a little chuckle as blood pours out of his mouth but then winces.

"Y-you're a w-wise w-woman. I-I l-lost t-this t-time."

I wipe the tears that build in my eyes. Though he taunted me for as long as he did, this was still a man I almost fell in love with and shared a part of my life with.

He's the reason I do what I love today. Protecting the safety of women.

I kiss him on the forehead.

"I told you that I'm the master of mind games."

He lets out an aggravated chuckle again, pressing down harder on the wound. He starts to turn pale at the blood loss.

"Y-you did. C-congrat-tulat-tions. I l-love y-y-ou..."

Those are his last words. He slowly slips to his demise, his semi-amused smile transforming into an expressionless face. Closing his eyes, I place another kiss on his forehead.

When I'm confident that he's dead, I stand up, get dressed back into my clothes, and phone Violet.

"How'd it go?"

"He's dead."

She lets out a sigh of relief. "That was fast. Did he put up much of a fight?"

"He was 200 lbs of muscle. I think that speaks for itself."

"What do you need from me?"

It's a good question. The thing is, I'm not certain I need anything from anyone right now. I'm leaving the country tomorrow. In the last eight months, I've found out that the States has nothing for me. My worst years were here. My best years were when I was training overseas to be an assassin in my early twenties. My past and identity will forever be linked to Port Rockwell, Massachusetts.

"Can you be here in ten minutes? I need a ride to Meredith's apartment."

About ten minutes later, Violet lives up to her promise of picking me up and driving me to Meredith's side of town.

I get to her place moments later and knock on the front door of her condo. The redhead opens the door with a boot on her leg. She looks me up and down before giving me a pleased smile. I haven't looked at myself in a mirror yet, but I'm sure I'm bearing some wounds.

"You did it, didn't you?"

"In true Siren Assassin fashion."

She chuckles, nudging me inside. Her condo has slowly become a second home. She took me in after Dad died and has always been there for me through the tough times. She's my best friend. I don't know what I'd do without her.

We end up in her living room, and she winces, sitting down.

"I just took my pain meds, so I'm feeling kinda sleepy."

"How are you holding up?"

She shrugs indifferently. "I feel like I've been in a hit-and-run."

"Fair enough."

She sits back, relaxing against the sofa.

"So what's next for the Siren Assassin?"

"Certainly not Port Rockwell, anymore."

She looks as if she's trying to read me. "So you're leaving."

I can't stay here anymore. So much has happened. And now that I have Kinsley out of my life, I can live freely now. But there's an entire market in Europe that needs my services more.

"There's just nothing here for me anymore. I feel like my entire identity will be tied to killing wealthy, abusive men. And that's not the legacy I wanna have here."

"So what do you intend to do, Low?"

My shoulders tense at the question. There's no easy way to tell her this. We both left Kill Elite after they scammed me out of a kill job years ago, and Meredith never got her paycheck for a big hacking job that a client hired her for. It just felt right at the time to part ways with the organization.

"Kill Elite reached out to me before I faked my death."

Her jaw tenses, and she looks down in contempt.

"Low, what the fuck?"

"I know, Mer. But I don't have a choice. There's a healthier market overseas than here in the States. I'll forever be the Siren Assassin and a menace to the people of Port Rockwell. Once I'm seen alive, I'll never be able to live it down."

"So you're leaving me. Your best friend." Her voice cracks.

I don't miss the hurt in her eyes.

"I don't have to."

"What?"

"Come with me. I need my confidant with me, carrying out these jobs."

She shakes her head. "They fucked me over. There's no need for me to go back to that sham of an organization."

"I can't go without you."

"Then don't! Just stay here. Did you forget what they did to you? They gave a $500,000 kill job to another assassin that fucked up another job. Not to mention the job was supposed to be yours, and they gave a shitty excuse of that assassin having more seniority over you. Why in the hell would you consider going back to them?"

"I already told you why, Mer."

"And it's a stupid reason. There are other organizations to work for."

"They're offering me a $1,000,000 signing bonus to come back and be a master assassin."

She sighs, rubbing her hand over her face in distress. "I can't go with you overseas, Low. I can't go back to that life. I already have a project here that I'm working on."

"A project? What's that?"

"It's still a fresh idea. You're not the only one that can have an appetite for vengeance."

She just stares at me, and it takes me a second to understand what she means. She gives me an easy smile, and I return it. I hate to part ways from the people closest to me. I've had to do it twice, and now I have to do the same with her.

"I'm proud of you."

"I guess I'm proud of you, too," she teases. "No matter how much I disagree with the decision."

"And I'm sorry for bringing you down with me."

"Low—"

"I'm serious. All of this could've been avoided if I didn't use your room for sexting a freak and getting you involved in my mess. You wouldn't be in this predicament. You've been through so much already, and I made it worse."

Tears well in her eyes.

"It's not a big deal," she rasps.

"But it is. You were collateral damage in all of this. I'm so fucking sorry, Mer."

She wipes her eyes angrily. Meredith McKinley hates crying. She thinks it's a sign of weakness, even though it's a very healthy reaction to everything.

"You can make it up to me by staying here," she whispers. "If you leave me here, that's leaving me with the dangerous streets of Port Rockwell."

"Violet will be a phone call away. If anything happens, she'll help and will always let me know."

She doesn't look happy, but she shrugs anyway.

"I can't force you to stay here. Make sure you keep in contact at all times, please. Don't be a stranger."

"I'll never be one. I've already sought out a two-bedroom place in Moscow. Whenever you guys wanna come visit."

She finally breaks into a genuine smile before nodding. When everything's all said and done, she walks me out.

"Let me know when you're leaving. I'll go with Violet to drop you off at the airport."

I give her my word and one last hug. Violet's been hanging out in the car, being my lookout. I hop back in the car, and she looks to me.

"Where to next?"

I have one more apology I need to make before I leave tomorrow. Caroline. Vinny's widow and the lady that's taken the place of my mother for the last decade or so. She'll be, by far, the hardest apology to make because something tells me she won't forgive me easily.

But before I try to make that attempt, my stomach growls. Killing Kinsley was a bit of workout, yet a huge feat.

"Right now, I feel like a burger."

She gives me a knowing look before starting the car and pulling out onto the street. On the way to the closest burger joint with a drive-thru, we pass my old apartment complex. It'll be a while before they find his body. Mainly because it's in the creek behind it. Violet already called for an underground cleaning company to get rid of the mess in the apartment. Time is ticking. I need to make quick work of getting the hell out of Dodge.

If there's one message killing him will send across metropolitan Boston, it's that, they may have run the Siren Assassin out of town. But her legacy is here to stay. And this is only the beginning.

AUTHOR'S NOTE

Thank you for joining me diving into Willow Harding's psyche and going on a journey with me. Willow Harding is such a special character to me. While her method of overcoming her trauma is not ideal, she managed to take her power back. She's not perfect in the slightest. But I love writing about perfectly imperfect characters, and writing her story has been an amazing journey. There's beauty in being human. It's a jarring headspace I've had to put myself in during the process of writing this story, and I couldn't be prouder of it. It's a message to fellow women that are dealing with troubling thoughts that they are not alone. As a fiction writer, I only aim to create worlds where readers feel understood and have the luxury to find their escape from the craziness that the real world offers. Writing romance is my first love, and I greatly believe that stories and themes of female empowerment and overcoming trauma (regardless of gender) deserve to be told.

With love,

Ally Lee

OTHER WORKS

King Larson (#1 in King Larson Series)
After Larson (#2 in King Larson Series)
The Home I Knew (#1 in Rose Valley Series)

COMING SOON

No One Talk: A 2094 Ruin (Summer 2024)
The Home I Lost (#2 in Rose Valley Series) (Fall 2024)

SOCIAL MEDIA

Instagram:
allyleeauthor